Acid Christmas

CHARLOTTE DUNE

OCEAN FLOWER BOOKS

Distributed by Ocean Flower Books.

This is a work of fiction.

To request permission to use any part of this book for any reason other than reviews, and to read more books, essays, and poems by Charlotte Dune, or to listen to her additional audiobooks in *The Psychedelic Love Series*, please visit CharlotteDune.com.

Ebook ISBN: 978-1-7343089-6-9

Paperback ISBN: 978-1-7343089-7-6

Hardcover ISBN: 978-1-7343089-8-3

Cover art by Cherie Chapman

To Mohita, for I'll never forget our first taste of Canada, and to Kayliegh for setting me off on this tale.

Hello Cellular Earth World Traveler,

Acid Christmas is a work of fiction. I do not condone illegal drug use or driving in blizzards. This book is not designed to educate you. It is written to entertain you.

The characters and events in this novel are entirely fictional. Any resemblance to actual persons, living or dead, is purely coincidental. I have taken creative liberties with the portrayal of historical events, locations, government organizations, and cultural references for the purposes of storytelling.

The views and opinions expressed by the characters in this work do not necessarily reflect mine, and any similarities to real-life individuals is unintentional.

DO NOT GET WET.

DO NOT MIX WITH BEETS.

Enjoy your Trip. See you Coolside."

Sincerely,

CHARLOTTE DUNE

"I have always loved blizzards, if only because of the driving experience—which is definitely an acquired taste."

"As for LSD, I highly recommend it."

— HUNTER S. THOMPSON

Teddy with the Crooked Tooth Begins the Ballad of Acid Christmas

The wind blows, the oil bubbles; I'mma scoop out this glazed dough and tell you 'bout the world's troubles. This is a tale that happens in Toronto, Canada—city of skyscrapers, traffic jams, maple leafs, rambunctious raccoons, deadly icicles, and tiny donut balls called TimBits. (Trademarked, 'tis, like everything else.)

I'm Teddy With The Crooked Tooth, and I hate the cold. Sometimes, I wonder why I left my little Caribbean home. It sure wasn't for this scenery. It's ALL gray here, almost every day; gray, gray, gray.

I left for the money, I suppose, but the dough turns out to be for someone else while my food is as bad as microwaved beef.

In the Pearson Airport, Terminal Two, I scoop up and serve your yummy Bits from morning to night, dear traveler, while you wait for your plane, while you soothe your crying bébés, while you shop for mugs that say, "Go Blue Jays!" With these gloppy, sugary glazed and original donut holes, I make your journey a little sweeter. I give you caffeine, plastic knives, and cream cheese, sometimes with a smile, but mostly not.

I hope one day I can make enough money to fix my crooked-ass teeth, but them rubbery braces trays ain't cheap.

Maybe I should've stayed back home, where the only snow I knew was served in cones.

Dreams don't always taste like pictures, you see.

So, sit back and enjoy the sleigh ride; eat a guava triangle or nine. Get out your crochet needles and sew me an ugly sweater, and let's begin this tumultuous tale together.

(Wink, wink, clown face, Santa, snowflake, schnauzer, raccoon, rat, and of course, magic.)

Part One

ARRIVALS

Chapter One

CANDI BOARDS

There are always those who can't, won't, or don't follow the rules. Some are oblivious and others are assholes. On an airplane, it becomes real clear, real quick, which is which.

The early morning of Black Friday, as dawn arose and stretched its pink lips over the simmering neon Las Vegas city strip, Candi Burns flew to Honolulu, to Austin, to Miami, to New York, to London, to Portugal, to Amsterdam, like blah blah, blah. For days. Destinations repeated. Two weeks passed. She came home and left again, lost track of her circadian rhythm and ran out of makeup remover. Then finally, her return plane arrived in the Netherlands. This would be her last leg. After a layover in Toronto, she could sleep at home, surrounded by the umber sands of Nevada... albeit alone.

In the Schipol airport, she restocked her skin wipes and went to the lounge's bathroom to smooth her lightly-rolled, auburn hair, its ends a perfect curve. She reapplied pressed powder, bronzer, and a light maroon matte-lip, only enough makeup to freshen and enhance her natural features. The sink's cold water washed over her manicured nails, Santa-suit-red for Christmas, and, in the mirror, with tired hands, she blended a light blotting of beige concealer to the blue-tinted half-moons under her pale, hazel eyes.

Despite a schedule perfect for a possum, Candi strove to appear as polished as a Macy's holiday window display. It was her job, after all, sort of, to be pretty and pleasing to customers, and if she let one thing slip, reduced her rituals even a little bit, well, she wouldn't. Changing herself would betray him, betray their past. Nothing should be different, not her makeup, not their house, not even his underwear drawer, nothing.

Back in the lounge, she sipped a venti black coffee and struggled not to yawn.

They boarded fifty minutes late. Passengers carrying winter coats and shopping bags roamed the aisles, chatting and moving luggage, stuffing books into backseat pockets and adjusting neck pillows. Candi answered questions and counted missing names.

They taxied at the gate for another thirty minutes before receiving the necessary clearance to leave, but as the captain announced their impending, belated departure, halfway down economy, a misshapen black duffel squeezed out from an open bin like a constipated turd.

Gosh darn it. Who put that there? She thought. I already closed those bins.

The lumpy bag loomed over the silvery head of a sleeping lady, and threatened to tumble.

This would not do. Why, oh why, did people think it was fine to stuff their shit where it didn't fit? There wasn't enough caffeine on the planet for this.

The duffel and Candi's mental stamina teetered on collapse. She'd wanted to go home for hours, for days, for Jasper's... She clipped off the end of her thought like a hangnail. Focus on the current task. Move the bag. One thing at a time—that's what her Zoom therapist said. But this wasn't supposed to be the current task. Jasper's mother needed her to prepare...

The bag creaked out a smidgen.

The dangling luggage could be a symbol for her entire year,

maybe her whole life, and the desire to yank it out and fling it around like a medieval flail, to throw it out the airplane's emergency exit door with a triumphant scream, almost overcame her, but Candi resisted, like she resisted 99.99999% of her in-flight emotions.

She could force it in the bin or find a different spot, but where? The plane was as full as a chipmunk's cheeks in pumpkin season.

A hungry, stale breath of recirculated air escaped her mauve mouth, and she made her way to the un-securely stowed item. A few multicolored, iron-on patches decorated the dark fabric. Before reaching the bin, however, she bumped into a stray limb. It blocked her entire path, extending from row to row. A bright green sneaker the size of a bowling ball connected to a lengthy leg in red track pants. Silver reflective stripes ran from the owner's ankle to his jacket, then to his collar, and finally to his face, and a cloth mask which said, "minimally compliant" in big white letters on a black background. Over his eyes, he wore a satin purple eye mask fashioned as a unicorn's head, complete with a stuffed, pearlescent, protruding horn, something straight from a bargain rack at Claire's Boutique. Candi frowned, though her expression was nearly as frozen as her emotions, only with Botox instead of avoidance; this person was 100% the owner of the vagrant luggage.

"Excuse me sir, can you please move your leg?"

The overgrown teen showed no signs of registering her polite request. Massive red headphones bedazzled with faux diamonds covered his ears. Quite tall, possibly the tallest person she'd ever seen on a plane, he was like an NBA player compressed into a grocery cart. He'd also already reclined his seatback in an unapproved fashion prior to takeoff.

"Sir," she raised her voice, "I need to secure your bag."

He didn't stir. Beside him, an overweight man slapped at a laptop, oblivious, and in the row behind him, the stray sack inched above the elderly woman's head like a guillotine.

"Sir, move your leg," Candi repeated, allowing exasperation

into her tone. "We're preparing for takeoff."

Nothing.

"Sir," she practically shouted. Techno music streamed from the youth's headphones. His cologne contained the undertones of a forest-dwelling skunk. She wanted to pinch her nostrils shut. His knee was so high that if she stepped over him, it would force her to hike up her skirt. Instead, she nudged his calf with the side of her shoe. "Sir, wake up."

"Mmhhhmm."

She wished she could gate check his bag—gate check it straight to hell.

The plane rolled toward the runway. Before she was able to muster the nerve to 'accidentally' stomp on the kid's foot, someone poked her—hard—from behind.

Candi let out a high-pitched "yip," and whipped around.

It was Chad, the A flight attendant. "Step aside, my lady," and with a brush of his hand, he pivoted her hips, moved the young guy's leg, and yanked out the bag, then slammed the bin shut.

The tall kid shifted his lengthy body and returned to the same position. Chad sauntered up with the bag and a coy smile. His boyish, gingerbread eyes flickered with amusement. "Can you find a spot for this?" He shoved the duffel at Candi, and she stumbled backwards, clutching the heavy thing with both hands like a full-grown golden retriever.

"Tsk, Tsk," Chad shook his blonde head, "Girl, you gotta get to the gym; work those arms." He took the sack from her and strolled off.

Candi scowled at his buoyant rear. She was pretty sure he'd gotten a butt lift. No man could have an ass that perky. Why am I always two seconds behind everyone else? She wondered.

The young guy roused and removed his unicorn sleep mask. "Oh hey," he said in a preppy British accent, "Could I trouble you for a glass of cold Chardonnay?"

Are you fucking serious? Candi screamed in her groggy head, then pretended not to hear him and left.

"Excuse me," the young man called.

She knew his type: nineteen and entitled, treating every female like their own personal maid—exactly how she never wanted her own son to act, except she would probably never have a son now... She would have named him JJ. Jasper Junior... Ugh, those thoughts again. They were worse than lousy passengers. At least passengers went away. Why couldn't she go an hour without wanting to cry?

Her mother thought she needed a hobby, to travel more, to do fun things, but travel more than she already did? When nothing was fun anymore... She involuntarily yawned. What would be fun would be a nap, for like a year. Which was basically what her therapist had prescribed. Unlike her mother, he believed she didn't get enough sleep, but that was easy for him to say. He worked from home with his cat, not with the scourge of humanity she served Diet Cokes and SunChips to on every flight, morning, noon, and night.

"You could change jobs," her therapist had suggested, "You could benefit from a stable, 9-5 schedule."

"What job would that be?" she'd asked, genuinely curious if he had a specific idea for her. He didn't.

"Whatever you want to try next."

Like it's all so simple, she thought.

Back at the front of the cabin, Adrienne, the B attendant, offered her a stick of gum. "Saw you with that tall guy; I think he's an actor or something."

"Why?" Candi took the gum with gratitude, letting the cherry taste replace her frustrations.

"He was taking selfies with girls at the gate."

Chad joined their conversation. "The big guy? I'm amazed he made it through airport security. He stinks like a stoner's butthole."

Candi stifled a laugh. Even with his blond crew cut, fake rear, and steroid-filled arms, at least Chad knew how to crack a butt joke.

"I thought that was his cologne."

"Oh God, Candi, you're so sheltered. That's the smell of some sticky icky mari-ju-ana."

Adrienne smacked her bubblegum. "He's *stocking cute.*" She emphasized the words, as if saying "fucking cute," but Candi clearly heard "stocking."

"Stocking cute?"

"Yeah, like you want him to slide down your chimney and stuff your Christmas stocking, and stuff ya' real good with his big candy cane, if you know what I mean?" Adrienne's mask was off, and her glossed lips glittered like a 90s slap bracelet.

"Santa's gonna put you on his naughty list," Chad hissed.

Candi rolled her eyes. "I'm old enough to be his mother."

"Girl, no woman can resist a handsome, tall man. He's over twenty-one; that's legal," Adrienne said.

"I'm almost 40," Candi said.

"35 is not *almost 40.*"

"Close enough. Fine, almost 35." Hardly any difference, Candi thought.

"Oh my God, see. You're still young as cum."

She blushed, good lord Adrienne could get crass.

The plane slowed to a stop, and the pilot apologized again; they were fifth in line for takeoff. More waiting.

"I'm getting a better look." Adrienne unbuckled her seatbelt and cat-walked down the aisle, hips swinging.

Chad watched her go. "Adrienne thinks every flight is a wedding, and she's 'bout to catch the bouquet."

The overhead speakers announced an even longer wait, and Chad instructed her to serve more drinks to first class.

She obliged and hid the coach section with the slide of a curtain, a still-remaining clear line to divide the haves from the have nots. How she'd love to delineate her own past like that, to separate it from her stupid brain.

Most of the guests in the privileged seats took their hot towels and drinks wordlessly, more interested in their phones than reciprocity. No one said "thank you" anymore. Since the last pandemic, people avoided each other.

She passed flutes of Champagne to a middle-aged man and woman, and their microscopic white and gray teacup puppy barked at her.

"Oh, he's so cute," Candi said because honestly the little pup was adorable, though he probably cost more than her entire wardrobe.

"This is Terry Fox," the woman said, petting the dog's ping-pong ball-sized head. "But we call him Foxy."

"What kind of dog is he?"

"A teacup schnauzer."

"Hey, Foxy, can I pet you?"

The pup backed away from Candi's outstretched hand.

"You're playing hard to get? Well, hold on. I'll be right back." She went to her seat, and from her purse, retrieved a plastic pouch of dog treats. The peanut-sized artificial sausages flew with her on every flight. Candi offered pet owners the yummy goodies to appease their often-stressed furry companions. Yet their meaty scent triggered a hollow sensation in her throat; they reminded her of PumpkinChai, her beloved schweenie.

Candi swallowed, suppressing the melancholic swell. PumpkinChai had passed away a month after Jasper and their deaths connected in her mind, forming one long stretch of time, of tears, of wiping off streaks of mascara in the bathrooms of different airports, of nights spent sobbing, unable to get through a single television episode. Oh, how she missed Jasper and their little spicy ball of apricot fur.

Treats in hand, she returned to the southern couple. With their pandemic masks lowered, they happily drank Champagne and flipped through the inflight entertainment. The gray and white puppy posted at attention on the woman's lap. It barked at her again.

"I've got a little something for you, Foxy," Candi said in a baby voice and opened her hand to reveal the mini wiener treat. "Would he like a sausage?"

"Of course," the woman cooed.

Foxy sniffed the air and strained to reach the treat, then gobbled it up.

"See, we're friends now," Candi said. "Though you will have to stow him soon for takeoff."

"He's a good boy. He'd be better off on my lap. He's not a fan of the case."

"It's for his own safety. Here," Candi gave the couple a few more treats. "Use these to entice him."

"Could we get another drink?" The husband asked, as if suddenly entitled to additional treats like his designer dog. Candi said sure and returned with more Champagne. Best to keep the rich folk satisfied, especially given the delay, she thought.

After another thirty minutes, the plane's chance to depart finally arrived. They lifted off the Netherland's snow-dusted terrain. In seven hours, she'd land in Toronto, then suffer a six-hour layover before flying home to the Vegas airport. Almost no longer awake, Candi served dinner, cleaned up trash, and ran through her required paperwork, but before she could finish her duties and relax, a passenger's emergency button flashed. She sluggishly went to the call signal, but as she waded closer to the button, a piney fragrance met her nostrils. It was the tall guy pressing it. You've got to be kidding me, she thought. Business class nerve on an economy budget.

She switched off the button. "Can I help you?"

In his hoity-toity accent, he said, "Yes, do you have any sleeping pills?"

Her painted lips parted with surprise. Sleeping pills? What, the weed wasn't enough?

"I've been trying to sleep, but I can't." He batted silky black eyelashes.

"No, we don't give out sleeping pills."

"No? Some flight attendants have them. Wine then? Umm,"

he looked at her name tag. "Candi?"

"We're not serving drinks in economy right now."

"So, not in economy, but in first class?" He didn't wait for her answer. "Are you saying I should sneak up to first class with you to have a drink?"

Candi was glad her mask hid most of her reaction.

"We can live a little, right?" He winked.

Is he flirting with me? She wondered, thinking—GenZ has no shame.

He stood and his body unfurled into the aisle like someone shaking off a picnic blanket. "If there's an empty seat in business, I wouldn't mind moving." He towered over her. "It's pretty cramped here. I'll follow you."

Under him, Candi understood why normal people committed assault. Though Adrienne was right, he was *slightly* cute. The accent, the unusual tallness, his tan skin, thin nose, high cheekbones, dark, onyx eyes—the combined package at least rendered him memorable.

But the unicorn mask was a no-go. Nope. Also, if he was famous, why wasn't he in first class already?

"Sorry sir," she said.

The plane lurched, and the guy crammed himself back into his chair. Candi widened her stance.

Chad's voice came over the loudspeaker. "We're heading into some turbulence. Please return to your seats and fasten your seat-belts." The seatbelt sign flashed on with a ding.

The plane jolted again, and the smelly tall guy clutched his arm rests and squeezed his eyes shut, mumbling as if counting out a game of hide and seek.

She held in a chuckle; Mr. Messy Bag was afraid of flying. No wonder he wanted sleeping pills.

As she returned to her position, Chad pulled her aside. "Word from the captain—unexpected high winds, strap in tight. We're rerouting over The North Pole and we're in for a very rough flight."

Chapter Two

GRETCHEN GREEN GETS BAD NEWS

Granola bar wrappers, an empty package of mustard pretzel twists, an IPA can, and multiple used disposable cups rested on Gretchen Green's hotel room dresser, like a shrine to the pursuit of snacking. With her travel schedule paused, she furiously typed on her laptop. She was supposed to be on her way to cover a mining conference hosted by the Canadian Minister of Natural resources, but the airline had canceled her flight to Ulaanbaatar via Korea at the last minute due to an impending snowstorm. With the trip taking twenty-eight hours, and with few flight options, the issue would likely make her miss the key conference events, and therefore the story. Though, would anyone else miss her story? Debatable.

Typing, always typing, Gretchen chewed on the end of a sour cherry licorice rope. All was not lost. She adjusted the blue satin hair wrap she slept in to keep her short, black curls less tangled and more refreshed. Instead of her usual economy beat, she sent "easy money" messages to various magazine editors, hawking her reserve of unpublished essays with saucy headlines like "Why Bad Moms Love Christmas Movies," determined to rush out as many paid articles as she could before the holidays slowed the news cycle, turning her freelance income to zilch. With the advent of artificial intelligence, she could easily churn out 100 such articles a day, and to her disbelief, people still bought them—at least for now.

Her cell phone rang. Hoping it was Sam calling to say she'd made a mistake, that she still loved Gretchen, that she wanted them to be together forever, Gretchen snatched up the phone, then groaned; her mother's picture flashed on the screen. She almost didn't answer, but it *was* the season of giving...

"Hey mom," she said, her mouth full of candy.

"Sweetie, how are you?" There was something stiff and staged in her mom's voice.

"I'm fine. What's going on?"

"Well, I have some bad news."

Gretchen's stopped chewing. With her parents in their seventies, any call could mean the worst. She tensed her hand around the phone. "Is everything okay? It's not about dad, is it?"

"Oh no, no, he's fine. We're both fine."

Her parents weren't dying. Disaster averted. Maybe her mom was watching TV again and freaking out. That was a favorite hobby of her parents—watch cable news and get riled up about the economy, then call Gretchen with recession questions.

"It's your brother," her mother continued. "Not to panic, I'm sure everything will be fine, but Kevin is in the hospital."

"What? Kevin? Why? Was there an accident?" Kevin in a hospital? He was the healthiest of all of them.

"He's a strong guy, you know... But... ugh... we're heading to the hospital. Kendra's sending us updates."

Goodness gracious, her mom had a way of not getting to the point. Gretchen raised her voice. "Mom, why is Kevin in the hospital?"

"Um, well, he's had a little heart event."

"A heart event? What kind of event?" Adrenaline ran through her like a sugar spike. She jumped from the bed to her sock-covered feet.

"Just a little heart attack. Very minor."

A little heart attack? A HEART ATTACK? Gretchen steadied herself. “What? Why?” Kevin is only thirty-two. Kevin isn’t on drugs. Kevin ran around the neighborhood. Kevin juiced kale. Kevin could NOT be having a heart attack. No. Not her baby brother.

“Wish I had better news.”

“I don’t understand how you can be so cheery,” Gretchen snapped, pacing around the hotel bed.

“Would you prefer for me to cry? Someone in this family has to keep it together. Don’t be hysterical.”

“I am NOT being hysterical.”

“It’s okay. Your father and I are on the way,” her mother said, as if Kevin was simply a child in need of an after-school pickup.

“Why would he have a heart attack?” Gretchen’s left hand waved in the air like a pastor at the pulpit. “Are they 100% sure? When did this happen? Where was he? What was he doing?”

“I’ll explain later. I’ve got to make some more calls. It’s probably this new variant.”

“What?” Gretchen halted her march around the carpet. “A variant? I haven’t seen anything about it on the news.”

“Oh, you know, another one is what Kendra said, but your father doesn’t think so. It’s very upsetting though. Kevin’s unconscious.”

“Unconscious? Like in a coma?” Her face contorted.

“I wouldn’t call it a coma. He’s just... in a deep resting state while his body recovers.”

Gretchen’s mind could barely process the words coming through the phone. “Should I come home?”

“No, no, don’t be silly. He’ll be fine. I’ve gotta go.”

“Hold on. If it’s a variant, what if Kendra’s infected, or the kids?” She softened her voice so her mother couldn’t accuse her again of being hysterical. “Maybe you and dad shouldn’t go.”

“My son is in the hospital, of course I’m going.”

“I’ll fly home. Seriously, mom. I’m not covering this conference, anyway.”

"Well, we're going to help with the kids." Her mother said this like she thought Gretchen couldn't handle watching two kids under five, which she believed was probably true, but it still stung.

"I can help with the kids."

"I'll keep you updated. Send me your flight info."

Were they really having this conversation? As if her schedule mattered when Kevin was in a coma.

She hung up and called Kendra, Kevin's wife. The phone rang and rang. Gretchen searched online for information on new variants; there wasn't much. She typed in "causes of a heart attack," suddenly aware of her own heart's incessant pounding. How many beats was that per minute? What was someone's heart rate supposed to be? *Dang, I need to get one of those smart watches,* she thought. What did a heart attack even feel like? What were the symptoms? The treatments? The survival rate?

Gretchen grabbed a bag of M&M's and ripped in, hoping chocolate extinguished panic, but as she read up on myocardial infarctions, ischemias and fibrinolytic agents, fear twisted in her gut like garland round a Christmas tree, and outside her window, walnut-sized snowflakes began to tumble from the sky.

Chapter Three

CANDI PLANE, CANDI PLANE

"Strap in," Chad commanded Candi with a grin fit for the Christmas Grinch. "We're in a major low-pressure system with northward winds. I can feel it!"

"What?" She never fully understood these types of weather comments, which maybe was why Chad had gotten promoted and not her.

Adrienne buckled up too. "Great. Let's leave the seatbelt sign on for the whole rest of the flight."

The plane rocked and the lights flickered.

"Hope everyone wore their Depends," Chad cackled.

"We've got four hours left; I'm sure it will clear," Candi said. Only four hours—and in four more hours, plus another day, plus another week, plus another weekend—her first Christmas without Jasper would be here.

"Don't say that." Adrienne swatted at her. "We need them all seated."

"Are you ladies sleeping in the lounge tonight?"

"Sleeping? We're flying out."

"Oh, Candi, you didn't hear? Big, big snowstorm. Huge. Rescheduled for tomorrow evening at best."

"You're kidding me." The last thing she wanted was an overnight stay in Canada.

"Haven't you been working for like 100 hours?" Adrienne asked.

It was true, it did feel like 100 hours, or even days. "At least I'm on triple overtime pay."

Adrienne raised her coffee, "Drinks on Candi!"

"I'll probably treat myself to a hotel room then, if we're staying. I'm exhausted."

"No, no, come to the lounge with us!" Chad put his arm on her shoulder. "Think of all the money you'll save. Toronto hotels aren't cheap."

That was true, and what was the point of working overtime if she spent all the money on a hotel room? Then again, she knew she needed a real bed, not cocktails.

Chad shook his blond head, "You're no fun. I miss WildTina."

WildTina was a flight attendant from Atlanta that usually ran the European routes with them.

"She's always ready to go out... and go down." Chad puckered his lips like a fish.

"Gross." Adrienne made a puke face.

"Bathroom's right there if you need to barf." Chad smirked. The plane jerked. "Uh oh, okay, make a plan for our evening. I'm going to ask the pilot something." He sauntered off towards the cockpit.

Adrienne blew a pink bubble with her gum. "He thinks he's hot shit since he got promoted."

Candi agreed. The plane lunged up and down. Chad's voice came over the loudspeaker, reminding everyone to stay buckled up.

Ten minutes of minor bumps went by and despite her fatigue, Candi was able to clear a chapter of her novel before the plane suddenly jolted, hard, like it was being punched from below.

What on earth? She put down her tablet. That was not

normal, she thought. She'd never felt such a hard thrust. What was the pilot doing? Then, it happened again. The force of the last change in altitude pushed her backwards against her seat. Everything on the plane quivered. Lights flashed on and off. She strained to check the window. A bolt of lightning snapped the night in half. Alarms sounded like ambulance sirens. The business class bathroom door swung wildly back and forth revealing a large man on the toilet seat. Why was he up? He was supposed to be in his seat! The man lunged forward and shut the door, but it only flew open again. Candi swallowed a scream. Others did not swallow; shrieks erupted from the rear of the plane. Oxygen masks sprang from overhead.

Another man shouted, "What's happening?" A woman pulled off her mask and threw up in the aisle.

Cracks of white light pulsed outside the plane's window, and she wondered if it was lightning. It didn't look right to her. Her breath came in fast and shallow as the plane kept bumping from below. She gripped her own seat, just like the tall guy had done. God, he must really be freaking out, she thought.

"Why did the masks drop?" Adrienne whispered to her. "The masks shouldn't have dropped."

It was like being inside a piñata. They pitched and jerked. A few overhead bins opened and tossed out bags this way and that.

The dogs onboard went nuts, barking and howling. Babies cried.

It's going to be fine. It's going to be fine. It's going to be fine. The pilots know what they're doing, she told herself. But as the plane slammed through clouds and loud rumbles, her internal dialogue lost its conviction.

Adrienne hyperventilated beside her.

Even Chad strapped himself in and gripped his chair, wide-eyed and red-faced.

The pilot's voice came over the loudspeaker, "We're experiencing unusual weather. I'm moving us to a lower altitude. Please remain calm. Everything is under control. Flight attendants assume the position of—" Static clogged the intercom.

The plane dove like an aluminum arrow, then straightened out and hurdled through the air like a truck driving over bodies.

Stay calm. Don't scare anyone. That's what she'd been taught to do. Follow protocol. From her aisle seat she pivoted around to glance at first class. The curtain slid open. A woman prayed in the last row. The plane dove again and right before her eyes, the gray and white pup from first class flew up into the air and slammed into the ceiling with a pain-filled yowl. Her instincts kicked in; on autopilot, she unhooked her seatbelt and ran to the dog.

The pup ricocheted from the ceiling to a screaming man's lap who tossed the tiny animal into the aisle. It collapsed with a crack and slid toward the plane's nose.

"Candi, no," Adrienne called.

The dog's mom shrieked. "No! Foxy, Foxy!"

The plane shook sideways, and Candi tumbled to her knees. Grabbing a nearby seat, she reached for the dog, but it growled and bit into her pointer finger with its tiny little teeth. "Ouch!" She screamed and yanked away her hand.

The dog scurried under the next row. Candi clutched her wounded finger. Little Foxy managed to puncture her enough to draw blood.

The schnauzer's mom screamed again, "Foxy! Foxy!"

At the sound of its master's voice, the injured pup scurried to his mother, and the husband grabbed the dog from the aisle.

Still on her knees, Candi crawled to her seat and hoisted herself beside Adrienne, who was braced stiff, gripping her armrests. Candi's finger ached and she thought about putting it in her mouth to suck up the blood, but she'd been touching everything on the airplane. There were too many germs. How had a little dog done such damage? Instead, she held her own hand and turned her attention to the nearest window.

In times of stress, since Jasper's death, she'd learned to soothe herself with the memory of him. Like an imaginary friend she would conjure him to sit beside her. He would hold her hand. Yes, he was beside her now, telling a joke.

Jasper, his olive skin and dark, intellectual eyes, he leaned in with his ever-present, bad-boy grin. She could almost smell him. Almost feel his body heat. His voice was always warm with mirth like a mug of wassail in the winter.

"I've got one for ya," he said, as they bumped and dove, shook and swerved, like the sky was a bobsled luge. "A plane crashes on the border of the U.S. and Canada. Where do you bury the survivors?

"I don't know," she said to him in her head.

And the punchline was, "You don't bury survivors."

Sadness swelled in her gut like sloshing cold water. Back on the plane, she was the survivor. And Jasper, he... he was buried now... How could it be? How could it even fucking be? Like her thoughts, her stomach tilted and lurched. The plane dipped down, almost in a nosedive. It was less and less these days that anything seemed real to her.

Another canine screech rang out, and she hoped to God it was the sound of Foxy being stuffed back into his carrying case where he should have been all along. That's what happens, she thought, when you don't listen, when you go where you shouldn't be—you get hurt.

Chapter Four

CANDI LANDING

The plane heaved through plaster skies all the way to Toronto before smacking down on the Pearson airport runway. Finally. God, how frazzled the pilot must be. She'd never experienced so much turbulence in her life. Candi's tummy slid left and right like a cat on ice. If she didn't get out of this chair soon, she would pee her pants.

"Sorry about that, folks. Hope everyone's okay," the captain announced, offering zero explanation for the three hours of relentless turbulence.

Cleared to move around the cabin, Candi bolted up and sprinted to the bathroom. Without bothering to wipe the seat or put on the flimsy paper ring, she ripped off her tights and panties and relieved her overflowing bladder.

As she urinated, she exhaled, and her eyes fell to her underwear. A misshapen circle of crimson stained her skin-toned, lace panties. Crap. Of course, this is happening now, she thought, of all the times. No wonder she'd been feeling so blue, so teary. With all the travel, she'd lost track of her cycle. Her period used to remind her that she wasn't yet pregnant, but now it reminded her that Jasper was dead. She'd probably never be pregnant. Any remaining relief she felt from landing was sucked away like the blood-soaked toilet paper released into the airplane's metal commode.

With as much of a scowl as her Botoxed face would allow, she cleaned herself up and washed her hands, examining the half-moon tooth marks left by Foxy. He sure had a strong bite for such a small dog. What terrible timing. Menstrual cramps would soon commence; they always did. I'm definitely getting a hotel room now, she thought.

"What the fuck was that about?" Adrienne asked her as she exited the bathroom.

"My period just started."

"I mean the fucking flight." And with a frazzled expression Adrienne disappeared into the bathroom.

As the shaken passengers gathered their luggage, Candi checked on the couple with the dog. It was in the carrier case as she'd predicted and though he'd smacked hard into the plane's ceiling, he didn't appear to be severely injured. The couple thanked her profusely for trying to help. A woman in coach had either broken or sprained her ankle, many had puked, most had prayed, but otherwise, everyone was fine.

After the last passenger exited the plane, Chad turned to Candi with raised eyebrows. "That was the fucking worst flight of my entire life."

Candi could only manage a nod. Her uterus twisted like challah bread.

Adrienne approached holding a trash bag. "I need a martini or five."

"Let's wrap up and get the hell off this cursed plane," Chad said.

Before Adrienne or Chad could pressure Candi to hit the lounge for drinks, she finished her tasks and bounded up the exit ramp. Earlier, she'd wanted to ask the pilot about the bright lights outside, was it lightning? But at this point, she didn't care. Like a zombie, she merged into the throng of passengers traversing Pearson airport.

Tired parents, whining kids, college girls in sweatpants, Quebecois seniors, Asian businessmen, and women in black hijabs rushed past her. Of all the airports she'd visited, Pearson Airport was possibly her least favorite. It was the only airport Candi knew of where everyone went through U.S. Customs *before* getting on their plane, which caused a lot of congestion and delays. Now with the holidays and winter, everyone was traveling south. She almost missed the peak pandemic times, not the no-pay part when the airline furloughed her, but the no-crowds part. With travel fully open again, the scramble for warmer temperatures, less rules, and more palm trees was what cable news called "The Snowbird's Revenge." Every seat was occupied at every gate. There were no available phone chargers. A bottle of water cost as much as a sushi dinner back home. Passengers drank beer and wine, packed in at different bars. She passed a Tim Hortons coffee shop with about forty people waiting in line. In her exhausted state, Pearson felt like the New York Subway at rush hour.

Then, her brain stopped thinking and her body went into autopilot, reaction-less beyond its necessary duties to function. Her only mission: find a hotel room.

She walked for what felt like a mile through the packed terminal, searching for a spot where she could get a signal on her phone to look up a hotel. Stopping to lean against a wall near the gift shop, she suddenly felt so alone, though very much not alone. Before, she would have called Jasper when she landed. She would have told him all about the crazy flight.

A TV flashed the news headline: "Storm Catches Canada Off Guard." Surely it was freezing outside. She couldn't remember if there was a hotel attached to the airport, but that would be ideal, as she just wanted to lie down, but hadn't brought a heavy winter jacket or gloves. What was she thinking, flying through Canada so unprepared in the winter?

One bar of signal appeared on her phone, but it wasn't enough to open either a browser or a map. She wandered on, checking for a stronger signal. Outside, snow drifted by the airport's large windows, giving the building, decorated for the holidays, the feeling of a Christmas snow globe. She passed a giant suitcase branded with Coca Cola logos, people on iPads, and a massive Christmas tree.

Still no signal. The thick crowds seemed to be affecting her cell service. The visual stimuli, her period, and the throngs of people made Candi feel nauseous. I've got to get out of here, she thought, even if it means facing the cold and taking a cab to a hotel.

A young guy in a lime green sweater with dirty blond corkscrew curls, and baggy, tattered jeans weaved towards her. She slowed down. He appeared to be in a daze. His green eyes were fixed on her yet looked through her.

"Hey," she said, but he bumped into her brusquely without seeing her. He whispered something like, "With one drop, the ocean freezes." She faltered for a second on her heels. Swaying like a drunk, he then vanished into the roving throng.

An uneasy feeling rippled through her body, something akin to *déjà vu.* What was that about? She wondered. He didn't seem right. But as she stood there, confused, her eyes caught a sign mounted to the airport's ceiling: *Luftel*, with an arrow. Thank God. A hotel. Luftel, she knew from her travels, was a nice but economical Swedish hotel chain. Forgetting the strange young man, she followed the arrow and reached the breezeway connecting to the hotel.

Luftel's lobby buzzed with travelers, but the first thing Candi saw was Foxy, the teacup schnauzer from the plane, once again out of his case and unleashed. This thing is following me, she thought, or rather, I'm following it. The husband and wife waved. Candi forced a smile and waved back, while hoping that their room was as far away as possible from hers. The last thing she needed was a barking dog.

Reaching the counter, the receptionist informed her their booking system was down. Candi would need to book on the mobile app. She wanted to pound her fists and cry. Why did everything have to be so hard today? She wondered as she went to the front window of the lobby and leaned against the cold glass, hoping the change in position would provide a better signal. Taking another deep breath, she thought again of her Zoom therapist. Take it slow, he'd say. One thing at a time, and with her dog-bitten hand, she stabbed at her phone until it downloaded the hotel's stupid app.

Chapter Five

GRETCHEN GREEN'S GOTTA GO

The more she learned about heart attacks, the more she wanted to leave Toronto. And the more she wanted to leave, the harder the snow fell. Sam still wasn't answering her calls or texts. She had no holiday plans other than the mining conference and a half-baked idea of going to Tokyo after it was over, mainly because she liked to eat fried chicken, and that's what people in Japan did for Christmas. But really, what am I doing here? She wondered. My family needs me.

Or did they? She wondered as she smeared ChapStick on her dry lips. Obviously, her mother hadn't wanted her to come. Or was her mother just being defiant and stoic? Whatever Gretchen suggested, her mother proposed the opposite, as if agreeing would degrade her parental authority or some shit. It was so annoying. Like any child, sometimes she'd obey her mother, and sometimes she wouldn't. Her compliance depended more on her own rationale than on what her mother said.

Stomach aching from too much chocolate, she scrolled the net and watched YouTube videos about heart attacks on fast forward, then paced around the room again. Realizing that she certainly wasn't doing anything helpful for Kevin by staying in the hotel, she sent an email to the editor that had booked her for the mining conference, explaining the situation, but didn't wait for his response. Instead, she found a flight to Arizona leaving the next day and paid for it. Done. Confirmed. She'd keep her hotel room for the night and depart the following afternoon. Hopefully, the weather would ease up by then.

Trying to calm herself, Gretchen splashed water on her face and changed out of her pajamas and into regular clothes. She unwrapped her hair and fluffed up her short, tight black curls. I'll go to the hotel bar for cocktails to pass the time, she thought, but as she approached the elevator, a notification popped up on her phone: *Pre-Boarding for flight 2121 to Phoenix begins soon. Arrive three hours before your boarding call for international flights departing from Pearson Airport.*

She stared at her phone. *Boarding*? A sinking sensation rattled her core. Did I accidentally book today's flight? She wondered and looked at the confirmation again. Fuuuccccckkkk! The flight was leaving today.

Gretchen kicked into overdrive and bounded to her room. God, how could I have been so careless, she thought, but then again, maybe it was better to just go. It was too late to change it now and even if she could, was tomorrow even available? "Shit, shit, shit," she murmured as she shoved her remaining snacks, laptop, and toiletries into her bag, trying to ignore her growing sense of panic, and now she'd also wasted money on a hotel room for the night.

She took one last scan around the room, hoping she didn't forget anything important, then grabbed her suitcase and rushed out. Down the hallway, back to the elevator, and then through the breezeway connecting the building to the airport, Gretchen moved as fast as her thick thighs could deliver her without her boots sliding on the slick marble floor, wet with snow other travelers had tracked in. Her thighs burned and her bookbag bounced against her bottom. Crowds clumped at the baggage check station. She whirled around, trying to figure out where she was supposed to go, then finally spotted the U.S. preclearance—the Customs and Border Patrol area that every passenger leaving Toronto for America had to pass through. Fuck, she'd forgotten about customs.

Ever aware of her heart pounding in her chest, she filled in the last spot in the long line. Her wrist hurt from dragging her heavy rollaway. She'd packed for a week in Mongolia and a week in Japan, not for Arizona, but that couldn't be helped. She'd have to buy summer clothes after she arrived, maybe grab a rental car and hit a Walmart before she went to the hospital. Thoughts jumbled in her head as the clock ticked and she shifted on her feet, poking her head above the snake of passengers young and old, all on their way to the customs counter to scan their retinas. With almost everyone in black jackets, the experience felt grim, like she was about to board a Depression-era train.

At least the slow-moving line gave her a chance to catch her breath. There was still an hour left before her flight. Surely that was enough time to go through customs.

She waited. The line moved two steps forward.

Ahead of her was a door, and beyond it, the main preclearance area where the U.S. security guys manned rows of kiosks and processed travelers. If she remembered correctly, she'd have to scan her information on a screen, then show her ticket to the officer, then go to security and wait in another line to have her bag screened, then she could make it to her gate. God, she thought, why does everything need to be so complicated? It isn't this complicated anywhere else. Why do airports think they're so special?

"Excuse me," Gretchen said to a passing airport employee, "My flight leaves in less than an hour, can you help me get up to the front, so I don't miss my flight?"

The airport employee ignored her. Gretchen considered bypassing the line, but there was a tight bottleneck and another attendant at the door. She turned to the woman behind her, "I'll be right back. Can you hold my spot?"

An attendant blocked the door to the next room.

"Hi, could I go ahead?" Gretchen asked, approaching him with her head slightly cocked and a polite smile, "My flight is leaving in less than an hour."

"You have to go to the end of the line. Everyone has flights leaving," the attendant scowled.

But Gretchen didn't move, instead she gaped into the next room, beyond the door, a room full of more lines, curving and winding through roped off paths. No customs officers, no kiosks, no eyeball scanners. She hadn't even reached the right room.

"Please, my brother just had a heart attack and I'm trying to get home," she confessed to the attendant, a stocky, older man. "I don't want to miss my flight." Though it was terrible to say, with a rush of guilt, she added, "He might not make it through the night. Please."

The man sighed, but waved her on into the next room, giving another attendant a signal.

Gretchen exhaled and went all the way to the front of the line.

"We pay all this tax money, and our own country treats us like refugees," a white lady said.

"I've just never in all my life seen anything like this," another woman shook her head.

"This is worse than the airport in Haiti," a man added. "You don't expect this from Canada."

"It's always like this," an older man grumbled.

Gretchen's throat constricted. Always. Like. This? What the...? Who knew Toronto would be so bad? She thought. She'd flown through hundreds of airports and hadn't ever seen a line like this.

Babies cried. Kids whined and young women wearing too much makeup put on more makeup, looking at themselves on their phones. The mess of puffy fleece clothes and snot-covered noses barely budged.

Gretchen checked the time, praying that her flight would be delayed. It was thirty minutes before boarding.

She was about 50% of the way through the next room when a man in front of her started arguing with an airport worker. "This is ridiculous," he shouted. "I've been in this line for over an hour."

She couldn't hear what the worker said, but a lady beside the protesting gentleman also piped up. "Can't you let the Americans go through? Why do they need to check us too?"

Murmurs ran through the crowd. Indeed, it was a mix of Canadians, Americans, and other nationalities, all trying to get into the U.S.

A young woman behind her mumbled, "Typical Americans, always wanting special treatment. Canadians should have their own line."

Gretchen tried to tune out the crowd but couldn't. This isn't good, she thought. Everyone around her was tense, disgruntled, frustrated. Then a woman screamed. A fight erupted. The two men yelled and shoved each other, and three attendants jumped in. An overhead alarm went off. Other passengers tried to scatter, but there was no room. Some managed to duck under the ropes and force their way into the next room, dragging suitcases. Gretchen tried to do the same, but she couldn't. Irate travelers pushed and bunched together, trying to get through the door, but blocking it instead. She backed against a wall. The fight intensified. A man's head smacked the ground.

Security guards ran in and tackled the other angry men to the ground, along with a woman who had gotten involved. One man managed to throw the officer and run, but the airport officers stopped him and body-slammed him down like the rest. Gretchen again heard a thwack as his head cracked against the tile floor. People gasped.

"This isn't right! You can't do this," a tearful woman shrieked. The camera phones came out now, everyone under 50 and over six was filming the scene. Blood flowed out of the man's head onto the white floor. I've got to get out of here, she thought. Sweat pooled under her heavy breasts, dampening her sports bra. Her jaw locked and she gripped her bag. Keeping her eye on the door, she waited for an opportunity to bolt to the next room. Only had one room to go. She had to get to Kevin. She had to get to Arizona.

Chapter Six

CANDI KISSES

Finally inside her hotel room, Candi hoisted her rolling suitcase onto a rack, stripped naked, and took a long, hot shower. It was such a luxury to stay in a hotel instead of the lounge. After drying off in the thick hotel towel, she slipped on silk pajamas, ate some crackers, drank water, pulled the curtains shut, set her alarm clock, and watched a bad TV series about animals that went crazy from pesticides and attacked everyone at a zoo.

In the show, a zoologist overcome with desire—ignited by the apocalyptic animal vs. human war—passionately kissed her male lab assistant. Watching them make-out made Candi's breasts tingle. Will I ever make out with someone new? She wondered. Counting back, it had been twelve years since she'd kissed a new person; Jasper being her last new kiss. The thought bored and pleased her at the same time. I guess that's how it should be, she thought, remembering their awkward first kiss, tipsy off 22s, in his student apartment. It wasn't very romantic, but after she left his room, all she could think about was him. She held onto the memory, replaying it.

Maybe it would be her last first kiss. She couldn't imagine kissing anyone else, nor could she fathom going on a date. It had been way too long, and dating apps intimidated her. Guys only wanted casual hookups anyways, that's what Adrienne said.

Her mind flashed to the young man from the plane with his red headphones and huge feet. He'd flirted with her, sort of, but passengers often flirted with flight attendants. Plus, flirting on airplanes was different from talking to potential dates. Airplanes were like small countries, with their own rules and customs, separate from reality. Sometimes all the planes and destinations and check-ins and check-outs made her feel like she was 100 years old, like she'd lived many lifetimes, and been in too many places, yet always inside the same place: the airplane, the airport, taxis, hotels. And what have all these flights done to my fertility? She wondered. This question nagged her often. Are my genes not meant to replicate? Though without Jasper, does it even matter?

She ate a melatonin gummy and re-brushed her teeth. Smoothing her auburn hair, she examined her skin: dried out. After the corner of 33, and then 34, the changes in her appearance were undeniable. Crows' feet. She was no longer young. No matter how much she slept, new lines formed, and dark circles lurked under her eyes. The Botox only resolved so much. Even her breasts weren't as perky as last year. Not too long ago, she'd caught her first gray hair, glimmering in the bathroom light and complained to her mother.

"You're lucky," her mother had replied with a hearty laugh, "My gray hair started as soon as you were born, and I was only 29!"

"Did you dye it? I don't remember you having gray hair."

"No, I couldn't, because I was pregnant with your brother, and you can't use hair dye while you're pregnant. It's not safe for the babies."

"Is that still a thing?"

"It was in my day. They said no hair dye."

A clenching thought had seized Candi like a hand that wouldn't let go—what if I turn totally gray before getting pregnant? She imagined her belly protruding out under gray, wiry, stringy hair. At the time, the image had made her throat contract with an emotion that was hard to pin down—a mix of embarrassment, fear, shame, regret, and panic. She'd worried about it for days... until life had given her something much worse to consider. How she would love to still worry about hypothetical things, the concerns of a wife, not a widow. She'd gladly be a gray-haired pregnant lady now, if only she could still hold Jasper's hand.

Before the first pandemic, she and Jasper had bought a house together, near the Hoover Dam, on a cactus-lined street, with a backyard, trails, and a community pool. It was an average home, surrounded by steaming hot desert that damaged your feet in the summer, nothing too extravagant; his software job more than covered their expenses, but now, even with their savings, she'd soon have to sell the... No, she couldn't even consider it. The whole situation was unthinkable. She refused.

She yanked out two more gray hairs with her fingers. At least she had thick hair.

The zoopocalypse show went on. The zoologist and the assistant were working as a team to cure the animal's violent behavior. They had frantic sex in a broom closet. Candi got up one last time, inserted a fresh tampon, switched off the show, and let her thoughts drift again to the past, to Jasper washing his truck, spraying water, beaming, his tan skin, tattoos, black hair, thick arms. In a parallel universe, she'd grab him and kiss him like the lab assistant. Maybe that's what I'll dream about tonight, she hoped. As she imagined the scene, exhaustion overcame her, and Candi slept like she'd crossed nine time zones and back in 24 hours, which she had.

Chapter Seven

GRETCHEN GREEN CAN'T GO

Despite the brawl, customs didn't close. Gretchen shifted on her feet scanning and rescanning the area as security removed about fifteen people, everyone involved in the tussle. With the extra bodies gone, she inched up to the front of the line and finally entered the next room. An exhale escaped her lips. She could still make her flight.

At the counter, the machine snapped a photo of her brown eyes: identity verified.

"What brings you to Toronto?" the officer asked.

She explained the mining conference and he waved her ahead. Prepared to run to the gate, she picked up her pace, but her hopes dropped like a tossed snowball. A couple hundred people were in another line just as long as the one she'd left. Now, bags were getting scanned and checked. Everyone was slipping off their shoes and taking out laptops.

She glanced at the time on her phone: 15 minutes till boarding.

There was one open line. With chest high and chin raised, she strolled confidently to the attendant guarding the VIP or staff entrance. "My flight is about to leave, and I'm with the press," she said simply.

The lady gave a look that said, "sure you are..." but let her pass.

"Thank you, thank you so much," Gretchen rushed to the front, took off her shoes, scanned in, put them back on. It all seemed like so much hassle for no good reason. She collected her belongings and ran to her gate, her breath coming in short, hot gasps. I'm gonna make it. I'm gonna make it, she thought. And she did, just as the crew announced priority boarding, but before she could relax or catch her breath, a screeching sound cut off the announcement. Everyone looked around, including Gretchen. Then an even louder sound, almost like a car crash, then sirens. She covered her ears. People bolted in all directions. More alarms went off. Men shouted. Bodies shoved past her. Paralyzed with confusion, her eyes found a window.

Outside in the snow, a plane skidded into her plane and spun it away from the gate, then lit into flames. The airport lights snapped out. Gretchen dropped to her knees and covered her head before the first explosion, instinctively, from her duck and cover training that she'd done while in Iraq.

Another boom, another crash. Screams.

Her heart sped. She couldn't think. She couldn't breathe. Is this a terrorist attack? She wondered with her hands over her head, face to the ground. A thought whipped through her mind —I survived all that war reporting to die in Canada? Another deafening roar, then a third explosion; splintering glass and wood, parts of the ceiling fell on her. Children howled. The smell of smoke and fire entered her nose.

No. NO. NO. Hell no. She didn't survive air raids in Iraq to die in vanilla-ass, boring Toronto. With a surge of adrenaline, she pushed herself up and brushed the drywall dust and debris off her face. With one hand on her carry on and the other over her head like a shield, she ran as fast as she could, through all the people, past darkness and whirring red lights, the sirens, and medics—through the chaos, fear, and panic of disorder—all the way back through security, through customs, and to her hotel room door.

Chapter Eight
CANDI DREAMS

Snow spread far and wide, across an open field, a pale landscape. Candi stood in a cloud of cold fog. In the distance, a figure floated towards her. A shrouded human form, its red robes blew in the wind like a Bedouin traversing a desert; only this was tundra.

Through the haze—a man's voice, "Candi," he called.

"Hello?"

The figure ran towards her. It was Jasper. But before she could reach him, he crumpled in a heap.

"Jasper!" Candi screamed. She ran to him through a gale of snow. It burned her cheeks. "Are you okay!? Jasper!" She stumbled to his body, but the motionless form was only empty clothes, a mound of damp, velvet fabric.

"Jasper," she screamed again.

A warm hand touched her shoulder. Candi whipped around. It was the weird boy from the airport. His eyes burned an alien, fiery blue.

"It's time," he said and grabbed her shoulders.

"No," she screamed and turned back to the pile of fabric on the ground, but it was gone. "Jasper," she cried.

The boy spun her around by the shoulder. "Look!" He

pointed a black handgun at her. Her eyes opened wide and panic filled her throat.

"Don't be afraid," he said, "Just do as they say." Then he turned the gun around and shot himself in the chin. His head exploded and his body dropped into the snow. Blood splattered red on white.

A sound blasted overhead like a bomb exploding.

Candi fell spine-first into the cold snow. Had he shot her too? She kept falling, falling, and falling. But she felt no pain. She gazed at the sky. The sun was no longer the sun. It was a groaning, globular, electric blue mass.

Chapter Nine

CANDI CRASH

Like an elementary school teacher on a snow day, Candi lay under the hotel's white feather duvet and scrolled her cellphone. She'd had a terrible dream, but the details were fuzzy now. Airline updates showed her return flight further delayed. There was also a text message from WildTina: "Girl, are you okay!?! I saw the news! Shit is crazy!" followed by several "mind-blown" emojis.

That's weird, Candi thought. Tina rarely texted her. What news? The message had come in last night while she was sleeping. She responded: "I'm in an airport hotel in Toronto, actually. Where are you? Chad and I were just talking about how we missed you!"

Tina responded, "Oh thank God. Is Chad with you? He's not texting me back."

Candi got out of bed but didn't answer Tina. Whatever her and Chad had going on, she didn't want to know. Not in the mood for chit chat, she wandered to the window and pulled open the drapes. A dense, opaque sky poured snowflakes, thick and steady, heavy; they coated the urban airport's landscape in a cold, dull cream, like someone had dumped shredded, bleached plastic over everything. Her green eyes widened to drink in the scene. How had it already snowed so much in one night? She wondered.

The winter weather blocked her view of Toronto's skyline, only the parking lot's street lamps and multicolored Christmas lights showed through the storm. She returned to bed, to fret over the situation. There wasn't much time until Christmas, and she was supposed to work again next week, on a domestic route. If winter stuck her long enough in Toronto, she wouldn't have time to prepare for Christmas, or for Jasper's...

She wondered if she should ask for a late checkout, but what she wanted was to get on the next plane and leave. That would be ideal. Then I'll be home, and I'll go to the grocery store, she thought.

Wait, she thought, is that really what I'm looking forward to? The grocery store? God, I'm really getting old...But she wanted to batch prepare different types of holiday cookies, to put them in lovely red boxes, to dole them out as gifts to neighbors, friends, and family. She wanted to feel normal, to get cozy at home and play the Nutcracker soundtrack. She'd make Jasper's favorite cookies, the peanut butter ones with Hershey's Kisses in the middle, just like every year.

Another hour slipped by. So much of her job, her life, her entire existence, it seemed, was waiting. Still no flight update, so no need to get dressed, but maybe there was a robe she could put on. She opened the room's mirrored closet door. Indeed, two white robes hung beside a long, black, quilted winter jacket. Oops, someone must be missing their coat, she thought, and held up the weighty garb. It felt unusually heavy, like a weighted blanket. She considered calling the front desk to report it missing, but didn't. Instead, she slipped on the jacket and pulled the fur-lined hood around her face. In the mirror, the expensive coat made her look like a scientist in Antarctica. Though it was big, she could use it to go for a walk outside, to get some fresh air. Then I'll take it to the front desk and return it, she decided. Fresh air will be so nice. She also hadn't experienced snow in quite a while. Maybe she would take a selfie outside in the jacket and send it to her parents.

It was an expensive coat, that was for sure, and very warm, with enormous square pockets. Feeling like a woman swallowed by a bear, she stuck her hands into the fur-lined pockets. In the deep left pocket, her fingers felt something hard, a rectangle.

Curious, Candi drew out the unknown object. It wasn't a box at all, but a book; blocky, with a dark green, velvet cover and gold edges, like an antique Bible. How odd, she thought. Was it a diary? She opened to a random page and wonder engulfed her.

The textured paper contained a painting of a snow-covered dome burrowed in a pine forest. The windows of the dome glowed with yellow light, leaking like liquid into the bluish, snowy scenery. The strokes of paint were exquisite and small, like pin lines and intricate Van-Gogh-esque swirls in the night sky. Traces of star formed beings and outlines of constellations sparkled in the sky amidst swaths of green, northern lights.

Wow, this is a work of art, she thought. Someone made this by hand. She flipped through the book. All art, but as she looked closer, she noticed perforated lines. The pages were quilted like the jacket, like a book of stamps.

Another page showed a colorful treasure map like something out of a children's fairy tale collection. Strange. Maybe this was someone's artistic sketchbook, she thought, but closer inspection revealed it printed on actual stamps. She turned to another page; it went on in the same fashion—a blank page, followed by a page of stamps with painted art. Some of the pages were actual paint and some were prints. Each piece had machine-cut, perforated edges. What a weird, but cool book, she thought. It must be a collector's item. She studied the colorful, psychedelic images, then flipped to the beginning.

On the back of the cover, where an owner might write their name, it was blank, as was the first page, but on the second page, Candi found a verse of text, in fancy, emerald-color cursive letters with a border of blue diamonds:

"Hello Cellular Earth World Traveler,

To begin: eat one tab at a time.
Don't be greedy. Greed is for weeds. You're a tree.
If you must, wait one hour before eating more.
DO NOT MIX WITH BEETS.
DO NOT GET WET.
Enjoy your Trip.
See you Coolside."

What? Eat one tab? Oh god, she realized, they weren't postal stamps at all. The book was full of LSD!

As if clutching hot coals, Candi dropped the drug-filled thing. It hit the floor with a soft thud, and she gasped. The pages fell open to a picture of a grinning, black-skinned Santa Claus with candy corn teeth, swirling, pinwheel peppermint eyes and his hat on fire.

Candi threw off the jacket and ran to the bathroom and washed her hands. Why would anyone leave this in the room? It must be a mistake. Did the LSD get on me? Was it really LSD? She vigorously scrubbed both hands and wrists with soap. *Cellular Earth Traveler...* What kind of weirdo had made this?

She'd tried acid once when she was 20. The beginning was fun, but the end was bad. She'd felt like a paranoid crack addict on the come down. That part of the memory came back to her as if it were yesterday. Thinking she needed a drink, she'd gone into 7/11 with her friends, but it had felt like being in the looney bin. Too bright. Everyone was watching her. She didn't understand their faces. The noises and their words jumbled together. She'd panicked and run into an alley; then she'd gotten lost. Her friends got frustrated with her. No one, including herself, understood why she'd freaked out so hard.

Since then, she hadn't touched psychedelics. How many years ago was that? She wondered. 12? God, what an awful number.

Was college really that long ago? She couldn't remember how LSD worked besides that you put it on your tongue, but could it also go through skin? That's the last thing I need right now... to start tripping...

She speculated on the stamp book's owner. Maybe they'd come into the hotel, hung up their winter jacket, and slept, but overslept and rushed to their morning flight, forgetting their jacket in the closet? Bold move—to fly with a book of LSD disguised as a diary. Then again, why would anyone search inside someone's diary? It was genius to put it in the most personal kind of book. She'd only been looking for a bathrobe, not for all of this. Annoyed, she washed her hands again, then splashed water on her frazzled face. Returning to the bedroom, with her sock-covered foot, she flipped the book shut, but instead of closing, it fell to a page with yet another holiday scene—a cozy living room, complete with a rosy fireplace, only long, fat red and black snakes hung from the chimney where the Christmas stockings should be. "Fuck." Candi said and kicked the book under her bed.

But then she felt stupid. Jasper would be laughing at me right now, she thought, he'd be rolling with laughter, probably clutching his stomach, making fun of me for being afraid of a book, of all things.

Jasper loved to tease her. Tears formed in her eyes. She stared at the spot on the brown carpet where the book used to be. Jasper was never going to laugh or hug her again, at least not in real life. The realization made her sadder than she ever thought possible. She wanted to call him right now and tell him about the book. She wanted to laugh with him. She wiped a bulging tear before it could drip onto her cheek, then got a towel from the bathroom and used it to cover her hand. She fished the book out from under the bed and put it in her bedside drawer, like a Bible, then rethinking that idea, slid it under her mattress. She didn't want housekeeping to come in and think she had a book full of drugs.

She called Jasper's number. She still paid his cellphone bill, though she didn't need to waste money, but she couldn't bring herself to disconnect the line. It rang 6 times, like it always did, then went to his voicemail.

"Hey, you've reached Jasper Burns. Please leave a message. Ciao." Beep.

She squeezed her eyes shut, as if holding in tears would turn the room into a different one, as if when she opened her eyes, Jasper would be on the bed.

"Babe," she mumbled into the phone. "I found a crazy book in my hotel room. I miss you."

She hung up and bawled into her pillow, crying until her tears ran out.

The afternoon passed as wearily as the morning. Snow continued to fall, and the airline sent another message. Her return flight was now canceled. She stared at the message. That never happened. The airline always provided details on the replacement route in these situations. She texted Chad and Adrienne, but neither responded. Maybe their phones weren't getting a signal in the lounge. Employees could book hotels at the airline's expense, it said. But canceled? She tried calling her supervisor in the airline admin office, but no one answered.

Well, at least touching the book hadn't triggered an acid trip. That was clear now. Duh. But ugh. She just wanted to get home. Is that too much to ask? She thought, switching on the TV. She flipped through the Canadian channels in search of an update on the snowstorm until she landed on the local news. The bright image showed a reporter and emergency vehicles. Then the camera cut to a plane, or rather, what was left of a plane. Candi's mouth went slack, and her eyes locked onto the screen. She turned up the volume. WildTina's text suddenly made sense.

The news story wasn't about the snowstorm; a plane had crashed. The male reporter in a long black jacket, very similar to the one in her hotel closet, stood in a blustery white gale on an airport runway. Behind him steamed the rear of a blackened, burnt, snow-dusted jumbo jet. The camera panned to reveal the plane's front tip smashed into the side of a terminal. To the side of the terminal's gaping hole was the outline of a red maple leaf, still visible like a cattle brand through the blowing snow. Then the clip switched to security camera footage; people stampeded and screamed through an airport.

It was Pearson Airport, the journalist said.

Candi blinked like a ream of short-circuiting Christmas tree lights. With shaking hands, she typed another message on her phone to Adrienne, "Omg I'm just seeing the news about the plane crash. Are you okay? Are you with Chad in the lounge?" She inhaled and exhaled big gulps of air as her fingers tapped the phone's letters in rapid succession. Which terminal was the lounge in? Which terminal had the plane hit? Why weren't they answering their phones?

The television coverage cut back to the journalist on the runway. "The search continues for missing passengers, as well as flight crew." Ambulances, fire trucks, and snowplows drove around the terminal. The reporter yelled into his microphone, while holding onto his own knit cap with his other hand, trying to combat the forces of nature around him. "A flight from Phoenix landing at Pearson last night lost control on the icy runway, and in the unexpected high winds skidded into another plane and then into the terminal, causing damage to several gates, to the terminal one shopping area, an executive lounge, and multiple bathrooms and restaurants," he went on to explain. "Reports are still coming in, but at present thirteen people are reported dead and more than fifty are injured."

A headline scrolled on the bottom of the screen: "The government of Canada has issued a state of emergency for all of Ontario, Manitoba, and Quebec in response to the unusual blizzard conditions."

Stretchers and medical personnel filled the demolished airport news scenes. Candi clutched her phone. The message to Adrienne showed as undelivered. She called Adrienne's number. It went straight to voicemail. She called Chad; it rang, but no answer.

"All flights incoming and outgoing to Toronto are grounded

until further notice," the reporter added before the catastrophe footage switched to the main news desk, where two other journalists shook their heads in disbelief. "Now, we turn to Najib with the weather update," the woman anchor said.

A chill slid down Candi's neck like skin rubbed with melting ice. Goosebumps rose on her arms and legs, and she curled under the covers of the hotel bed that probably saved her life.

Part Two

BAGGAGE

Teddy's Cold News Chorus

I am Teddy, coming again to you straight from Timmy Cratchit's International Canadian airport coffee production line.

This Hortons was spared, but my head is gashed.

A plane crashed and turned to ash.

I'll stop the bleeding with Band-Aids and pressure, but the people, oh the people, they won't stop eating.

"Pumpkin Spice Donut."
"Double Double."
"Two raspberry crullers and a bag of bits!"
"Would you like sugar with that?"
"A chocolate muffin."
"MAYBE TWO?"

But I've stopped listening. I suck on a watery Ice Capp. I toast another cinnamon raisin bagel and think, hmm, what does the working man or woman really want? To get to her destination? To finish for the day? To get paid? To be a mother or a father? This? Or this? Or that? Who died on that plane and why?

These people here, they come from everywhere,

but they aren't all alike.
I imagine if we were all dogs.
Would the airport be a kennel or a park?
So many colors, shapes, dispositions, and teeth.
There's a Beagle, Terrier, and Poodle.
An Afghan Hound, a Bichon frisé, a mutt.
Do I see any Labradors? Retrievers? Great Danes?
No, it's mostly Doodles, Schnoodles, and Shih Tzus,
Not a Pitbull in sight...

Yesterday, a strange fellow came to my line. He handed me a bag of tings. The boy with the blond curls.

Zed was what he called himself. He had a lot to say. It started with a page, simple instructions, a picture of a rainbow in a snowglobe...

He said *they* had a lot to say.

I gave him his latte and his change. His change... as if a few loonies and toonies could cause a metamorphosis. Then he left me here at the Timmy's. He had other places to be. I wish I did.

"Don't forget to roll down the rim!" I called to him as he walked away. "You could win!"

And what's the opposite of winning?

Freezing to death or burning in flames?

Maybe.

At least I wore my long underwear. My bum is toasty roasty like two oxtails in a pot and this grease is hot, and oh the smells — the holiday smells, the feet smells, the Christmas smells, the ringing bells, the rats with nests of peanut shells.

Aren't we all like these deep fried balls—a little guilty and a little great?

When's lunch?

Jerk chicken and hibiscus tea, please.
Wish I had me an island wife to cook saltfish and callaloo.
But alas, this corporate cappuccino will have to do.
Though my tummy is rumbling so loud I can barely hear the orders anymore.
In the army, when you can't hear the orders, people die.

Please no more orders, please no more bad news...

What's that old song again?
You can check in if you like, but you really won't want to stay...

But, hey, I digress.

Let me continue this Christmas yarn before the weather really turns to shit. In the snowglobe, you can see it too. Call me clairvoyant, call me Mr. Cleo, or just call me your poetic friend.

The rest of the folks here, they come and go. Are they victims or vixens? Something in between? What about the ones you don't even see, the ones who change your life so radically that you'd kill them if you only knew... but you don't, and you never will.

Life is full of 'em.

And how do people eat these sweet, sweet pastries at all hours of the day?

For the love of God, it's only 5am...

Now, back to scooping dough.

I'll talk to you soon.

'Cause this isn't the only scoop.

While your flights are boarding, please take warning—this year's Christmas surprise may lead to your demise.

Chapter Ten

GRETCHEN'S TIPS

Giant yellow and gray cubist machines combed the airport's grounds, pushing snow. To where? Gretchen wondered. Wind whipped across her face like paper cuts. The blizzard worked faster than the plows. With her still-valid boarding pass for her delayed flight, no one had stopped her from reentering the airport, going back through security, locating the damaged terminal zone, and walking the temporary rescue ramp connecting the gate to the scene on the ground. Everyone working at the airport was busy with more important things than her. She didn't fully understand why she'd come back, seeing the crash site wasn't going to get her home any faster, but still, something had compelled her. Something told her this was more than just an accidental disaster; it was a story—the one thing she couldn't resist.

Charred metal, blood, and suitcases spilled and sunk into the thick snow like macabre sprinkles on a vanilla cupcake. The chemical, almost iron smell of burnt plastic and leaking jet fuel wafted in the cold air. Vehicles and airport personnel roamed the white scene and it made her remember a storybook from her childhood about a red snowplow named Katy with human attributes. Katy saved a town from a blizzard, but this was not that.

There wasn't a happy ending for the people on the planes. The news said the death toll had risen to thirty.

Smoke lingered in the air and it was quieter than it should be, almost too quiet, too much space for her to think. The snow dampened the sounds, choking them down.

Brrr. She contemplated going back inside, getting a coffee, parking it somewhere and calling Sam, but Sam hadn't picked up any of Gretchen's calls or texts since their last fight. No, better to stay here and survey the damage, take some photos. Then she could write her crash piece from a spot in the airport, ingesting the chaos, mixing it into words. There were plenty of things to write about, that was for sure.

A group of Canadian police officers trudged by in knee-high boots. EMTs milled around the wreckage like black ants in a sugar bag. The fire department wound up long hoses. She pinched her nostrils shut with a gloved finger, tired of smelling burnt things.

A Canadian police officer spotted Gretchen and waved her over.

She hesitated for a second, then obliged, moving towards him in the wind.

The police officer eyed her, "You're with CBP?"

"Reuters."

"You shouldn't be out here."

"No worries." Gretchen raised her black gloved hands, "I'll head back."

The officer nodded and pointed to a makeshift entrance with plastic sheeting, leading to the damaged terminal, "Walk around from here to the press entrance."

"Gotcha. Thanks." Gretchen pulled her hat tighter over her short, curly hair and lumbered in the direction the cop had pointed.

As she headed inside, her thoughts returned to her brother Kevin. Was he out of the ICU? She still hadn't seen anything about a new Covid strain in the news. Then again, all the Canadian news was focused on the *Snowpacolypse*, as they called it, and the crash. She'd sent texts to her mother and Kendra, asking for updates, but neither had responded.

More emergency personnel streamed past her in heavy jackets and blaze orange vests. News crews with cameras on black tripods formed a ring beyond where the Canadian police encircled the crash site, creating a separate corral with yellow tape. From her days of working embedded with the military in Iraq, she recognized that the scene wasn't actually secure. Media were all over the place, as were workers from different organizations. Didn't the airport management realize that nefarious elements could wander in and out if they didn't keep a close watch on the crash site's access? Canadians could be so laissez faire compared to Americans, so worried about some things, like being sensitive to everyone's emotional needs, yet oblivious to real threats. Though post-pandemic, no amount of government incompetence really surprised her.

Thankfully, customs had been spared from the crash damage. What a mess it would have been if the plane had hit customs. All those arrivals could have run inside or even left the airport and just entered Canada. Then they'd really have a problem on their hands. She wondered if some still had. Surely there were deportees, criminals in transit, and asylum seekers who had jumped at opportunities caused by the crash's disorder.

Near the entrance, two men and a woman in civilian clothing opened another door, off to the side of the plastic sheeting. Gretchen squinted at the figures through the dense snowfall, then decided to follow the trio. Maybe there was a separate press room. But the door was locked. Dang, she thought. I walked all the way over here for nothing? She brushed snow from the arms of her jacket. Shaking off her boots, something blue, sticking up in the snow caught her eye. It pointed up in the snow like a golf-tee next to an abandoned baggage cart. She walked over, then recoiled. It was someone's two fingers.

"Hey," she yelled, backing slowly away from the frozen hand. "Hey, I need some help."

The person was totally submerged in the snow, though it was less than 24 hours since the crash. They'd been reaching out or maybe tried to dig themselves out. Perhaps the crash had knocked them out. She shuddered inside her coat. How many other bodies were out here, buried in the night? Some injured people must have escaped the crash. She didn't want to think about what they would find when the snow melted.

Gretchen considered digging around the body, to check if the person was alive, but it seemed impossible for them to have survived. She needed to find an EMT or the police. Slipping off her right glove, she snapped a picture of the icy digits, as evidence. The cold bit at her own pink fingers. Soon, she knew, even these tips would be submerged, lost, like blue fossils in the ceaseless cascade of white.

Chapter Eleven

CANDI WALK

The lobby's revolving glass jowls spat Candi into a landscape as welcoming as a polar bear's throat. Winter air snatched at her beige sweatpants. Careful not to slip on ice by the door, unclear of her destination, she navigated through the dense gale of snow which shrunk her visibility to only what was right in front of her.

She strained not to imagine the dead bodies of her friends, yet her mind wanted to conjure it, to create a fictional horror film, though at least the true image was only fictional. She hadn't seen the crash. Chad and Adrienne might still be alive. Her projections and worries would eventually fade. She hadn't really seen anything, not like what happened to Jasper. His death—she'd never unsee it.

The baggy stranger's coat kept her torso warm, but her face tingled, and her cheeks burned. Without gloves, she shoved her bare hands into the fur-lined deep pockets, just as she'd done when she found the book of LSD. At least she'd packed boots, though they were more for fashion than warmth—the fake, black leather kind you wore with a dress in New York City in the fall. The hotel staff had made an attempt to clear and salt the sidewalk, but it hadn't worked; the snow fell too fast. She pulled the oversized jacket's hood over her face, and pulled up her sweater, covering herself up to her eyes. Maybe I should go back inside, Candi thought, followed by another thought—one that replayed —I almost died. I almost died. I almost died. I almost died. I almost died. She shuddered and shut down her dark, twisted thoughts. Forging ahead, she vowed to enjoy the fresh air, but the extreme chill made it impossible.

With a sense of defeat, having only gone about three blocks, Candi turned back, but as she did, a shrouded figure trudged towards her, closing in, a human form hunched in the blizzard wearing a dark green jacket, brown fur trapper-style hat, and a long black scarf that blew like a cat's tail wagging and twitching. Candi squinted at the short figure. Surely a child wouldn't be out here alone, she thought.

It moved closer and called out in garbled, strange syllables that Candi couldn't understand. It wasn't a child, but an older woman with her arms held out, spewing a string of unknown words, her expression panicked.

"I'm sorry, I don't understand. I only speak English," Candi said.

More alarmed sounding sentences came out and she waved her hands around, animated, as if she was trying to warn Candi of something. Frustration contorted the woman's expression and her black eyes watered. "*Naneun geudeul-eul boassgo ulineun modu jug-eul geos-ibnida*," the woman raised her voice and pointed at the sky.

"English?" Candi repeated.

The stranger grabbed her arm and tugged her away from the direction of the hotel.

"Hey." Candi twisted her arm away. This was uncalled for. Had she come from the hotel? Or the airport? Parking lots and highway ramps surrounded them and you couldn't see beyond a few feet.

"We need to get inside," Candi yelled. "It's too cold."

The woman waved her hands. Candi caught the word

Toronto, and the lady pointed to the city, then trudged into the cloud of white and disappeared.

Instinctively, Candi called out, "Hey, come back." But there was no answer.

She needed to get inside now. Her toes were going numb. Toronto was a 30-minute drive at best, and in this storm... She blinked the snow off her ginger lashes. Without mittens, proper footwear, and a balaclava, the relentless blizzard was too much for her. Walking as fast as she could, she went back to the hotel to find someone to help the older woman.

Disgruntled passengers packed the noisy lobby. Candi waited in the concierge's line, shivering with stinging eyes and red skin. She squeezed her hands, trying to wake them, to recirculate her blood. She shook out her feet. There were no feelings in her toes; they had fallen asleep.

The man at the desk didn't bother smiling.

"Hi, I — I'm staying here and I'm concerned. I'm not sure who I should talk to." She leaned against the counter and lowered her hood. "I-I went outside, and there was an older woman, a senior citizen, wandering around in the snow. She seemed very confused. I think she needs help."

"Outside the hotel?" The man's blank expression shifted to worry.

"Yes. Someone should help her. I tried, but she walked away, and I don't have the right winter clothes."

The concierge took down a few details from Candi and assured her that they'd send security to look for the woman.

The older lady's terror-filled black eyes and screeching voice stuck with her, gave her chills as Candi rode the elevator up to her room. Surely, no one could survive for long in that bitter cold. If it was her own mother, she'd want someone to help. Hopefully, the hotel would find the woman, but maybe she should also call 911. Did Canadians have that?

She dialed the number on her room's landline but got a busy signal. Weird. Restless, she considered her options. The stroll outside had done nothing to diffuse her stress. No news on her flight home. I'll check out the gym, Candi thought. Go for a walk on the treadmill. That would wake up her cold feet and exercise always calmed her, but she didn't have sneakers. Maybe she could go back into the airport and buy some? Even with the crash, some stores must still be open. Plus, she still had Christmas gifts to buy. Then, after, she could return to the lobby to check on the status of the missing woman.

With the stranger's coat under her arm, she returned to the terminal. As she walked, her toes throbbed and tingled. Finally, they're waking up, Candi thought.

She breezed through security with her flight attendant pass and found the shopping area just as busy as the day before. The Tim Horton's line was just as long. In a duty-free store she grabbed a bottle of red wine, then added a second bottle, and a bottle of Canadian whiskey in a special edition holiday box for her brother. She also picked out a Blue Jay's hoodie for her nephew, and a fancy holiday package of Ontario Ice wine for her mom and dad, as well as some maple syrup and cookies for Jasper's mom and dad, and chocolate CN towers for her niece and nephew.

Moving on, she found a clothing store with yoga gear that had a pair of gray and teal sneakers in her size. Though it felt weird to try them on with her feet still half asleep, and the nerves in her toes fired sharp pains through the arc of her foot, causing her to wince. Shouldn't she be thawed out by now?

She also bought herself a pair of yoga pants and a matching fitted top, then gasped at the bill's high total, over two hundred Canadian dollars, but swiped her card anyway. She figured she'd randomly cheated death, so she may as well treat herself.

In the gym, stranded businessmen, middle-aged women in sweats, and young gym rat types occupied every fitness machine. As she scanned the room, a bolt of bright color jumped out at her —a tall man running on a treadmill in a neon orange track suit wearing giant red headphones. Candi almost groaned out loud.

She'd recognize those headphones anywhere. It was the guy from the plane with his leg in the aisle.

She looked away and caught the eye of another man, older than her, in a snug gray t-shirt, with short, gelled black hair, tan skin, and a face like a brown James Bond. He offered her a sly smile from a weight machine. His skin shimmered with sweat. Candi blushed and looked away, only to meet the eye of the young guy from her flight in the gym's mirror. He waved at her and his expression lit up, excited. She raised her hand with the most uncommitted greeting possible, then quickly left. No point in staying with all the machines in use. Ugh, I bought this stuff for nothing, she thought.

Returning to the lobby, Candi inquired about the missing woman, but the same concierge was no longer there, and no one else knew anything. With a twinge of guilt for not doing more to help, defeated and hungry, she wandered to the hotel's restaurant, but it was closed.

"There's a Tim Hortons in the airport," a cleaner outside the restaurant offered.

"Any other places? The Tim Hortons' line was really long."

"Figures." The cleaner's eyes reconnected with her vacuum, no doubt as unhappy as Candi with current circumstances. Like fuck off white lady, at least you don't have to suck dirt off the floor.

Candi retreated to her room, yanked off her new sneakers, then squealed. Her toes still felt weird. She flung herself on the unmade bed and hoisted her feet up like they belonged to someone else. Ten minutes went by with her just looking at the drab ceiling while her sock-covered toes throbbed. Still feeling unusually cold, she turned up the room's thermostat and wrapped her lower body in the hotel's duvet. Thankfully, her fingers had returned to their normal, beige color.

She called Chad again. Now his phone was completely off. After reassuring her parents that she was still alive, she called Adrienne ten, twenty times. WildTina called her, but she didn't answer. She couldn't bear the awkward conversation—or the possibility that Chad and Adrienne might be dead.

With a heavy exhale, she retrieved the art book and let it fall open to a random page. The stamps revealed a mountainous forest scene with falling snow and a naked, purple-skinned woman facing forward, floating above the pines with her tongue stuck out and a third eyeball open on her forehead. Silver snowflakes sprouted from the woman's ears and lavender hair. Rays of blue light streamed from her outstretched fingers. Luminous beings floated around her like giant, translucent sea creatures, like the mountains were under water.

Candi traced her fingers over the art, no longer worried about drugs seeping somehow into her skin. Who cared? There was nothing good to eat and no one she wanted to talk to.

Looking at the art in the book, she thought again about the time she'd taken LSD. She'd been with Jasper and his friends, Jake and Jenny. Jake. She hadn't thought about him in a long time. Was he the last person I kissed before Jasper? She wondered. They'd called themselves the 3J's, like a gang, and she'd always felt slightly less glamorous than the rest of them, slightly less cool, like a five amongst 10s. Jenny was especially beautiful and tall, like a model, very chic, from Sioux City and half Native American. Candi closed her hazel eyes and remembered the better part of her last acid trip.

> It was close to dawn in Death Valley, the sand like a frying pan. They found a swimming pool and listened to the clouds tell stories. She and Jasper weren't dating yet. They were just friends, but Jake had walked with her well past the campsite, to the moon, he said. He took her hand, and kissed her cheek, a timid kiss, to see if she'd comply, and she did, more out of intrigue than desire. The acid made her float and of course kissing your friends felt perfectly normal when everything else turned unreal. His lips on hers. The heat of the landscape. The wide sky. The world

> stopped. She had gone to the moon. But worried Jenny would see them, she'd also felt nervous. Jenny had a crush on Jake, so kissing him seemed wrong. Still, she'd let Jake slide his tongue in her mouth and stroke her breasts through her bra... But she put a stop to things, wandering off without an explanation, when his hand moved to unzip her jeans. Then that was it—their one and only kiss. A few weeks later, she started dating Jasper, and she never looked back, at least not until now.

Atop the hotel's white duvet, she wanted to remember more. She visualized the bright blue sky, cotton clouds, the LSD, the joy, Jake in cutoff jeans, the taboo of kissing her best friend's crush—but even more than that, she remembered Jasper's carefree happiness. He was the one she'd always wanted to kiss, not Jake. She'd wanted Jasper since the first time she'd seen him, in the dorm's elevator. Around their campfire that night, his large brown eyes sparkled, his shaggy dark hair and olive skin, his half unbuttoned, oversize men's shirt, he resembled an Italian movie star, like he should be out in a vineyard picking grapes.

God, she'd had a good time for most of the trip. It was only later that she'd started to feel bad.

The evening of her memory spiraled off in different threads, in a simple, but sad way, as one relives things they can never experience again. The last time she'd seen Jake or Jenny was at Jasper's Zoom wake, as the pandemic had prevented any in-person gatherings by the time Jasper's mother had relented to having the wake. Candi had barely said anything during the online event— "Thank you." Or "I know." "Yes." "Okay". The whole affair had been so, so hard, and so detached. Many people had turned off their screens. No one knew what to say. A woman she couldn't identify hadn't put her zoom on mute and they could hear the TV in the background. Was everyone just supposed to listen? The sound quality glitched during Jasper's dad's final words. She eventually muted her mic and turned off her own screen because she hadn't wanted anyone to see her cry, but then Jasper's mom criticized her for it later. No one had remembered to press record, though maybe this was a good thing. She could cry just thinking about it. Many of their friends were mutual, but after his death, as if stifled by the tragedy, those friendships sputtered out. She disliked seeing anyone connected to him. For months, she had retreated into a deep introversion, spending her free time with Netflix dramas and tortilla chips. But now she regretted pulling so far away, because the pandemic had also done something weird to everyone. Friendships felt almost unrecoverable. Unspoken conversations loomed like dirty dishes in a sink.

She could text Jake and Jenny right now, tell them about the book of acid, tell them she missed them both, tell them that she wasn't okay, but she didn't.

Chapter Twelve

GRETCHEN'S DISASTERPIECE

Hands in her pockets, Gretchen slinked through the airport. The police really weren't nice, she thought. They should've thanked her for finding the dead man's body, but instead they'd acted like dick wads. Then again, why was she surprised? It's not like the police and Black journalists were buddy-buddy these days.

Other reporters swarmed a roped-off area lined with lightless, duty-free stores and vacant perfume kiosks. They segmented the terminal to contain the press, emergency crew, and government agency personnel. The collective mission was to assist with rescuing missing people and repairing the damage caused by the crashed plane. Gretchen shivered. With the multiple holes in the building, cold air couldn't be denied entry. Everyone kept on their ski jackets and hats. Another female reporter typed on a laptop in wool gloves. Maybe she'd have to go back to the hotel. No way she'd get anything constructive written without heat.

She was also hungry. A snack from Tim Hortons could work, then lunch at the hotel later. She'd love a large Double-Double and a warm crueler, though her pants already felt tight, and Christmas hadn't even begun. If only the yummiest foods didn't also make you chunky. Wouldn't it be great, she thought, if I could eat a donut a day and not turn into a glob of goo? By New Year's she'd probably need a size up in jeans. Thank you, Thanksgiving. Not to mention all the fights with her on-and-off-again-girlfriend Sam that kept her in a perpetual state of stress eating.

Gretchen texted her mother and Kendra. Neither had anything new to report about Kevin. Her brother was in the same condition. No visitors were allowed into the ICU to see him given the fear around a potential new Covid strain.

"I'm at my wits end," her mother replied.

Gretchen's thoughts roamed in all directions. She imagined Kevin with tubes in his throat, needles in his arms. She went to Tim Hortons, waited in line and got a chocolate chip muffin and a Double-Double. Fuck it. Kevin had been vaccinated. This wasn't supposed to happen. She cursed the snow and she cursed the pandemic, as she'd done 1,000 times before, cursed it for existing, cursed it for making the world a worse place. Right when she was getting back to traveling for stories... a variant? Come on... Enough. Don't start that crap now.

Into the scrum again, Gretchen tread slowly with her large coffee, sucking out the energizing liquid with a rapidly disintegrating straw, munching on the muffin and avoiding eye contact. At a security area with metal detectors, and lines in both directions, Gretchen stopped and studied the scene. After years of working for different publications, she could pick out fellow journalists from a mile away. They all had a certain look—a certain entitled vibe, but also a weariness, and a pushiness, the demeanor of someone used to rushing, no makeup for the writer, non-camera women, frizzy hair, and the guys wore glasses and scraggly beards. She wished she had a briefcase or a press badge, anything to make her appear more official.

A young male reporter at the rear of the exit line, with brown hair in a ponytail that stuck out from under his winter hat, turned around and gave her a nod as she filled in behind him. Gretchen returned the gesture. She maybe recognized him and he maybe recognized her. But she couldn't remember from where. Single file, they approached the checkpoint and moved through the gun-detecting arch. Three army men arrived, escorting an official. Gretchen raised her eyebrows. It was the Mayor of Toronto; she recognized him from the winter storm news.

The men ushered the mayor and his entourage, a gaggle of staff in suits past the reporters. Then the mayor shook hands with a tall man in a heavily-decorated Army uniform and beret.

A few people filmed the mayor on their phones and others snapped photos on DSLRs. I can't wait to tell Sam about this, she thought, once they made up, which they would probably do tonight. They always made up eventually. She pulled out her cell phone, and also videoed the mayor from the side, zooming into his plump, rosy, smiling face. Sam won't even believe it.

Security cleared the way for the mayor like he was in a parade. Alongside the army commander, he departed the area at a brisk pace.

Gretchen rose on her toes to get a better look. That's where I need to be, she thought, and sensing an opportunity, she accelerated her step and slid in behind the guy with the ponytail. They followed the mayor. Her heart thumped like a dog's hind leg when you scratch its tummy. The mayor was probably about to give a press briefing. Now, this was luck. She could get soundbites without doing interviews.

Her vision narrowed to the person ahead of her, a squat man in a black jacket and suit pants. Gretchen tightened her position behind him, overtaking the guy she maybe knew. No one stopped her. Be confident; act like you belong wherever you want to be—that was something her father had taught her from a young age. Be a confident Black woman, walk and talk like a white man and you'll get far, act like a nervous cat and you end up in an alley scrounging for trash. You are whoever you want to be. Her dad had decided on a dentist—she on a journalist, and she wanted to, needed to, embody her chosen role. Double down. Triple down. You don't get a Pulitzer by writing about cake recipes, something her father had also said recently, and boy it had stung. She sucked in her stomach and lifted her chin. From disaster comes a *disaster-piece*; this was her chance. Focus.

They reached another, narrower checkpoint. An airport officer opened a swinging side gate and Gretchen followed the mayor's group in—unquestioned, undetected, unexamined, un-judged, and un-arrested—a few steps closer to the story, to the truth.

Instead of a press briefing, to her surprise they filed into a conference room and shut the door.

Gretchen, trying not to breathe too hard, took a seat against the wall beside the younger staff, possibly interns. There were about thirty people in the room, and no one was checking IDs or badges. Must be a bunch of organizations in here, she thought, and that's why they aren't noticing me. No one already knows everyone.

The room settled and an airport official opened the meeting and briefed the mayor on the crash, the storm, and the airport's emergency action plan. She turned on her cell phone's audio recorder and suppressed a grin, though it soon became apparent from the presentation that her good mood would not last.

Chapter Thirteen

CANDI BOYS

The elevator smelled like wet mittens. Candi pressed the button for the floor that linked to the airport, but before the silver doors closed, a hand reached inside, and the young guy from the airplane exploded onto the elevator like a grenade, in the same outfit from the flight, with his weed smell, red shoes, track pants, and bedazzled headphones. On his heels was the older man she's made eye contact with in the gym, now in a gray cashmere sweater and jeans.

"Oh, hello." The young guy said, grinning at Candi like he'd snuck into a club underage. His brown eyes twinkled, and his full lips maintained a permanent smile.

Was he wearing lipstick? Or gloss maybe?

"You're the flight attendant without the sleeping pills." He winked. "Small world."

Candi minimally nodded. She glanced at the older man from the gym. He sort of resembled the younger one; were they related? The older one leaned against the rear of the elevator and ran his fingers through his silver and black hair.

"Where you headed next?" Her former flight mate asked as they ascended toward the airport gateway.

"Las Vegas."

"What!?! Me too, I was also going to Vegas."

Candi again offered a miniature nod, then averted her eyes. She didn't want to make small talk with this yahoo; she wanted lunch containing fresh vegetables. The door opened and she exited the elevator first, hoping to leave the guy behind on the carpeted tunnel to the terminal.

The older man increased his pace to walk next to her. "So, you work for the airline? I heard this storm will last a week."

Candi slowed her pace and glanced at him again. He was handsome and also had an unusual accent. Was it British? Or French? She was terrible at guessing nationalities. "I'm actually hoping they'll allow flights out tomorrow."

"I highly doubt it."

They reached the entrance to the airport. She stopped and glanced in both directions. There was a Tim Hortons or a hallway. A long line or head closer to the crash site... Neither option seemed good to her.

"There's a decent pub down that way." The older man said, gesturing away from the Tim Hortons. I've eaten there before. I'm Franck, by the way." He pronounced it *Fronck*, like "bonk," and not with the hot dog "Frank" hard-A sound.

"Did I hear the word *pub*?" The younger man was upon them like a blister.

Franck raised his thick eyebrows, "You heard correctly."

"I'm Vybes," the colorfully clad youth stuck out his hand to Candi.

"Vybes?" She gave him a quizzical look.

"Yep. Vybes with a Y. V.Y.B.E.S. Vybes Von Bibi to be exact."

Vybes Von Bibi...? Now she'd heard it all. Of course he had a ridiculous name.

"I'm just getting some coffee," Candi said. "Nice to meet you both."

"Ahh I was there earlier," Franck said before she could walk away. "The line is like 2,000 people long. Come to the pub with us. Drinks on me."

"Yes," Vybes said with his wide, perma-grin, "Come with us Ms. Delta."

The last time she'd turned down drinks, it had saved her life. Though a real, sit-down meal did sound much better than microwaved sandwiches and sugary drinks...

"Follow me," Franck said, relieving her of the obligation to answer. "And also, tell us your name."

"Candi."

"Oooh candy girl! You are my world," Vybes cooed. "Candy girl, you look so sweet. You're a special treat!" He sang the words and then the notes, in a high falsetto voice, like he was a one-man cover band.

Franck and Candi exchanged raised-eyebrow glances.

"That's enough of that," Franck said.

Vybes stopped singing, "Where are you from man, by the way? You didn't tell me where you were headed either."

"From Belgium and heading home to Belgium."

She definitely would have never guessed Belgian. And they obviously weren't related. How racist of me, she thought, assuming every brown guy I see is from the same family.

The trio proceeded to the bar which was less like a pub and more like a panopticon of touch screens and plastic chairs. Slammed, there were no open spots.

"Should we go somewhere else? This place looks shit," Vybes said.

"Yeah, I must be remembering wrong. The place I went to before was like a real pub you went inside. Let's keep looking."

They walked past another five or six gates and then spotted the right pub. It buzzed with people, winter jackets, rolling suitcases, and conversations, but at least there was space at the bar and real human servers instead of iPads.

Franck pulled out a stool for her in the corner of the large bar and she leaned her elbows on its sleek, black marble top, comforted by the normalcy of the environment. Dark wood paneling, with light fixtures made of empty wine bottles gave the pub a cozy feel. The older Belgian man wedged himself between her and the wall. Then Vybes wedged himself on her other side, like she was in a man-sandwich, or on a subway. They both felt too close to her body, but there was no other space. She wouldn't have sat this close to men if Jasper was still alive. If he was still alive, she would have insisted on waiting for a table. Was she slowly changing? The realization felt heavy, and her split second of comfort evaporated; she wanted to leave.

"Well, this is certainly cozy." Franck chuckled, breathing hot air onto her cheeks, as if he'd read her mind.

"Drinks!" Vybes exclaimed.

They waited ten minutes for the bartender to finally take their orders. Candi's stomach growled. The men each tried to entertain her. Only quasi-listening, she focused on the hope of eating a meal that wasn't wrapped in plastic and sold at a convenience store.

Two glasses of white wine and a cranberry walnut raspberry vinaigrette salad later, and she'd learned more about both men while offering little of her own backstory. Vybes was actually not Indian at all. He was mixed-race, with a British mother and a Ugandan father. He'd gone to school in England for computer programming, but had instead become a fashion influencer known for his tall stature, colorful clothes, and original headphone and sneaker art. He was traveling to Vegas to attend a friend's nightclub opening.

Franck worked for the investment arm of a Belgian bank and had been in Toronto for a finance conference.

Vybes scarfed down a bacon cheeseburger, while Franck inched closer to Candi and told her all about his Toronto hotel for the conference, which he'd thought would be nice, but wasn't and blah, blah, blah. She maintained polite attention.

"Would you like another?" Franck gestured to her near-empty glass of Chardonnay and raised his thick silver-threaded eyebrows. "Or some dessert?"

A little tipsy, she said, "Umm."

"I'm going to switch to a whiskey." He added. "Then sleep away the rest of the day and wake up with a departure time."

She laughed. "Okay. good idea."

They ordered another round of whiskeys. She glimpsed herself in the bar's mirror and noted that despite everything, she was looking pretty good in her fitted tan sweater and a basic application of makeup. With the jet lag subsiding, and a real bed, at least life was returning to her visage. The drinks also warmed her up and took the painful edge off her feet. All her toes stung and pulsed on and off, depending on how much weight she put on them.

"God, you're making me want a cigarette and something t'a snort." Vybes said, sipping his third drink.

Franck raised his whiskey glass. "To partying in the airport."

"To all types of snow!" Vybes fake-snorted air up his nose.

"You know, speaking of drugs," Candi giggled, lowering her voice, "I think I found a whole book of LSD in my hotel room."

"What!" Vybes almost fell off his bar stool, which he'd finally snatched from another departing patron. Franck tilted his head closer to her body, "And how many did you take?"

They all laughed.

"Do I look like someone who goes around taking LSD?" Candi giggled again, now tipsy. "No, of course I didn't." She described the book to them.

"That's crazy," Franck said. "I haven't done LSD since the late 70s."

"Wow, the seventies." Vybes said. "Must have been so cool back then."

Franck rolled his eyes, "Yes, and you weren't even a fetus."

Feeling brazen from the three drinks, Candi asked Franck his age.

He leaned back, as if to let her look him up and down. "How old do you think I am?"

"I'd say 60." Vybes said.

Franck shot him a scowl. "No one's asking you, Bibi."

Candi pretended to inspect him like a doctor. "Forty-five?" She lied, thinking he had to be at least 50.

He smirked, "Try again."

"Fifty?"

"I'm fifty-two and you are very kind."

"Wow, what's your secret?"

"Genetics and chocolate," he winked.

"So, back to this LSD. Can we come see it?" Vybes put his gigantic arm around her shoulder.

"I mean, I don't really know what it is."

"Let's test it," Vybes said.

"Oh no." She shook her auburn hair, "That, that would be too crazy."

"Could be fun. I mean we aren't leaving anytime soon." Franck shrugged.

Candi couldn't believe the older investment banker was suggesting they ingest a stranger's LSD. Europeans were so wild. "Honestly, the moment I can leave, I'll be the first one out. I've got a lot going on at home."

"What do you have going on?" Vybes asked.

"I—"

"Guys, look at the news," Franck interjected, pointing to a TV, saving her from answering the question.

Behind the bar the news flashed the headline: "Climate Crisis Halts Christmas Travel." The newscaster predicted the storm to last three more days. Snow in Toronto was now up two feet and the death toll from the storm was up to 60 in Toronto alone, mostly elderly who had died trying to shovel the snow, plus a small number of people whose electricity had gone off in the night and their children who had frozen to death inside their homes. Why did they put stuff like this on the news? She looked away and shuddered at the awful idea of a frozen baby.

"And I thought England was too cold," Vybes brown eyes widened. "Remind me to never come to Canada in the winter."

After another whiskey and a slice of cheesecake with canned

strawberry goop on top, Franck cleared the bill. She and Vybes protested, but he ignored them.

"I should get to my room," she mumbled.

"I'll come with you. I want to see this LSD," Vybes jumped up.

"Me too, I'd love to see it," Franck downed the rest of his whiskey.

Candi, feeling the need for distraction, agreed to them coming to her room and tried to act like she wasn't drunk. Vybes launched into a story about his Kenyan friend who'd flown from Paris to Nairobi with a bunch of acid.

On the crowded elevator, Franck positioned himself next to her and whispered into her ear, "I'm glad you agreed to lunch."

She could feel his body heat through his sweater. Could he feel hers? More people got on and they moved deeper into the corner together. The alcohol swam in her bloodstream. Guests emptied out floor by floor until it was their turn.

"You guys are lucky you got rooms," Vybes said. "By the time I made it here, they were all full."

"You don't have a room?" Candi balked, "But I saw you in the gym."

"Yeah, I slept in the airport, so I was feeling really uncomfortable, and like nasty, so I snuck in to shower in the gym, then figured, well, I may as well also work out, ya know, since I'd been sitting for so long on the plane."

"Wow, that sucks. Maybe something will open up."

"I've got two beds in my room," Franck offered, "You could stay with me if all else fails."

"Really? Thanks man, I really appreciate that."

What a nice guy, Candi thought. She wouldn't have made the same offer. Or maybe he was just as tipsy as she was.

They paused outside her room as she fumbled in her purse for the key card, again thinking about how she'd never do this if Jasper was alive. Her room was kind of a mess. But she did want a second opinion on that LSD. It's okay, she told herself. Franck and Vybes are just friendly guys, killing time. But inside felt too intimate with the duvet rumpled and the sheets exposed, as if they'd stumbled onto someone's romantic tryst. She wished she'd made the bed.

Franck went to the window. "Nice view. You can almost see the city."

Candi removed the book of art from under her mattress.

"Hey, instead of the Princess and the Pea, you're the Princess and the LSD!" Vybes exclaimed.

She sure didn't feel like a princess, far from it. "I didn't want the hotel cleaners to find it."

"Wouldn't they make the bed though?" Franck asked.

"Oh yeah, you're probably right." Candi felt silly.

"Maybe put it in your safe," Franck suggested.

"There's a safe?"

He walked to the TV and opened the cabinet doors. There was a small safe. Candi felt even dumber.

Franck relaxed on the end of her bed, his dark clothes and skin contrasting with the white sheets and the bleak scene beyond the window. Vybes plopped beside the older man, and stuck his long legs off the bed. They really could be father and son, she thought, as she opened the velvet green book to show the two men its inner contents.

"Wow," Vybes said. "This is incredible. Fucking incredible. Have you searched for this online? Or looked for the art? People share blotter art and post drugs. Maybe you could find out who made this."

"Really? People do that?" Candi blinked. She hadn't thought of searching for the book online.

"People do everything."

"Can I get a closer look?" Franck touched her shoulder. Her lips parted at the touch. His hand was so warm.

She passed him the book and he lay it open on his lap. "I don't know." He turned a few pages, stopping at an image of a menacing blue wolf in a winter landscape. "We can't really tell if it's acid without testing it." He moved the book to the window to get a better look in the natural light. "Someone must be missing this though, that's for sure."

Silhouetted in the window, Candi thought he looked like an Indian George Clooney.

"I'll eat one," Vybes said. "If you don't want the book, I'll take it."

She hesitated, then thought, why not. She wasn't about to take LSD.

"Though I'd hate to tear out any pages; the book is so exquisite." Franck said.

"Actually, you should keep it," Vybes told her, "It was meant for you to find. And, I should see if the hotel has any more rooms."

"Yes, go check; you never know," Franck said.

Candi noticed he didn't offer his room again. She could understand why. Vybes was a lot.

Vybes raised his lengthy body off the bed, "Will you guys be here?"

Candi saw Franck hesitate, then he said, "I'm in room 708. I should probably go back to my room as well."

"Okay, I'll let you all know what happens. I'll be back."

Her eyes met Franck's once Vybes was gone.

"He's a wild one," Franck said.

"It's very kind of you to offer him a bed."

"Surely the whiskey talking."

They both paused. It was weird being alone by an unmade bed in a hotel room with a strange man.

"Speaking of whiskey, do you have anything to drink? I could do one more."

Candi hesitated. Did she want him to leave or stay? She couldn't quite decide. Though she would like another drink herself... and better not to drink alone. "I have some wine," She pulled out one of the wine bottles she'd bought in the airport. "Oh but, actually, I don't have an opener."

Franck pointed to the bottle, "It's a twist."

She blushed again. Gosh, she kept doing dumb stuff today. "Oops. Well, maybe that means I don't need any more wine."

"Nonsense." He filled their disposable cups, but as she reached for hers, he touched her arm, guided her to him, and kissed her on the mouth.

At first, she entered a lucid dream of soft, warm lips. He tasted like whisky. Blood rushed to her extremities. He pressed her body to his. Her heart pounded, but then her adrenaline kicked in, breaking the spell. Startled, she pushed him away. "Sorry, I'm with someone," she stumbled backwards, grateful she hadn't accidentally spilled wine on the carpet.

"Oh, sorry. I didn't know."

"I-I'm married."

"You don't have a ring." He motioned to her hand.

What was she even saying? She'd only recently stopped wearing her wedding ring, after Adrienne had called her on it—as if life could be restarted by removing a sliver of metal.

"I... I don't wear it on trips." Another lie. She'd always worn it. She wished she'd never taken it off.

"Well, this is embarrassing. My apologies. You're a very attractive woman. I suppose I got carried away." Franck took a swig of wine. "Perhaps I don't need this drink either."

Her heart was an engine now, but instead of takeoff, she was ready for him to depart. She struggled to collect her scattered thoughts.

"I better go nap this one off." He sat his wine cup on her TV stand. "Really, my apologies. I thought you were interested."

Her face flushed. Had she given the perception that she was romantically interested in him? Maybe she had flirted in the restaurant a bit, but she was just being nice... "It's not a big deal. I should have mentioned I'm married." Again, a lie, though she did still feel with Jasper, always with him, but she never was, never would be.

He studied her, "Well, I definitely need to go then, because I want to kiss you again."

She almost spat out her wine. The words hung in silence, suspended midair as her heartbeat throttled. She didn't know what to say.

"But I won't. Candi." He enunciated her name. "It was lovely to meet you."

She slid her hands in her pockets, palms like damp napkins.

Franck grabbed his winter jacket off the bed and in a completely normal tone, as if nothing awkward had just happened, announced, "Room 708, and here is my number. Call me if you need anything." He passed her his business card, and she took it. Then, without hugging her goodbye, with only a wave, he left.

Candi flopped on the bed and caught her breath. What just happened? She wondered. Why did I invite him to my room? Then another voice in her head said, you brought this on yourself, last night, thinking about being kissed. Now you got your new kiss, didn't you?

"Shhhh," she told her own brain. It wasn't like that. She wanted her last kiss to be Jasper, not some random airport man. Ugh. She shouldn't have had so much wine.

This was how she sometimes talked to herself. Conversation after conversation with no one but her own mind now that Jasper was gone. Or sometimes, she would play out dialogues with him, imagining what he would say. But today, it wasn't Jasper's voice that came to her, rather she remembered a random video clip Adrienne had sent, part of her friend's efforts to convince her to move on. It was called "Why Women Need New Shaft," and the thumbnail was a giant picture of an eggplant. Candi hadn't watched it. Adrienne had said that after women have sex with the same person 100 times, they get bored and want other men. But what if you could never have sex with the man you loved again? Then, surely... but no. She didn't want a new shaft, not yet, maybe never.

Feeling guilty, yet slightly aroused against her own will, she flipped on the TV for some distraction.

There, on the bright screen, was a picture of Adrienne's smiling face. Her mouth went dry. Adrienne had been found dead, one of the victims of the crash in the lounge. Candi almost screamed. Fearing they might show her friend's body, she switched off the TV. No, no, no, not Adrienne. This wasn't really happening.

Before she could freak out further, there was a knock on the door. "Hey, it's me, Vybes," a voice from the other side.

She didn't answer.

"Hello?"

"Just a minute," she called and hauled her weary body out of bed like an over-packed suitcase, full of grief instead of clothes.

Of all the people to be here, Candi thought, why him? Why is he here and not Adrienne? Adrienne should be in the hallway with her suitcase, not this fucking guy. She opened the door and explained that Franck had returned to his room.

"Hey," Vybes put his oven-mitt sized hand on her shoulder, "Whatever it is, it's all going to be alright."

She stared at him. How did he—was it that obvious that she'd been upset?

"Do you want to talk about it?"

Confused, she just kept staring at him. He shut the door and waited for her response.

Her lips quivered. ""My friend Adrienne—the other flight attendant on the plane—she... She... was in the lounge..." Unable to control herself, tears came and she bent forward and cradled her head in her hands.

"Hey, hey there." Vybes hugged her and she folded into his vast body.

"It's okay, I'm fine," she said to his chest.

He kept hugging her. "Everything will be alright."

She couldn't speak more about Adrienne; it was all too much. "I'm fine, sorry," she repeated.

He held his hug until she finally calmed down and pulled away.

"Sorry, but thank you," she said, rubbing her eyes. "I don't know what came over me."

"Anyone would feel the same," he gazed at her and it was clear to Candi that he wanted to say more, but she was grateful he didn't. They exchanged phone numbers and she agreed to update him if she heard any news about their flight. The hotel still didn't have any rooms. He'd stay with Franck. They'd fly home soon, he assured her and left. She went to bed and pulled the covers over her head. She would sleep and when she woke up, her plane would land in Vegas. This is all a dream, she thought. It must be.

Chapter Fourteen

GRETCHEN AND THE BIG WIGS

The author of the airport's emergency action plan droned on about safety, supplies, and the maintenance of order. Gretchen, her recorder running, scanned the room. No one appeared alarmed. The storm would likely end soon, the man explained, and in the meantime, they would study the crashed plane and repair the terminal and lounge. He discussed budgets, public relations strategy, and snow removal. Gretchen yawned and considered leaving. This meeting was too by-the-book. She, like many in the room, snapped pictures of the PowerPoint slides on her phone—maps, protocols, and contact numbers, maybe something would prove useful.

A manager spoke about food deliveries, another on the heating system, and another discussed the possibility of using an unfinished underground tunnel connected to the airport to bring extra supplies from a depot on Lake Ontario where the Canadian military stored dried meals and medical equipment. The hotel and airport restaurants would remain open for as long as possible in the blizzard, and the military would bus in airport staff from the subway and GoTrain station if necessary.

An older man in a navy suit with thinning gray hair and a red face spoke up. He introduced himself as the U.S. Consul General to Toronto. "We've received indications from the State Department that this storm involves unusual features which may extend its natural duration."

Gretchen's ears perked up like a kitten at supper.

The Toronto mayor interrupted, "What kind of unusual features?"

"We've provided reports from the U.S. Department of Defense and NASA to the Prime Minister's office and to the Premier, who asked me to attend this meeting. It's very technical, but in simple terms we're predicting a storm that may last several weeks."

A hush fell over the room. Gretchen checked that her phone was still recording. Several weeks? How can they predict that, she wondered.

The Consul General cleared his throat. "I don't want to alarm anyone, but we're expecting record snowfall with a heavier-than-typical-mass, making it more difficult to remove. Temperatures are predicted to decline into the double negative digits leading up to Christmas. The State Department and DOD have offered to assist given the high number of U.S. and dual citizens stuck at this airport and in Ontario."

A murmur spread through the room. Gretchen studied the man speaking, this politician turned weatherman. She willed herself to remember his face, to look up his name later. Finally, something juicier than blueprints and emergency operating procedures. Later, she'd call the U.S. Embassy, NOAA, and NASA for statements.

The mayor stood up, "I don't think we're at the point where we need foreign assistance aside from your cooperation with preclearance and the crash investigation."

"I agree," the Canadian Colonel beside him said, "But please keep us informed."

"Yes, in regards to that..." The Consul General cleared his throat. "We are going to shut down U.S. preclearance from tomorrow until further notice, for the safety of our U.S. personnel." The Consul General gestured to the woman beside him, "The CBP chief will be available for any questions."

Gretchen's brown eyes widened. Close preclearance? This was serious. She checked the airport's Chief of Operations' expression for a reaction, but there wasn't one. He must have already known.

"Of course, we will reopen DHS and preclearance as soon as the weather permits," the consul added. "We're also issuing a statement urging American travelers with vehicles to proceed to a U.S. land border immediately. We will keep the land border open for as long as we can with the snow accumulation, for U.S. Citizens to re-enter from Canada and for Canadians to return, but tourism and immigration is paused until the storm ends. We will announce the change on the news this afternoon."

Her spine stiffened. The U.S. Government was concerned enough to risk a cluster fuck at the land border?

"Is that really a good idea? To order people to drive? Why not close the land border if it's that serious?" The Toronto mayor spoke out of turn, now clearly flustered. "Things are bad on the highway as is. It's already pandemonium at the rental car lot. We've issued an order this afternoon to halt all rental of cars. We can't have Americans on the roads having accidents requiring emergency personnel while Canadians are told to stay home."

"I understand," the consul nodded. "However, we would like to instruct American citizens without permanent residency in Canada to leave by land as soon as possible." The American man leaned forward. "The U.S. rental car companies at the airport have offered to allow one-way rentals on vehicles between here and New York State and to Michigan to help folks get home for the holidays."

Gretchen's shoulders relaxed a bit, so this was a PR stunt on the part of the big rental car companies, and they'd asked the consulate to intervene on their behalf in face of being shut down by the Canadians. "Let's get Americans home!" She could see their ads now. Typical corporations, always trying to make a buck off disaster.

"There are plenty of nationalities stranded here, not to mention Canadians from other provinces and other parts of Ontario. We can't prioritize Americans taking rental cars over everyone else" The mayor was curt and the whole room tensed, waiting to see how the U.S. Consul General would respond.

"New York State, Michigan, Ohio, and the National Guard will send plows and manpower to clear main routes to the border."

"That we can discuss with the provincial government," the mayor said. "Let's break and I'll meet you one-on-one in fifteen minutes in the airport's secure briefing area. Meeting adjourned. Thank you everyone for attending."

The onlookers broke their attention and people spoke to their colleagues in hushed tones, gathering up their papers, pens, and folders.

Gretchen scrunched her face. This was getting crazy. Secure briefing area meant classified, but this was public interest.

The consul general spoke again, his voice booming over the den of whispers. "One more thing, the U.S. Consulate will also close temporarily, though our emergency line will remain on for calls and we will continue to assist Americans and American companies in the Greater Toronto Area as best we can."

The mayor and the consul's teams exited the room. Gretchen hurried behind them. There was no time to waste.

In the hallway, she caught up with the Consul General. "Excuse me sir," she said, "I'm an American journalist working for Reuters. I'd love to get your comments on the crash and storm and why you're urging Americans to evacuate the city."

He shook his head, scowled, and kept walking.

"Why are you taking this to a secure briefing room? Isn't it the American public's right to know what's going on? Why do you think the storm will last longer than normal? Are you evacuating State Department employees from Toronto?"

"No comment," he snapped and beckoned to one of his staff before turning his back on her.

A tall white woman with skeleton-like legs in white tights and a black pencil skirt suit moved in. "Who are you with? No press was supposed to be in that meeting."

"Reuters," Gretchen swallowed. Fuck, which agency was this lady with? She looked like a scary bird.

"What's your name?" The woman scanned Gretchen's body with her eyes, looking for a badge. The consul general and his group continued on, leaving her alone with the hawkish Karen. Two other men came forward, both in dark suits.

Shit, was this diplomatic security? Airport security? The secret service?

"Your name and ID ma'am." One of the men said.

"Jancy Crawford," Gretchen lied, using a name that came to her out of nowhere.

"Jancy Crawford," the woman repeated, "Which agency are you with? I need to see your ID."

Gretchen took a deep breath. Nope. She wasn't getting caught up in this crap. "Actually, the Toronto mayor's press liaison invited me to the meeting." Her heart rate increased as she lied. Then she gave the woman a patronizing, sickly sweet smile. "Sorry, I've gotta run. My ride is outside." Without waiting for a response, Gretchen pivoted and booked it towards the terminal's exit, zig zagging through the crowd, praying the suits weren't following her.

The lines for the rental car offices in the terminal were thirty people deep. A security guard told her there were several more car companies in another building beyond the terminal. She could take a shuttle. Was the shuttle still running? He didn't know. She'd have to find out.

Confident she wasn't being followed, she surveyed the busy airport scene. Should she stay and try to dig more into the story? Or try to leave by land? The prospect of getting stuck weighed on her. She needed to get home to see Kevin. This was no longer a matter of waiting it out for a day or two, as she'd thought before. This was a potential transportation crisis of epic proportions.

Returning to her hotel room, out of breath, Gretchen grabbed all her belongings and stuffed them into her suitcase, bookbag, and purse. Working abroad for as long as she had, befriending several U.S. Diplomats along the way, she knew the State Department didn't make rash moves. They kept to their standard operating procedures, and rarely ordered American citizens to leave. They only did that if shit was about to get bananas. They obviously knew something she didn't. Maybe the crash was an attack, she thought. This couldn't be just about a blizzard.

As fast as she could move her short legs, Gretchen dragged her rollaway bag to the elevator, her thoughts full of questions. Maybe this whole evacuation was about the pandemic, the variant her mother had mentioned. She fished a facemask out of her purse and put it on. Might not do much good, but it made her feel better and it couldn't hurt.

The shuttle buses were no longer running to the rental car offices, nor were taxis. Every ride share app on her phone had wait times over an hour.

Almost growling, she left her luggage with the receptionist and bundled up for the cold. Outside, the intensity of the weather shocked her. It was worse than the morning. How? She wondered if she was being crazy, or rash, dramatic like her dad would say. Should she just wait things out in her room? But no, something in her gut told her that things were about to get worse, much worse. She lowered her head to the wind and moved like a determined machine, only looking up to check the signs leading to the rental cars, lugging sore thighs through the thick snow. At least she didn't have to worry about falling on ice. The powder covered everything.

The parking lot for the rentals was almost empty. No one else was around. Out of breath and freezing, she scanned the lot. This wasn't good, but maybe there were more vehicles on the top levels?

Passing through the lot, she went inside one of the offices and joined the line behind two weary looking men. Minutes passed that felt like hours. Both men walked away with keys.

Finally, it was Gretchen's turn.

"Do you have a reservation?"

"No, but I'd like an SUV," she said to the attendant.

He clicked on his computer a few times, then a few more times. "Yes, the earliest I have available is next week, provided the vehicle is returned on time, Monday at 10 AM. Shall I book that for you?"

Gretchen dropped open her mouth. Next week? "No, I really need something right now. What about any cars with snow tires? I'll pay for a premium SUV or whatever you've got, a truck? Do you have any trucks?"

He shrugged, "I'm sorry ma'am. We're really completely out of everything but the sedans. Even if you had a reservation, we wouldn't be able to give you a car suitable for this weather."

She curled her gloved hands into fists, "Are you telling me those dudes in front of me took the last SUVs?"

He nodded.

Gretchen grabbed her bag and ran out to the parking deck. Maybe one of the guys could give her a ride. But there was no one there. They were already gone. Fucking men, always taking everything. She let out a bearish groan that echoed through the lot and returned to the rental car office only to find the employee locking up.

"I'll try a sedan," she said.

"Sorry, my boss just called and told me to close."

Gretchen clenched her fists. Oh no. No way. She had to get a car, any car.

"And a sedan wouldn't be safe." He zipped up his coat.

"Please. Could you give me a ride? I'll pay you."

He hesitated.

She continued, her voice now pleading. "My flight is canceled, and my brother is in the hospital. I need to get home. I need someone to give me a ride to the border, to the Buffalo airport."

"Sorry, I have to get home to my own family. Good luck." He put on his winter gloves.

"Or at least give me a ride back to my hotel?"

He gave her an exasperated look. "Having a car in Toronto is too expensive for me. I'm taking the GoTrain."

Gretchen's shoulders sank. Of course he didn't have a car. Most people didn't own cars in Toronto. Parking was limited and insurance was astronomically expensive in Ontario; she'd heard people talk about this before. Folks took public transport or used ride shares. She considered for a moment following him to the GoTrain station, but she'd be heading away from the US border, and then what? Most restaurants, schools, and stores were probably closed already for the blizzard.

"Sorry. If I could help you, I would. Flights are never delayed for too long." He shrugged and left her alone.

It would soon be dark. Without much choice she followed him out to the road, but instead of walking back to the airport, she stuck out a gloved thumb, determined to head south, even if it meant hitchhiking the whole damn way home.

Chapter Fifteen

CANDI BUBBLES

According to the weather channel, the snow accumulation in Toronto was as high as 10 feet. Ceaseless drifts blew cold across highways, rivers, and city parks. Candi watched the news half-hoping, half-terrified of seeing Adrienne again. Unread messages filled her phone. On TV, a journalist broadcasted from his home studio, a pinkish man in front of a well-arranged bookshelf. "Twitter is buzzing with speculation surrounding the so-called "1000 Year Blizzard, the Snowpocalypse," as citizens question if the extreme conditions affecting Eastern Canada, Michigan, Ohio, Upstate New York, and New England are caused by climate change, or something more sinister. The non-stop snowfall has left many wondering if North America is experiencing a man-made weather attack."

Candi's heart chomped at her chest like a hungry goat. A weather attack? She stepped out of bed and winced. What the hell? Her feet were on fire. Laying back on the bed, she slid off her socks. Blisters bulged, big as chewing gum bubbles all over her toes and the bottom of her feet like her body was not her own. She stared at her bubbling toes. Some pockets of skin were clear and some were filled with blood. Yes, her feet had been hurting, but surely the new shoes wouldn't have caused these blisters. What on earth was happening to her feet? She threw the duvet over her monstrous toes, then dialed the front desk.

No answer.

She searched for her doctor's phone number and called their office back in Vegas. "Please," she explained to the receptionist, "I really need Dr. Targas to call me. Something's very wrong and I'm not able to come into the office. I-I've woken up with blisters all over my feet and I don't know how I got them."

The receptionist said she'd pass on the message, but told Candi to go to the nearest emergency room.

Hanging up, Candi lay in bed and stared at the ceiling for a good ten minutes before mustering the courage to hobble to the window, to check the storm. Tears began to squeeze from her eyes as she limped, holding onto the furniture. God, what have I done to my feet? She wondered. Closer to the cold glass, goosebumps perked on her forearms. Frost coated the glass like intricate, antique lace. As if inside a giant cotton ball; there was nothing to see but snow. Fuck. She returned to her bed and curled into a fetal position.

She wanted to go to the lobby to look for a doctor, but putting weight on her feet for that long seemed impossible. The blisters might burst. Her stomach lurched at the thought. Instead, she took Advil and dragged herself to the bathtub, ran cold water and stuck her feet in, hoping it would numb the pain. It helped a little, but the cold also hurt.

She searched the internet for blisters. Nothing looked as bad as her feet. Sickened by her own toes, she photographed them, and posted the picture on a Reddit doctor's forum, explaining her situation. Did anyone know what this was?

Almost instantly, someone responded, asking if she'd spent a lot of time out in the cold.

Candi's heart pounded. The cold? Yes, she had.

"You may have severe frostbite," the user, DoctorOuchOuch replied. "You need to seek medical treatment asap."

The phone shook in her hands. She couldn't type. Frostbite? *Frostbite?* But she'd only been outside a short time...

She called 911 again. Her panic level rose.

The line was busy.

Chapter Sixteen

GRETCHEN AND THE PARADOX

Gretchen shivered. Despite warm winter outerwear, the forceful storm tore at slivers of her exposed skin. No one drove by. She kept her hand out, one gloved thumb like a beacon of hope. How long could she stay out in this weather? The daylight waned. But her mom was wrong; she needed to get home. Kevin needed her.

Every couple of minutes she stuck her shaking hands under her armpits to warm up. Her gloves couldn't compete with the sinking temperature. She'd visited Canada off and on over the years and during winter, but winter had never felt like this. Her eyelid spasmed. Ugh. She rubbed her face and opened and closed her watering eyes. Her nose tingled, and her cheeks burned in the slapping wind.

With darkness impending, she kept her thumb out, but started walking, cursing under her breath. Her vision was blurry and teary, but she wasn't going to give up. Maybe it wouldn't work tonight, but she vowed to try hitchhiking again tomorrow, early, in the daylight. Her jaw trembled and her teeth clattered. As she neared the airport terminal and her hotel, a voice called out to her. Gretchen scanned the landscape but didn't see anyone in the dimming light and snow. The voice cried again. "Help me."

Gretchen increased her steps, moving toward the sound. In the snow, something pink moved.

"Hey," Gretchen yelled.

The figure came into focus through the storm. In the blue and yellow light of dusk, a naked woman on the side of the road clawed at the ground on her knees. She had black hair and wore only boots, no hat, nothing. Gretchen ran to her as fast as she could, huffing and heaving as she waded through the snow.

"Help. Help me." The naked lady crawled to her and clutched onto Gretchen's leg, almost collapsing them both. The stranger's skin was more red than tan. White snow clung in clumps to the woman's eyelashes.

"Oh my God." Gretchen said, "Where are your clothes? We've got to get you inside."

The woman writhed and curled into a ball, crying.

"You've got to get up!" Gretchen screamed and grabbed the woman's arm, hoisting her small body onto her feet. The woman was so frail and thin, she flopped in the wind like a wet leek. With all her strength, Gretchen picked up the woman and tried to carry her like a baby, but she wasn't strong enough. As the woman whimpered, she let her down for a second and then grabbed her under the arms and dragged her towards the airport.

Adrenaline raced through Gretchen's core. She had to find help, and fast, or this woman was going to die. The lights of the airport twinkled in the distance, still so far away. The woman's head flopped around, but her eyes remained open. Gretchen huffed and puffed. Her chest hurt. Her arms ached from holding the woman's weight, but she couldn't leave the woman out here with no clothes.

She felt like her heart might explode, but, as she grunted with exertion, she heard sirens. Lights flashed. An ambulance drove towards them. Gretchen released the woman in the snow, and ran to the vehicle, waving her arms and yelling, "Help, help."

And thank God, the ambulance, with its sirens blaring, screeched to a halt.

Chapter Seventeen

CANDI BUMP

Against the elevator wall, Candi leaned her body and attempted not to cry. The Advil had done little to help the pain in her feet, but she couldn't stay in bed, calling phone numbers that just rang and rang. The doors opened and she limped to the lobby, tears edging down her cheeks. People passed but no one offered to help. She finally reached the front desk and put her weight against the counter, alternating from one leg to the other, gritting her teeth. The woman at the desk visibly backed away. She thinks I'm crazy, Candi thought. I must look crazy. "Please help me," she said, her voice shaking. "I think I have frostbite. I-I need a doctor. I've been calling so many times and no one is answering." She started crying.

They brought her a wheelchair and she waited beside the desk, grateful to be off her feet. After an hour, a nurse came.

"Sorry to keep you waiting; it's very busy."

She nodded and explained her situation. The man propped her foot up and took off her shoes and socks.

"I'm sorry, it does appear you have severe frostbite."

Candi's face contorted. "I-I was only outside for like fifteen minutes. Are you sure?"

"Trust me, you're lucky it's just your toes. If you'd seen what I've seen today..." the nurse trailed off.

"How long will it take to heal?"

He took a deep breath. "I'd recommend discussing it with your doctor, when you get home, but in the meantime, we can drain and clean the blisters and give you medication to help with the pain."

"My doctor is in Vegas."

"This phase will go away in a few days. Then, the blisters should scab over."

"This phase?"

"Normally, we'd take you to the nearest hospital for care, but given the situation with the storm, for anything minor, we're keeping people here." He wheeled her like an invalid to a makeshift exam room in the airport terminal.

Another nurse wiped off her blisters with antibacterial pads while Candi kept her eyes squeezed shut, but she couldn't stop her tears. "This is going to take a while," the nurse said. "Please try to relax."

But Candi couldn't relax, not while a stranger in rubber gloves stuck syringes into her feet. It felt more like a hundred needles than one the way the sensations traveled up her leg like she was meat defrosting and refreezing in real time. "What's going to happen to me?" Candi asked, her voice fraught with fear.

"Well, they may scab up pretty bad." The nurse fiddled with Candi's toes. "But if they start to turn black, come back right away."

"Turn black?"

"Yeah." The woman continued sucking. It hurt but wasn't unbearable, what was unbearable was not being able to go home.

Candi focused on the fluorescent lights above her. With her jaw clenched from the uncomfortable sensations in her feet, she quietly asked, "What happens if they turn black?"

The nurse didn't answer.

Chapter Eighteen

GRETCHEN'S NOSE KNOWS NO NEWS

Drained by the prior day's ordeal, Gretchen woke up very late. Discarded clothes and empty soda bottles cluttered her hotel room's floor. Outside the fierce snowstorm raged on, battering the windows and howling through the hotel's cracks. She felt a surge of anxiety and reached for a granola bar beside her bed. But what if she ran out of food? She tore into the chocolate oat bar anyway and finished it in under a minute. The more she ate, the better she felt.

Everything she'd experienced in the past 24 hours seemed like a dream, the naked woman, the ambulance, the rental car office, trying to hitchhike.

The EMTs had assured her that the woman from outside had a chance of surviving; a chance, not a guarantee. They'd praised Gretchen as they'd wrapped her in blankets, calling her a hero, and giving her hot chocolate. They'd also put warm washcloths on her face and heating pads for her hands. Her arms, legs, neck, and throat hurt, but at least they'd given her some pain meds.

Things could be much worse. That was always obvious to her. The more she traveled and saw the world, the more she knew America and Canada were some of the safest places for her to be. Still, the view outside her window filled her with dread. She could no longer feel her nose. Shivering, more from emotional shock than cold, she cocooned deeper in her bed. Exhausted, despite sleeping late, she wanted to go back to the airport and order a Cinnamon Toast Crunch Latte to wake herself up, but every small movement made her muscles ache. Dragging the woman and hiking through the storm had drained every ounce of her strength. Though her eyes also hurt, she checked the news on her phone. The weather radar predicted snow for the next seven days. The blizzard covered single story houses in Toronto. Thankfully, most of the people in the city lived in high-rise condo buildings, or narrow three-story houses, but some affected residents had attempted to escape in cars. Some were stuck. Some were missing. Others waved from rooftops and filmed themselves on cell phones wearing ski clothes, desperately signaling for rescue helicopters that never arrived. Many moved in with friends and family in taller buildings. The blizzard hit the homeless people the hardest; survivors huddled inside shelters or hid underground in subways. Others died.

I've got to find a ride out of here, she thought over and over again as she doom-scrolled the storm news with her mouth full of another chocolate bar.

But the idea of venturing back outside terrified her.

She touched the numb tip of her still-cold nose.

No, she'd have to wait. This wasn't normal winter; this blizzard claimed lives.

Chapter Nineteen

CANDI COLD PANTIES

The TV hummed commercials for local car dealers while Candi propped her bandaged feet on a pillow. Her toes felt way better with the blisters sucked dry, or maybe because the pain killers had kicked in. The nurse had also given her antibacterial cream to apply daily. Dressed only in the Blue Jay's hoodie she'd originally bought for her nephew, her only warm and comfortable piece of clothing, and wearing her last clean pair of panties, she studied the ginger stubble dotting her thin, pale legs on the white bedsheets; she wished she could shave. She hated feeling unkempt.

Military trucks delivered supplies from a nearby Canadian army base. Yet even these sturdy vehicles struggled in the almost-supernatural, abnormal storm conditions. Snowplows failed to keep main routes clear and per the prime minister, only emergency vehicles were allowed on the roads. Citizens who violated the stay home orders were taken to jail. She'd given up on driving south. Now, her only hope was for the snow to stop. Or for the US to evacuate citizens. Though since she was in a designated shelter, even if they evacuated people, she'd be one of the last to go.

A knock interrupted her thoughts.

"Who is it?"

"It's me, Franck," the accented voice called from the hallway.

"And me!" A different, more British accent. "Are you there, Candi girl?"

She grimaced at the silly nickname. She'd just gotten comfortable, but maybe they had some news about the storm. Plus, given her injured condition, having friends nearby couldn't hurt. "Coming," she called, and slipped on dirty sweatpants, smoothed her hair, and floated to the door. The pain killers were definitely working.

"Hi guys," she said, attempting to sound casual and upbeat as she greeted the two European men.

Puffy bags sagged under Franck's weary eyes. In a faded Oxford sweatshirt and gray sweatpants, he looked more disheveled than their last meeting. Then again, what did she expect? Their gazes linked and the air constricted around her. He really shouldn't have kissed me, she thought, or said he'd wanted to kiss me again. The incident returned like a thumbtack stuck into the bulletin board of her brain—one she promptly yanked out. As if the blizzard and the crash weren't enough for her to worry about.

"We wanted to see if you're still here." Vybes said, spilling into the room behind Franck.

He wore the same big red sneakers, fitted pants that looked like they were made from ten different sweaters, and a yellow and pink plaid women's housecoat. The outfit was so busy that it almost made Candi dizzy. "How would I leave?" She pointed to her feet and told them about the frost bite.

"Holy shit," Vybes said. "Like, that's crazy."

"How long were you outside?" Franck rubbed his chin.

"I'm not sure, but I think only for ten or fifteen minutes. It's just so cold, and the wind chill is what the nurse told me. It's really not safe to be outside."

"I can't believe this." Franck shook his head. "I've lived in Europe for a long time and I've never known anyone to get frost-bite unless they were like climbing Mount Everest."

"Yeah, well, here I am." She pointed to the corner. "At least they gave me a wheelchair."

"Hey, I was wondering how that got here." Vybes plopped into the chair.

"Sorry my room is a mess."

The colorful young man waved his oversized palm, "Our room is the same."

"The cleaning staff indeed seem to have stopped coming," Franck scowled and sat lightly on the side of her bed.

Candi wondered if her room smelled like trash to outsiders, she hadn't moved her garbage bags yet to the hallway. Despite the regretful kiss, seeing the two friendly men made her realize how isolated she'd been, leaving only to get food, now emergency meals in to-go bags delivered to the lobby of the hotel by Canada's version of the red cross. People stuck in the storm still packed the airport and hotel, clustered in different spots with makeshift beds of luggage and winter jackets.

Vybes said softly, "And I wanted to make sure you were okay, you know, since you're grieving."

Grieving? Candi blinked. The word flew at her like a knife thrown across the room. She clenched her jaw and bit her gum to keep from tearing up. How did he know about Jasper? She wondered.

"We're very sorry for the loss of your coworker." Franck added. "Vybes told me about it."

Oh, right, he meant Adrienne. She'd told him about Adrienne.

Vybes popped out of the wheelchair and hugged her. "I'm so, so sorry."

Over the young man's shoulder, stuck in his awkward hug, Candi noticed Franck watching them from her room's desk chair like a cuck, scowling. An uncomfortable, nervous energy surged through her body, and she broke away from Vybes' embrace, then went slowly to the closet, and carefully put on her sneakers. Her feet barely fit with the bandages. "I've been in this room for way too long." She laced up her new sneakers, realizing that their visit was an opportunity. "Do you guys want to come with me to the airport for a roll?" she gestured to the wheelchair. "The nurse said I should take it easy and not walk too much, but I'd love to check the actual airline desk for updates. No one is answering their phone and I haven't gotten anything by email in over a day."

The two men exchanged glances.

"Are you sure you want to go back there?" Vybes tilted his head. "That won't be too stressful?"

Candi realized he was referring to returning to the location of Adrienne's death, but she couldn't avoid the airport forever. "I want to find someone else working for the airline. One of my coworkers seems to still be alive, or at least he hasn't been reported dead. I want to check if anyone has any information on him."

"But of course, pro-roller at your service," Vybes winked and pulled the wheelchair up for her to sit down.

Franck's probing eyes penetrated her, questioning her in silence, almost like he didn't believe what she was saying. Candi averted her gaze.

Travelers leaned against the terminal's walls and frazzled moms entertained their kids with flickering digital tablets. Mounds of snow blocked all the natural light. The building rumbled with a sound that reminded Candi of an outdoor pool pump, a churning, droning machine roar.

"What's that noise?" Candi asked.

"I think it's generators running," Franck said. "The electricity must be out."

"This feels so apocalyptic," Vybes commented as they entered the main check-in area. It was hard for her to go fast on her own, so Franck pushed her. Airport security was closed now, as were the gates. The few coffee shops and restaurants before security were all shut down aside from one Tim Hortons and several vending machines selling non-perishable snacks and bottles of water. Passengers already beyond security were allowed to remain there, but no one new could enter, so they couldn't pass through.

A skeleton crew roamed the half-lit building with grim expressions.

The two men took Candi to the airline counter, but no one was there. Her heart sank in her chest. If no one was working, was anyone still looking for Chad? What had happened to him?

A woman in a TSA uniform came out of one office and went in another using a key fob. Candi tried to flag her down, but was ignored.

"Do you think the airport staff are living here somewhere?" Vybes asked.

"Maybe they're bussed in and out by the military," Franck said.

"We should try and get on one of those shuttles," Candi said.

"Why? To go where?" Franck frowned. "Do you know anyone in Toronto?"

None of them did.

The federal government had evacuated Canadian citizens from the airport, sending them home in vehicles designed for the arctic terrain. They'd all seen the trucks outside the hotel. Hotels, motels, and Airbnbs in Toronto were ordered to waive fees for stranded travelers until the storm ended. She'd heard on the news that Americans were instructed to leave by land, but how could they? No one had a car. She felt like crying again.

They traversed the length of the first terminal, then a long tube connecting the next terminal, where they found a vending machine with iced coffees and soda. She bought several cans.

"I'm going to the bathroom," Vybes said. "Give me a second."

Candi considered going too because she was nervous to be alone with Franck.

He pushed her to some chairs by the window and sat down beside her wheelchair. This must be what a person with a disability feels like all the time, Candi thought with her heart as heavy as the snowfall outside. Just seeing it piled up beyond the window made her feel nervous. Since the frostbite, the idea of going outdoors filled her with anxiety and dread.

Franck cracked open a can of Coke. "The bank contracts with a private company that predicts storms and forecasts risk. I spoke to them on the phone yesterday."

"What did they say?"

"That it's going to get worse, to leave now."

"Please don't say that."

He showed her a picture on his phone. A swirling, red, yellow, and blue radar cloud hovered over all of Eastern Canada. Her eyes widened. How could it be so big? "Do they think it's like..." she hesitated, choosing her words.

"Man-made? No, they don't think so. If it was a weather attack, someone would have noticed planes cloud seeding or the military shooting electric pulses into the sky, or something unusual, but no one saw that."

"Then, what is it?"

He shrugged. "Strange things happen naturally and we can't understand everything. I heard a podcast saying it could be related to solar winds."

Candi looked at her new sneakers and wondered what solar winds were, but she didn't want to look dumb by asking. And wouldn't solar make things warm? She didn't understand. "Where is global warming when you need it?" she mumbled. She thought about Chad again. Where was he? Was he buried somewhere out there in the snow? Was he in a hospital unidentified and unconscious?

"Unless there's a way to alter the weather besides cloud seeding, and the Chinese are doing something new, or the Russians, or the Americans." Franck frowned, leaned back in his seat and folded his arms.

Candi also frowned. "Why would Americans want to do this?"

Franck shrugged, "Who knows. Or maybe it was an accident."

It was all worrying. She couldn't miss Jasper's ceremony and his mother wouldn't want to change the date. So much was already planned. "I just wish it would stop snowing." She sighed.

"The bank is working on solutions for me."

"Well, that's nice, because the airline seems to be just ghosting me."

"When will your feet heal?"

"I don't know. They said to see my own doctor, but I can't really do that."

"You should find a doctor in the airport to examine you. There must be a stranded doctor around here."

"I'm supposed to host my entire family for Christmas." She didn't explain the other reason everyone was flying in for the holidays. Better to let Franck keep thinking she was married.

"This isn't clearing by the weekend," he pointed to the snow-blocked window.

"If the bank comes up with something, will you please let me know what it is?"

"Yes, of course. Though a guy in the gym told me they're going to move people in the airport to the hotel, to conserve generator fuel, and make it easier to deliver the emergency food."

"But the hotel is full." That sounded like a terrible idea to her.

He raised his eyebrows. "Don't I know. Speaking of which, where is Vybes? He's taking quite a while."

"Or maybe there is more room because the Canadians were evacuated?"

Franck checked what appeared to be an expensive watch on his wrist. "Probably he's in there talking to people. Vybes is a talker." He leaned forward, "I keep thinking, I should have invited you to share my room instead of him."

Heat rushed to her cheeks, but before she could stammer a response, Vybes reappeared. "Sorry, that took so long, I met this weird guy in the bathroom, and he was asking me all sorts of questions. He's like living in the bathroom and is too afraid to come outside. It was crazy. I told him, no dude, just come out, it's fine, they have food and stuff. But he wouldn't."

Franck gave Candi a quick glance that said, "I told you so."

They left the airport, but before parting ways, she thanked the guys for checking on her.

"It's going to be fine. This mess will all be over soon." Vybes knelt on his knees beside her chair and hugged her.

Gosh, Candi thought, this guy loves hugs, but at the same time, it was nice. He really seemed to care about everyone, unlike Franck, who seemed to only care about getting in her pants. "That's what you told the crazy guy in the bathroom, I bet, too," she said, feeling silly that he was kneeling on the ground, yet still somehow taller than her.

"Because it's true."

"Well, bye," Franck said gruffly and left.

He's jealous of Vybes, Candi noted again. Jealous of a man hugging a frostbitten invalid in a wheelchair? Vybes was just being friendly. Franck had no right to act possessive. Candi made a mental note to avoid being alone with him again. Though, if his bank really arranged a way out of the airport, that might be worth putting up with more unwelcome advances.

Alone in her room, she hoisted herself out of the chair and limped around, drew a hot bath, and stripped off her clothes, overcome by the need to steam herself. She removed her bandages but kept her feet elevated on the edge of the tub. Despite the treatment, her toes weren't looking great. Now they were starting to bruise. Though she wasn't often religious under normal circumstances, before getting in, she closed her eyes and prayed: Please, God, make this storm stop. I've got shit to do. I can't be stuck in Canada in a fucking blizzard. I can't handle this. Please get me home. Amen. Then, balancing against the wall, she carefully stepped into the bathtub and gasped. The water was ice cold.

"Fuck my life." Candi said to no one.

She returned to bed, naked, cold, her nipples hard, with a pinched expression on her face, feeling bored, frustrated, and angry all at once. Without bothering to rewrap her feet, she pulled the covers over her head and screamed into her pillow.

She screamed until her throat hurt, then feeling a little better, applied the treatment cream, bandaged her feet with the extra wraps from the EMT, and put on a dirty T-shirt. None of her underwear were clean. Bare-assed, she turned on the tv, then turned it off and tried to remind herself that she should be happy to be alive and healthy. At least I'm not dead. At least I'm not dead. One thing at a time, she told herself. But the mantra no longer brought much comfort. In a bad mood as unrelenting as the snow, she poured wine into her disposable coffee cup, rolled to the bathroom, and washed all her underwear in the bathtub's icy water. She hung her damp undergarments around the room on the radiators and furniture to dry before returning to her bed to gaze at the colorful assortment of wet lace dotting her room. I should be at home decorating the Christmas tree, she thought, not here in Toronto hanging up cold panties. Honestly, she didn't know how things could get much worse than this. Not only would she have to spend Christmas without Jasper, but she might have to spend it right here in this stupid room, in cold, cold Canada.

A Pause, a Breath, an Oulipian Snowball Poem

BY TEDDY

Oh,
things can
always get worse.

Chapter Twenty

GRETCHEN'S HOT/COLD MESS

In her messy hotel room, surrounded by empty single-slice pizza boxes and candy wrappers, her once white sheets stained with chocolate and crumbs, Gretchen read every theory on the Snowpocalypse.

The main causes proposed were:

• Low pressure (whatever that means.)

• Warm air moving quickly into a cold area. (Makes no sense.)

• A large body of water nearby. (Well, that checks out: Lake Ontario.)

• Topography, like mountains. (Nope)

• Climate change...

The last one seemed obvious, yet made her the most nervous. Then again, there were examples of other crazy blizzards, plus rare events were labeled rare for a reason. In 1972, she read, a blizzard the size of Wisconsin buried Iran under 26 feet of snow, killing as many as 5,000 people. Likewise, a deadly blizzard in Afghanistan, in 2008, with -30-degree weather and 70 inches of snow killed 100,000 sheep and goats.

70 inches. How many feet was that? It was five feet. The Iran blizzard had been 10 feet, the worst in history and supposedly

caused by a mix of Siberian air, Caspian Sea low pressure, and Black Sea moisture. The death count for this storm was still under 5,000, and Toronto currently reported 17 feet of snow. She stared at the number. Could it really be true? She wondered and rubbed her eyes, tired from looking at screens. Her fingers felt something weird on her face, like bumps.

Disturbed, she got out of bed and went to the bathroom mirror. Holy shit. Were they zits? She looked closer at her cheeks and nose, then backed away from the sink, horrified. They weren't zits. They were blisters. Just as the EMTs predicted: frostbite on her face. Tiny blisters. She checked her fingers and toes, and they still seemed okay, so just her face. Great.

They'd said she needed to keep her skin warm to prevent damage, so she tried to soak a washcloth in hot water, but no hot water came out of the bathroom sink. Using her coffee machine, she heated up a cup of water, dipped the cloth in, and held it over her nose and cheeks.

How could she get out of here without freezing to death? Was there no solution? Kevin was still in the hospital. Her entire family was staying with Kendra, unable to go and see him. She needed to get down there too. There had to be a way. She couldn't just spend the holidays in this disgusting, smelly room!

She called Sam again. No answer.

She racked her brain, then checked her credit card. Maybe she had enough money to buy a snowmobile if she couldn't rent one, or buy a snowplow, or at least a pickup truck? Her mind cycled through possibilities, bad answers, and not so great ideas. Between her debit account, her savings, and her credit cards she could buy a vehicle, but from where? Was Carvana operating? Could she get a vehicle delivered? She went online and looked, but the website didn't even work in Canada.

Maybe if she staged an injury, or went outside and got herself into trouble like the naked lady, the Canadians would haul her out in an ambulance. Though they wouldn't take her to the border.

What she needed was a brave hick with a big truck. Did such a person exist in Toronto? She rewet her warm washcloth, pressed it to her blistered face, and flopped, backside first, onto the bed. She was running out of options and snacks.

Chapter Twenty-One

CANDI PANCAKES

Candi touched her hand-laundered panties. Still damp. The day's outfit would have to be yoga pants sans underwear, plus her nephew's Blue Jays sweatshirt. Not bothering to look at her toes or unwrap the bandages, worried they might be turning black, and then what? She dressed and rolled in her wheelchair to room 708. She needed coffee and she needed it now.

Vybes opened the door with an energetic grin, "Ready for cold eggs and stale toast?"

"I think I literally had a dream about a latte."

His attire, a lime green tracksuit with pink flamingos and silver stripes, resembled the straw in a fancy drink. His room was almost exactly like hers, but with two queen beds instead of a king. A rainbow assortment of clothes and electronics covered half the space. His rumpled duvet dusted the floor. The other bed was made and tidy.

"Where's Franck?" she asked.

Vybes cocked his head, "He was going to stop by and tell you."

"Tell me what?" Her eyes narrowed. Had Franck found some way to leave?

"He's doing a yoga class in the airport."

Candi exhaled. As if she could do yoga in her current condition. So that was the knock she'd ignored earlier. "You aren't a yoga fan?"

"I'm not a morning person," he laughed, jiggling his large lime-colored shoulders. "I'll get us both food if you want, and plenty of coffee and you can chill here, if that's easier?"

"That would be amazing."

He brought over the room's chair for her to elevate her foot, then left. As soon as she was alone, she regretted the decision, realizing that Franck could return any minute, and then they'd be alone.

Vybe's room faced the opposite side of the hotel, overlooking the airport. The crashed plane's carcass still jutted out of the terminal like a broken arm, albeit now snow–covered. When Candi saw it, her jaw locked, and her lip quivered. She imagined Adrienne sipping on a glass of wine, or on her phone, or taking a nap, and then suddenly, lights, and fire and... death. She shuddered.

Snow removal vehicles drove around the plane. A figure in the distance, a dark dot in the white haze, headed away from the crash. She followed it with her eyes until it vanished. It was someone leaving the airport on foot. Her heart pounded and her feet ached at the thought. Everything was surreal. Instead of being here, by this awful window, she should have been at home with Jasper, so that's where she went, behind closed eyes, she imagined breakfast in bed, the hair on Jasper's bare chest, his arms, his lips.

But her daydream didn't last. A man's voice boomed into the room over a loudspeaker. It was the hotel manager, he explained. After a welcoming preamble and a promise to return the hot water, he said, "Due to the current emergency and the flight cancellations, we're working with the Government of Canada to keep everyone safe. However, we may need to consolidate rooms in order to provide space to stranded families. Throughout the day, hotel staff will be coming around to single-occupancy rooms to make adjustments. Thank you for your cooperation."

Shit, Franck had been right. Her heart pounded. She hadn't believed it would actually happen. They must be expecting the snowstorm to continue if they planned to consolidate rooms. She really didn't want a roommate. Though she felt a bit guilty about being in a room by herself when there were families with kids sleeping in the airport, but she'd reserved a room; they hadn't. And bunking with a stranger was unacceptable.

The door opened and she pivoted to see Franck, his hair slicked back, wearing a gray t-shirt and sweatpants.

"Oh hey," he said, stopping mid-step. "I wasn't expecting you here. Did they move you here already? I just heard the announcement."

"No, Vybes just went to get us breakfast."

"Oh. Well, of course if they make us consolidate rooms, you'd be my first pick," He grinned and pulled off his shirt.

Candi tried to contain her surprise and quickly averted her eyes, but it was too late, she'd seen his chest and stomach, surprisingly toned for a man his age, and tan.

"I'm going to take a quick shower," Franck said, "And I mean quick."

She nodded and kept her eyes on the rug.

Vybes returned and they ate lukewarm, rubbery pancakes, tater tots, and containers of artificially sweetened yogurt.

"I'm assuming you heard the news?" He said.

"I did."

"You can move in with us, so you don't get a stranger."

"That's kind of you, but if they consolidate rooms, I'm finding whatever vehicle I can and driving south."

"In this?"

She nodded. Even though she knew it was pure fantasy, she needed pure fantasy right about now. The breakfast tasted like hospital food, which made her think of Jasper in the hospital, before he died, which filled her with sadness. It was like she would totally forget about him, only to remember him again five minutes later and get upset all over again, like she was a dementia patient. But now was not the time to cry. At least Vybes with his constant, running comedic interpretation of the weather was there to distract her.

Franck exited the bathroom fully dressed in what looked like fresh clothes. She was envious that he'd been able to retrieve his checked bag.

"How was yoga?" She asked, somewhat impressed that a man his age would voluntarily do yoga. She'd tried to get Jasper to join her and he always refused. He said it felt like taking a nap in different positions while strangers watched.

Franck ran his fingers through his damp, black and gray hair, which curled a bit in the front, giving him the air of a youthful political figure, or a painter. "Nice, very nice. I met a lady with a private plane connection. Her husband runs a mining company, and wants her and his daughter back home."

"Oh wow," Candi said. "Maybe we could get a seat on their plane?"

"I offered to buy us a seat." Franck flipped over his palms to say, *let's see.*

Candi almost jumped from her wheelchair. She wanted to hug him. "That would be amazing. I'll pay you back, whatever the cost."

He chuckled in a condescending way that made her glad she didn't hug him. "I'm sure it's a long shot."

"I don't think anyone can get too far in this storm," Vybes said, looking out the window at the ever-falling snow.

Franck shrugged, "I'm sure there are planes that can fly in this. She said they're trying to get to Florida."

"We're going to Vegas," Vybes proclaimed in his chipper British accent.

"You're in the aviation industry," Franck turned to her, "Why can't they just de-ice the planes and fly us out of here?"

"It's the high winds and the amount of snow on the runway.

It's not that simple and now everyone is paranoid since the crash."

"My office doesn't seem to care anymore if I stay. I think they like me being on Eastern Standard time for a change, or it's so close to the holidays that everyone has already mentally checked out."

"Do you celebrate Christmas?" Candi asked, suddenly wondering if Franck was Muslim.

"No. I was raised Muslim, but I don't practice much."

"I don't mind staying here for longer," Vybes said. "I'm easily adaptable."

Candi swallowed another lump of cold yogurt then said, "Well, that makes two of you, because I'm not fine with anything about this."

Franck rubbed the stubble on his chin. "Let's see how this offer pans out. I'm sure the mining people know what they're doing. They operate in Calgary and cold places."

"I saw on the news that NASA was flying planes around the storm."

"They fly over them. Not in them," Franck corrected her.

"It would be pretty funny to drive a snowplow all the way to Vegas." Vybes laughed. "I'd do it just for the videos, for the headlines. Like catch me DJ-ing in the snowplow." He sang the last few words and moved his hands back and forth like he was scratching records.

Franck rolled his eyes.

The idea was funny and for a second it made Candi smile. "Most people in Vegas don't even know what a snowplow looks like."

"Viva Las Vegas! I'll drive it down the strip!" Vybes pretended to steer a car with his hands while his long body lounged sideways on the bed, like he was Burt Reynolds by a fireplace. "I've always wanted to go to the south, like South Carolina or Alabaaama," he drew out the words.

"Alabama is not close to Vegas," Franck said. "Well, I'm going to get breakfast now. I haven't eaten." He looked at Candi, "Want me to push you back to your room?"

"Stay here." Vybes said to Candi, "You don't have to work; I don't have to work. We can watch a movie or something."

She swirled the remaining coffee in her styrofoam cup, "Thanks Franck, but I'll stay here for now."

"Suit yourself." Franck pursed his lips and left.

"He has the hots for you." Vybes said. "He's jelly donuts that I'm alone with you in his room." He rolled onto his back and laughed, "I sadly think he wishes he never met me."

"No, no." She felt her cheeks flush, embarrassed.

"I think so..."

"I'm old enough to be your mom."

"My mom? Really? Come on. How old are you?" Vybes sat up to inspect her.

"I'm almost thirty-five."

He broke out laughing again. "Darling, your math is a wee bit off; my mother is 62. You're probably closer in age to me than to Franck. Let's see, how old did he say he was?"

Candi scrunched up her face, "52."

"So, I'm 28, you're 34, and he's 52?"

"Wait, you're 28?" Candi was taken aback, she thought he was twenty-one or twenty-two.

"Yes, dear, didn't you know? Black don't crack. And I'm half black. SO, you and I are only seven years apart, and you and Franck are 15 years apart."

Candi's head spun like a globe. She couldn't do math that fast. Was Vybes correct? She felt more akin in age to Franck than to Vybes. God, she thought, why do I feel older than I really am? Then again, there was a world of difference between 28 and 34, wasn't there? But what exactly was the difference? Less happiness? More responsibilities? More bills? It's not like I have kids, so I can't use that as an excuse.

"Hello. Earth to Candi," Vybes waved his large, brown hands, his fingernails were painted pink now with black tips. "How many fingers am I holding up? Are you still there?"

"I guess you're right. I don't know, I thought you were younger. Nice nails."

He held his fluorescent hands to his chest. "Why thank you. I get that a lot and I hope it never ends. Keep me young forever, please! Young and dumb!"

Must be nice, Candi thought, to stay in the state of a teenager, to be so unconventional and vibrant.

"You don't look old either, by the way," he said. "I assumed we were like the same age, or close to the same. Like you don't have a *fupa* or anything."

Candi almost burst out her last sip of coffee. "That's a word you don't hear every day."

"May you never hear it," he laughed. "But even if you had one, I'd still be friends with you."

"Oh, well thanks, because between this wheelchair and the hotel food, I'll probably have one by tomorrow."

Vybes laughed and turned on the news. They watched scenes from the snowstorm. Most of the footage was shot on cell phones by random people in Toronto of collapsed roofs, children huddling together in jackets, and families collecting firewood to burn from Toronto's High Park.

"At least we have heat," he said. "It looks pretty bad out there."

It was true. She should feel grateful, but she didn't, not really.

"What we need is a monster truck. Just drive right over this mess, and I could give myself a monster truck driver name!"

Like the snowplow in Vegas, for a second the image of Vybes in a monster truck made her smile. "What would your monster truck name be?"

He bit his lower lip and his eyes flickered with delight. "Your monster truck name is your last Halloween costume plus whatever your dad did for work."

"What? How do you even come up with these things?"

"Mine is..." He thought for a second, "Vampire Gyno!" He grabbed his stomach and almost rolled off the bed laughing.

"Vampire gyno," she wheezed, laughing too. "Your dad was a gyno?"

"Yep, I'll never see as many vages as him! What about you? What about you?"

"I-I haven't dressed up in years."

"Oh poo, okay the last costume you remember plus whatever your dad did."

"Let me think." There was only one costume that came to her mind, she'd done it as a joke for Jasper; he'd thought she looked sexy. She stifled a laugh, "Schoolgirl Landscaper."

"Hahaha," Vybes howled, "That sounds so naughty."

At that moment, Franck came in from breakfast. "What are you two cackling about?" He sounded like a grumpy principal.

Candi sucked in her breath, trying to compose herself.

"Snowplows only." Vybes winked.

Ugh, he's gonna make Franck even more jealous, she thought and quickly explained the monster truck names.

"Haha. Very funny," Franck said dryly, not laughing or even smiling.

She wanted to return to her room now that he was back, and clearly in the mood to kill the vibe, but she also didn't want to be rude. With his private plane hook up, he was possibly her only chance of getting out of here. She waited fifteen minutes, while trying to keep all the conversation light, asking Franck questions and smiling sweetly then finally said, "Well, I should get back to my room."

"Yes, I need to work," Franck checked his watch, "I've been slacking off."

"I'll give you a push," Vybes offered as Franck opened his laptop on the room's desk.

At her door, the towering 28-year-old put his hand on her shoulder, an easy task since she only came up to his waist in the wheelchair. "Hey, before you go," he whispered, "I don't want to be presumptuous, but since I'm annoying the shit out of Franck, do you think I could move in with you anyway? And that way you also won't have to get consolidated with a stranger."

The question and his warm hand caught her off guard. She paused and swallowed.

He held both palms in the air like it was stick-up. "I promise I'll keep my hands to myself."

What could she say? She didn't want to share a room with anyone. And if Franck was jealous now, he'd certainly be jealous if she invited Vybes to move in... *Why wouldn't this situation just end?* But he was right, rooming with a stranger might be worse. Or would it be? Maybe she'd get another American woman, or another stranded flight attendant.

"I only have a King-sized bed," she said, avoiding the question.

"Franck yelled at me this morning like I was a little kid who needed to clean up his toys."

Candi stifled a laugh. Vybes' side of the room was ridiculously messy, and Franck was extra quiet and clean.

"Anyway, tossing it out there, and then we could take your LSD. Think about it." Then he bounced off, waving goodbye.

But there was no time to think. As Candi hoisted herself from wheelchair to bed, with a rap, tap, tap, someone knocked on her door. She scrunched her face. Vybes again? Had he forgotten to tell her something?

Another knock, louder.

"Candi Burns?" A female voice called from beyond the door.

Chapter Twenty-Two

CANDI FRIENDS

A woman with blond hair and an iPad explained to Candi that the hotel was consolidating single occupants on the floor to create space for families stranded in the airport. The hotel staff wanted to move her into a conference room they'd set up with cots to accommodate single travelers.

"It's not just you. We're relocating all the single guests on this floor."

A rush of adrenaline shot through Candi. A conference room? Use the public bathroom or gym locker room? The woman's sentences blurred together. She almost wanted to cry, though she knew she was being a baby. Things were probably worse for families, but why did it always feel like single people got penalized? It wasn't her fault she didn't have a husband anymore, or kids. A tear squeezed out her eye.

"I'm sorry," the woman said, "I know it's an inconvenience, you'll have any money you paid to the hotel refunded, of course. It's just temporary." The woman sounded so cheery, like she'd solved world hunger. "Should only be for a night or two."

"Really? Are flights resuming?" She'd almost forgotten that things could return to normal. Nature could solve their whole human mess.

"I haven't heard that exactly, but the hotel is working with the government to get folks home safely."

"I really prefer to stay in my own room."

The woman looked her in the eye, "I'm afraid that's not possible. If you want to gather your things now, I'll come back in an hour to take you to the conference room."

"Please, I'll pay extra to stay here. I'm a flight attendant. I may get called back anytime and then you can have my room." Gosh, she really was promising money she didn't have left and right today, but what else could she do. "Please, I can give the money to you. I could Venmo you right now."

The woman frowned. "We don't have Venmo in Canada. We have families of four and even five and six who need rooms. We have elderly people sleeping on the floor in the airport who haven't bathed in days."

Candi rolled her lips and flushed with shame. She shook her head. Her mind raced. Franck would probably get relocated too. He wouldn't want to do that. If they pretended they were a couple, maybe they could stay in his room. Then Vybes could sleep in the conference room. He was young and "adaptable" as he'd said, and he had no room to begin with. Though it meant being alone with Franck, at least he had two beds, and sharing a bathroom with one person was better than potentially sharing one with a hundred, especially since he was as tidy as a 50s housewife and possibly her only way home.

"Actually, wait. I've made a friend on this floor. Could we share a room? You can count us as a couple. Then the family can still have my room."

The woman sighed, "Okay, we can do that. Which room?"

Candi gave her the room number and Franck's name. The hotel employee scanned her list, but made the adjustment that Franck would move to Candi's room, since he had two queen beds instead of a King bed, and all the queen rooms were going to families with multiple children.

"But, um." Candi stopped. Her heart dropped to her peach

sneakers. They could not share a king bed. No way. He'd have to sleep on the floor.

Before she could speak, the woman gave her a look that said, don't even go there...

Candi felt cornered. Still, keeping her room was better than moving to a cot with a bunch of strangers like a refugee camp. Without any other choice, she latched onto the idea that sharing a room was temporary. Just for a night, she told herself as the hotel employee wheeled her along to Franck's room to finalize the switch.

Surprised, but as mild mannered as ever, Franck smiled politely and agreed to the arrangement.

Of course, Candi thought, he's probably thrilled.

The hotel coordinator left them, no doubt moving onto the next single person on her list.

"What about Vybes," Candi asked. He wasn't in the room. "Where is he, anyway?"

Franck shrugged, "I'm not his babysitter."

Again, a trapped sensation crept through her chest as she waited while Franck packed up his belongings, organizing all his clothes neatly into air compression pouches organized by garment type.

She sent Vybes a text and explained the move. He needed to come get his things before a new group moved in.

When they reached her room, Franck wheeled his suitcase inside and said, "Umm. Laundry day?" His finger pointed to a pair of underwear looped on the closet door knob. Candi's cheeks went cranberry red. All over the dresser, desk, and chair her lacy bras and panties hung out, finally dry.

Chapter Twenty-Three

GRETCHEN'S ROOMMATES

The dreaded knock came just before lunch. Gretchen rushed around the room, throwing her trash into an overstuffed bin, then opened her door to find a hotel employee, a man in his early forties, a tired looking woman, and two young boys under 10.

Consolidation, the hotel staffer explained.

Her face collapsed. How would all these people share her room? She was expecting another single person or maybe a couple, but an entire family? The coordinator explained that they'd be bringing in a double rollaway bed for the kids. The parents would take Gretchen's other queen bed and Gretchen could either stay or go to a conference room and receive a twin cot. Gretchen opted to stay. No way she could sleep on a single cot in a room full of strangers. The queen bed and a semi-private bathroom was preferable, or at least she thought. She tidied up more and shoved her belongings in the closet.

The family said hello, but eyed her wearily as they moved in their many bags into the room. The once luxuriously large suite instantly converted to cramped quarters. She introduced herself, but soon realized that no one but the older kid really spoke English. The family was from Angola, the elder boy, age eight explained in broken English. His brother was five and they'd flown to Toronto on their way to Vancouver to see family for Christmas. That was about as much as Gretchen could get out of the kid.

For the next twenty minutes, the mother fussed over her children. The younger one wouldn't stop whining, and the dad paced in front of the window on the phone, yelling at someone in Portuguese.

Fuck my life, Gretchen thought, and with her stomach growling, made her bed and left the disgruntled family alone, venturing downstairs to the restaurant in search of lunch.

Chapter Twenty-Four

CANDI CAFETERIA

As Candi scrambled around the room removing her now-dry panties and shoving them back in her suitcase, she noticed her feet no longer hurt as much. "Hey, I'm walking," she announced to Franck, almost giddy. "I'm walking and it isn't hurting."

He gave her a placid smile, "I can see that, but did they say you should use the chair for a specific amount of time? You should follow whatever instructions they gave you. Frostbite is a serious matter."

Candi frowned, why couldn't he just be happy for her. Instead, he critiqued everything she said. She shrugged, "They didn't say much. Anyway, I'm just happy they feel better."

He nodded and went back to hanging his work clothes in her closet.

Vybes arrived fifteen minutes later with his overstuffed duffel and nowhere else to go. The new residents, two older couples, had arrived in Franck's room. "Sorry," he sighed, "I feel like I've come to a birthday party with no gift."

If only this were a birthday party, Candi thought, but it's just about the furthest thing from it.

"You can get a cot in the conference room," Franck immediately suggested, but Candi jumped in.

"Nonsense, stay with us." She decided Vybes could be a buffer to Franck's advances.

The young man glanced at Franck, then back at Candi. "Are you sure?"

"Yes, yes." Candi gushed. She felt jittery like a spider lived in her shirt. "We can go to the lobby to see if we can get an extra cot. I can walk now. My feet aren't hurting."

"Oh my God!" Vybes jumped with glee and almost hit his head on the ceiling, then hugged her. "That is so so amazing! I'm so so glad!"

Candi couldn't help but smile, though she caught Franck scowling once again at the hug. Serves him right, she thought, for being such a downer. They left him to his computer and Candi and Vybes went down to the lobby to enquire about a rollaway for the room.

Of course, the hotel front desk had no extra beds.

"I can sleep on the floor," Vybes said as they headed together to the hotel's restaurant. "I don't mind at all. They say it's good for your spine"

"No, we can take turns, but I'm glad you can stay. It'll be more fun," Candi said, wondering if she should tell him about Franck's perpetual advances.

Weary guests thronged the restaurant, forming a long line out the door, and instead of a buffet, men in Canadian military uniforms distributed yellow styrofoam trays of food wrapped in blue plastic. She and Vybes waited behind a younger Black woman with short, curly hair wearing a University of Arizona sweatshirt.

"Oh hey," Candi said to the woman, "Did you go to the University of Arizona?"

"I did."

"My brother went there too."

The woman's face lit up. "Awesome. Are you from Arizona?"

"Vegas," Candi said. "Well, I am. He's um." She motioned to Vybes. "How do you describe yourself? British? Ugandan?"

"Yes, a proper hybrid." He stuck out his large hand. "I'm Vybes."

"Gretchen." The woman said. "Nice to meet you."

"And I'm Candi."

The line advanced one more person.

"What brings you to the frozen tundra?" Gretchen asked.

"I'm a flight attendant."

"Oh nice. So do you have any inside scoop on the plane situation?"

"I wish. The airline isn't giving us much info. What do you do?"

"I'm a journalist."

"You'd have the inside scoop then," Vybes said.

"Scoop of cold potatoes is all I'm getting around here."

"The food has really gone downhill," Candi sighed.

"We're trying to make the best of it though." Vybes added. "Quite the adventure if you ask me."

"Adventure is not the word I'd use. But with this garbage, maybe the silver lining is that I'll lose some weight."

"Don't look to me like you need to lose any," Vybes grinned.

"Why, thank you." Gretchen winked at Candi, "You got yourself a keeper."

"We're just friends," Candi clarified. "We were on the same flight. Then we got consolidated into the same room."

Vybes smiled at her and an unidentified feeling stirred in her stomach. They had become friends. What a weird thing to happen.

"Oh, lucky y'all. I'm staying with a family and no one speaks English except me and one of the kids. I'm considering moving to the stairwell." She shook her head. "The dad keeps yelling on the phone in Portuguese."

Candi listened as Gretchen went into more detail about her rooming situation, but her mind drifted. She imagined a real breakfast and clean clothes, an actual Starbucks latte...

As they finally reached the main table and grabbed their trays, Gretchen turned back and said, "Well, nice to meet you all."

"Hey, you should come by for a drink," Vybes said.

"A drink? You mean you have alcohol? Hell yeah, I'm dying for a glass of wine. Please tell me it's wine."

"Some wine. Mostly vodka and whiskey, and a ton of LSD."

Candi's mouth fell open. He shouldn't be telling people they had LSD, especially with all these military officers around.

"A ton of what?" Gretchen let out a giggle.

Vybes' brown eyes twinkled. "I think you heard me."

"We found it in our room," Candi quickly added, trying to act less mortified than she was that Vybes had shared her secret. "We don't really know what it is."

"Sounds like a real party. No wonder you're calling it an adventure."

"If we're still here for Christmas, we can all take it on Christmas Eve." Vybes' eyes kept dancing in the artificial light, "And have a holly jolly acid Christmas."

"Y'all crazy. Ha, acid Christmas. That's hilarious. Though, good God, I hope we aren't still here for Christmas. But sure, it sounds like more fun than what I've got going on."

Candi couldn't believe how casual everyone seemed to be about LSD. Did people just do this kind of stuff? She didn't have any adult friends who would have taken acid in a hotel from a stranger. Who were these two?

Vybes and Gretchen exchanged numbers, and again Candi felt a weird stirring in her system, a brewing, simmering anxiety, and a sensation of jealousy in response to the ease with which he carried himself, the way he made friends quickly, his casual confidence. She found it hard to make new friends. It wasn't like she wanted to keep Vybes all to herself, but they didn't know this woman at all. Though she'd taken the LSD in stride, she could have just as easily reported them to the authorities.

Vybes was having a fun "adventure" and chatting up strangers, planning an acid Christmas party while she spent her time stifling grief, fear, and dread.

A man's voice over the intercom interrupted their conversation. "Good morning, this is the hotel manager. We hope you're enjoying your stay during this difficult time. We are working to restore the hot water, however, we are needing to conserve fuel for the generators and heat due to the storm's impact on the electrical grid." The manager continued explaining the situation as the restaurant rumbled to life with conversation in reaction to the announcement.

"This isn't good." Gretchen said, stating the obvious.

"Could be fun," Vybes offered, clearly flirting with the journalist. "They say cold plunges are healthy."

God, he is the same guy from the airplane, Candi reminded herself. They parted ways with Gretchen and took the steps instead of the elevator with their lunch trays in hand.

"Are you okay?" Vybes asked. "You seem distant."

Candi lowered her voice, stopping on the stairs to face him. "Well, you told her about the LSD. What if she reported us to someone?"

"Reported us?" Vybes laughed. "She seemed cool. We should all go to the airport bar later, if it's still open."

Candi didn't respond. Her eyes fell down the long stairwell. Like her current situation, the conversation suddenly felt weird and overly familiar. Why the fuck was she here? She shouldn't be here. Jasper was like Vybes, the more the merrier—he would have said. He was always more trusting and open with new people than she was, but look where that had gotten him.

She didn't feel one bit merry. Though maybe now Jasper would be skeptical of everyone like she was, if he'd survived. He would have changed. He would have become like her, preferring his dog and a good book to airport bars and strangers. What happened would have changed everything. Would have... should have... She wanted to cry for the 100th time that day, but instead she mumbled, "I don't know, sorry," and resumed her climb up the steps, noticing that though she could walk, her feet didn't feel quite right. Her skin felt tight. Maybe she needed to loosen the bandages.

Chapter Twenty-Five

GRETCHEN'S GIRL SAM AND DANIEL FORD

After scarfing down her lunch in an isolated hallway on the hotel's top floor, a space she'd identified as potentially empty, due to the fact that it contained only two penthouse suites, Gretchen gave up her remaining dignity and called Sam once again. Though she knew Sam didn't deserve her calls, she couldn't stop herself. Sam probably wouldn't answer anyway. Her back against the wall, she brushed crumbs off her chest and listened to the phone ring. But then, a click... Time seemed to stop for a second. Was Sam actually answering?

"Hey." The familiar, raspy female voice sounded as excited as a half-asleep sloth.

Gretchen sucked in her breath. Sam actually answered! But the detachment in that tone... Maybe this was a bad idea. It took her a second to even think of what to say.

"Hello?" Sam sounded annoyed.

"Hey Sam," Gretchen said, "Are you okay?"

"Well, I'm trapped in a concrete stack in the midst of the second coming of the ice age, but sure, yeah, I'm fine. Netflix is still working, what more could I ask for?"

Gretchen's breath released. "Netflix is good. Boston knows how to deal with snow at least."

"No one knows how to deal with this."

Pause. Tense silence.

Gretchen rose like an eager groundhog to fill the gap. "I'm glad you're okay. When I kept texting you and you didn't respond, I got worried."

"And it seems like you're fine too, so we're both fine, so you can stop texting."

The coldness in her words. Gretchen swallowed, then shivered like she'd choked down ice cubes, which she kind of had. Where was the sweet, old Sam? The one who sipped homemade peach moonshine on rooftops and howled at the stars in tube-tops? The one she'd fallen in love with, even though she didn't often date women. That Sam somehow got replaced by this winter witch.

Gretchen took a deep breath, "No. I'm not fine actually. If you must know, I am in a bad place, not actually fine at all. I'm way less fine than you." God, she sounded juvenile, but this is what Sam drove her to. "I'm stuck in an airport. No one can leave. The snow won't stop snowing. I think my nose is frostbitten. I've got a blister on my face, and I've been stuffed into a single hotel room with an entire Angolan family and everything here is basically falling apart and it's freezing cold. So no, I'm not fine. Not at all."

"What? I thought you were at like a conference in Morocco?"

"Morocco?" Gretchen almost spit out her tongue. "The conference was in Mongolia!"

"Oh. So, are you stuck in Mongolia? I'm so confused."

"No, I'm stuck in Toronto."

"Toronto? Oh, wow. That's like the worst place right now, isn't it? I've been hearing about it. I have an old friend there."

Gretchen seethed. "What old friend? In the city? I really need to get out of this airport."

"Yeah, in the city."

Gretchen could almost hear the shrug in her voice, and she imagined Sam was looking at Instagram or something while talking to her.

"Who is it? Could they help me?"

Sam paused, "Probably not. Also, they're a cop."

Gretchen's mouth gaped open. She wanted to throw the phone against the wall. A COP? "You never told me about a Canadian cop friend."

"He wasn't always a cop. He used to be in the army. I knew him from Iraq."

"What guy in Iraq? With the Canadians?"

"Yeah. You never met him. He was before your time."

Iraq was the only thing that really bonded them together, Gretchen could see that now. And like their relationship, their days in Iraq were long over. "Please, I'm desperate Sam. I only called to check on you, but if there is any chance this dude could help me, I'll take it. It isn't safe here. It's going downhill fast. You know how it is—too many people in one place and not enough food."

Sam sighed, "But you hate cops."

"Thought you did too."

"Well, this one is cute. You'll probably like him, since you love men so much."

"Do you really think this is the time to be petty?" Gretchen snapped. God, why couldn't they go five minutes without fighting? The entire last month of their relationship, the only time they weren't bickering was when they were kissing or fucking, so why was she surprised? But still, in times like this, Sam's low blows were telling. She's just an unstable, PTSD bitch, Gretchen thought, then felt bad. That was too mean to say out loud, or even to think, regardless of if it was true or not. Why did she still love this moody, brooding, way-too-skinny Gemini photographer so much? Why she craved this bony bitch's attention made no logical sense. She vowed this would be their last call ever.

"Can you send me the cop's number?"

"He probably won't help."

"I'll pay him. I'm telling you; I'm not being dramatic. The

situation is bad. It's very bad. Why you don't care is beyond me, but I want to get out of here alive. This is life-or-death."

"God, okay, I care. I just doubt he can help you, but I'll send his number, sure. His name is Daniel, Daniel Ford."

"Thank you." Gretchen didn't want to tell Sam about Kevin. Sam didn't deserve anymore to know anything about her personal life. "Send his number right now while the phones are still working."

"Okay, okay, I'm texting it."

The text came through with a ding.

"Thank you. And you know what?" Gretchen said, "I really loved you, but we obviously weren't meant to be. So, goodbye Sam. I won't be contacting you again." Before Sam could respond. She hung up. Then, she put her blistered head in her hands and cried for a few minutes before she called the cop. He didn't answer. Gretchen dialed him again and again. She called his number eight times and on the eighth time, he picked up.

"Hello." A deep man-voice.

"Hi, is this Daniel Ford?"

"Yeah? Who is this?"

"Please don't hang up, I'm a friend of Sam Carlson."

Gretchen explained everything, more than everything. She wove the saddest sob story of her brother, her mother, the hospital, the yelling Angolan man, running out of food, Iraq, how her good friend Sam had spoken SO highly of the man on the other end of the line. And how Gretchen would do anything, anything, to repay him if he could just help her leave the airport.

By the end of the call, Daniel Ford promised to help her, his voice as sincere and as purely Canadian as a maple-flavored Tim Horton's donut hole. She'd struck the right damsel in distress strings of his little police officer heart. He had friends in the army, he explained. They had a sort of base, the armed forces college. It was northwest of the airport on a large estate where top level army officers from around the world studied military tactics and networked with Canadian generals. He would try his best to get her there. She'd be safe. He'd do whatever he could and if he couldn't get her there, then she could come and stay with him. He only had a one-bedroom apartment, but it would be okay, they'd manage. Any friend of Sam's was a friend of his. How was Sam by the way? She was the greatest, wasn't she?

No, she's a stone-cold cunt, a big giant cunt, Gretchen wanted to say, but she bit her tongue and praised her ex-girlfriend instead, thanked him, praised him as sweet as she could, in the highest, girliest voice one might muster.

We're all just one blizzard away from shacking up with a strange cop, she thought as she hung up the phone.

Without wasting time, she broke her own vow and called Sam again. This was important, she rationalized. Sam needed to be filled-in on Kevin and what she'd told the cop in case he cross-checked her story.

"Are you really serious right now?" Sam said when she finally answered on the fourth ring.

"I am serious." Gretchen replied. "Serious as an ice pick." And as she said the words, the walls and windows rattled. Gretchen rose to her feet and steadied herself on a wall. Her eyes darted around the hall. A thundering sound filled her ears and her heart rate floored to top speed. "Holy shit. I think we're under attack." She covered her head and sprinted to the stairwell.

Chapter Twenty-Six

CANDI DOWN

Candi reconsidered her options as she ate her limp turkey sandwich. The room already smelled too human. Maybe she should have moved to the conference room. Though at least the younger of the two men hadn't seen all her panties.

Franck broke out a bottle of wine from his bag. "Who's ready for a drink?"

God, was she ever. They all chugged the first cup, and the tension in the room reduced to a low simmer. Franck poured refills. "I keep looking out the window and thinking any minute the snow will stop."

"More military tanks are arriving," Vybes said.

Candi joined the men by the pane of cold glass, taking each step with care, still concerned about her wounded feet. Below, a caravan of dark green Army trucks followed an industrial plow. An icy sensation cracked across Candi's chest, under her sweater and over her breasts. Outside, the city, the airport, the highway—the entire landscape vanished beneath the rising snow, like they were suspended in a white, liminal space. Life used to be a familiar picture in a frame, one you could buy at Hobby Lobby, but now, on day six of the snowstorm, the image changed to a foreign science fiction film; she could no longer predict the next scene.

"They're probably bringing supplies," Franck said, putting his hand on his hip. "That's a good thing. Don't want to run out of toilet paper."

A loud noise erupted overhead like a cannon firing. Candi instinctively clutched onto the closest thing—Franck. An explosion followed the first deafening sound, then came a steady drone, like a jet rushing overhead. Franck grabbed her by the waist and pulled her away from the window. Candi threw her hands over her ears. "What is that?" she yelled. Terror replaced her chilly disassociation with a visceral, intense pulse rapping against her sternum. She dropped to her knees and crawled behind the side of the bed furthest from the window.

Vybes shouted something, but she couldn't hear him over the noise.

The sound boomed louder, like a giant pull-string lawn mower, sputtering and popping and the building seemed to shake. It sounded like a sky raining boulders.

"The hallway!" Franck yelled as he yanked Candi up by the arm. She clung to him and they ran out of the room. Other guests streamed out with fingers in their ears.

"What's going on?" Franck shouted to another man. Candi clutched his arm, terrified.

"Get to lower ground," the man called back. "It's coming from above."

At the end of the hall, a group clustered around a wide, floor-to-ceiling exterior window. An avalanche barreled down the side of the hotel, like a white waterfall. Military planes shot by spraying gas out of metal tubes. She gripped Franck tighter, and he held her close as they joined their frightened floormates, clumping and crowding together like fleshy magnets in front of the torrent of falling snow and the cacophony of the zooming aircraft.

"It's the Canadian military," Franck shouted in her ear. "Don't be afraid."

The rumbling and thundering sounds continued. She sucked in breaths of air, clinging to Franck, but adrenaline roared through her veins.

"We're under attack!" someone screamed.

And we're trapped, Candi thought. There's no way out. We're going to die. The hallway seemed to sway. The lights flickered. The ceiling and window shook. She couldn't hear herself think.

Franck's mouth was moving. He was yelling something, but it was too loud outside to hear him. He tugged on her, motioned back to their door and she followed him into the room, not knowing what else to do. The sounds and shaking continued.

Inside, Vybes lay on the bed like Sleeping Beauty, in a Zen state with his eyes closed, wearing his bedazzled headphones. She stared at him in disbelief, wondering how he could be so calm. Franck lowered his body to the floor, then slid himself under the bed. She did the same, scooting beside him on the carpet. Her body wanted to shut down. An alarm in the hotel went off and blared repeatedly. She could feel Franck's hand on her arm, a light squeeze, like she might leave if he didn't hold on, but she couldn't turn her head to look at him. There wasn't enough room. Her breath came in jagged gasps. The dust under the bed made her sneeze. The sound of the jets intensified. She lay perfectly still, waiting in fear for whatever came next. Tears pooled in the corners of her squeezed-shut eyes. I have to get out of here, she thought again. How am I going to get out of here?

Chapter Twenty-Seven

VYBES VIBES

In the ear-splitting tumult of the hotel's potential, maybe inevitable collapse, alone in the shaking room, Vybes found Candi's book and ate a tab of what he hoped was acid; then for good measure, facing imminent destruction, he ate another. If this was the end, he was dipping out Hunter S. Thompson style, in a fantastic blitz, with a noggin full of LSD.

Candi and Franck had run off somewhere. He put on his noise canceling headphones, turned up an old song by Bob Sinclair called "World Hold On," and set it to repeat. The man's voice sang, "Open up your heart. What do you feel?" as the acid came on slow, then sped up, heavy, like a chunky girl pretending to be your friend when she really wants the vitamin D, the pants-jammer, the hog dog, the *mbolo nene*...

The grinding, roaring torrential din continued. Sirens punctuated the beats, but he focused on ignoring them. His thoughts tumbled and swirled like rocks in a tornado. Colors pulsed behind his closed eyes. Marabou storks danced on pink sunsets. Lake Victoria shimmered, and he plunged into her waters. A glass egg rotated and glowed at the bottom of the lake. This acid is strong as fuck, he thought. After some time, his experience opened up, felt more free and his body relaxed. The whooshing jet sounds receded into the distance and he reopened his eyes. Franck and Candi were back in the room. Their presence startled him and he immediately shut his eyes again.

The shining glass egg was gone, and a rainbow snowflake vibrated on luminescent guitar strings. Time passed and again he felt a surge of energy, a desire to talk, a curiosity about the earlier uproar, and so he opened his eyes once more.

Franck was pouring wine. Candi looked like she needed a hug, or perhaps a straightjacket. The carpet transformed into the neon string things he'd just seen.

"I turned around and you were both gone," Vybes said.

"You sure took that calmly." Franck didn't look at him, but took a deep swig of wine.

"I thought we were all going to die," Candi pressed her palm to her collarbone like a necklace, rubbing her chest through her sweater, like she was urging her heart to decelerate.

"What happened?" he asked.

"We don't know for sure, but I suspect they were blowing snow off the building. Perhaps they feared a roof collapse. We're lucky in a way. No one is blowing snow off the houses out there," Frank gestured to Toronto, but Candi asked him to draw the blinds, saying she'd had enough of everything.

Vybes watched them. Candi glowed red and Franck looked green. Her feet hurt, she said. "I think I overdid it, running on them." She reclined on the bed beside him and he could feel her warmth. He wanted to hug her. Could he hug her?

Could he even think straight? His vision brightened. Wonder set in and everything around him electrified with vibrant colors, motion, sensations, joy.

He couldn't wait to tell Candi that the acid was real. It worked! But would she be mad?

The floor, the wall, textures swimming. He felt connected to a current. He wanted to take a walk, but he also wanted to see Candi's book again, to look at the art. A force propelled him, urged him to see it. He needed it with him.

"Can I look at your book?" he asked her.

She found it and gave it to him. Neither she nor Franck seemed to realize he was tripping.

Like a child sneaking sweets, Vybes fingered the velvet, forest green cover. Everything around him fluttered; that's how he felt too, in motion. He took deep breaths and willed himself to stay focused as he opened the book. "Looking is for free." That's what they would say in Kampala when you passed by a shop. "Come on in. Looking is free." The book weighed heavy in his hand, as heavy as a case of beer in a college kid's backpack. He flipped to a random page. There it was again, the strange inexhaustible images, each sparking with animated color. You could never see it all. A girl strummed a harp of multicolored and dripping, liquid paint that flowed into her blond hair. The strings of the harp vibrated beyond its frame, representing the vibrations of sound itself, like the girl's entire world was a psychedelic lake. The woman, instrument, and sound waves made a full circle, an orbit. What was this book's purpose? To be beautiful? Was that enough?

Candi came closer to him on the bed, also looking at the pages, and he liked the feeling of her body being near. He traced his painted fingernail over the harpist, a mix of young and old, a crone and a babe. Faint lines sprouted and pruned paths around her red lips and creases puckered at the joints of her lapis eyes, a trove of lifespans, a person overlayed with ages. Aren't we all? Though not everyone. Some are gone. *Nakimuli...* his little sister. He'd been thinking more about her since the storm. Maybe because of the state of uncertainty, she was with him again. His memory of her had fossilized, become mythological. More than his dead sibling, she contained his entire childhood, departed.

Nakimuli.... He believed she still existed somewhere. Like this painting that only he and Candi could see right now, someone could see Nakimuli. His mum said her soul lived in the most beautiful flower petals, because Nakimuli meant flower in Luganda, her first language. But flowers die, he'd always think.

No, he envisioned her in original form, on an alternate timeline, one where the medicine came fast enough. One where she'd never gotten sick in the first place. Hell, maybe one where mosquitoes never existed. Wouldn't that be nice?

The cold would do that, he realized. Another ice age and all the mosquitoes would die.

Poof. Bye.

He flipped all the way to the end. The tab he'd taken was from the middle of the second half of the book. No one cared about that part. The very beginning or the dead center or the very end would have aroused suspicion, but he was safe in the subdivision of a subdivision, a nothing spot, 3/4ths of 2/3rds or whatever. Even people didn't remember that part of their lives. Nostalgia begins at the end, but focuses on the beginning.

When would he die? Would he be 50 or 95? 33?

Or maybe by then, humans would live really long, like they used to in the Bible, up to 900 years, or even forever, so there would be no beginning of the end, only the continual, like the woman as a circle of paint and sound, not even a loop, but an infinite forward trajectory.

His grandma claimed the old ages in the Bible proved that humans used to be better designed, more perfect. Then, the flood broke them and everything changed. It deteriorated the pure DNA. His grandma would wink and say, "those were the Black Africans, the ones who lived that long. The perfect ones." It was a running joke that his Ugandan side of the family were descendants of Adam, as in Adam and Eve. His ancestors survived the flood, that's what his grandma said, and that's why everyone in the family was so tall. Humans were giants before those Noah's Arc times.

The thought of his grandma, like the memory of Nakimuli, turned his trip sad. Emotion welled up his chest and into his throat. His *Jajja* was still alive, but she wasn't doing well. She'd returned to her village, north of Uganda's capital, and spent her days on a worn outdoor sofa, staring at the banana trees and mumbling. Her hands never stopped shaking. A young cousin brought her hot tea every morning, which she struggled to swallow. She wouldn't live to 900 or even 90.

A tear formed in his eye. God, this acid has me all emotional, he thought. I just couldn't wait. Like that experiment where they told kids not to eat marshmallows, well, I ate them.

"Are you okay?" Candi asked, interrupting his thoughts.

He nodded and turned the page.

Another picture, a blue, luminescent river winding through glowing cedar trees. Haze filled the air, and beside the water squatted a green, yellow, and orange frog. The frog pulsed and breathed, grew and shrunk again. Vybes grinned. This one was cool. If it was a poster, he'd hang it on his wall.

Why do I even care if Candi finds out I've taken the tabs? He wondered. But he did for some reason. Taking it in secret felt wrong, yet somehow necessary. He didn't want anyone scrutinizing whatever was about to happen to him or waiting on it to happen. Nor did he want to hear Franck's snide comments.

The frog grew larger than the moon in the center of the sky.

Candi left his side.

He turned to the window, but the curtains were closed. This hotel room—no, too drab, not good. Must go. The walls contracted. It felt claustrophobic. He needed those curtains open, to watch the snow, but Candi wanted them shut. He didn't know how much time had passed since he'd eaten the tabs. If this is the beginning, how will I manage the peak? He wondered. *Banange.*

Franck and Candi poured more wine.

He looked again at the painted frog. It winked at him, and as clear as crystal, it said, "Look at your phone."

He almost dropped the book.

Then his phone rang.

Chapter Twenty-Eight

GRETCHEN STRESSIN'

She texted Sam, but with each response, found herself more upset. It was like Sam would never care enough. Her heart still hammered, and her breath remained uncatchable from her run down 20 flights of steps, and the panic induced by the unexpected roof-clearing. From a sofa in the lobby, she watched a trickle of angry guests complain to the front desk, all with the same complaint like they were running off a script. Watching them over and over again made them seem like they were actors or video game NPCs. The hotel employee also ran their script each time and the scene repeated. Bet she is rethinking her career choices, Gretchen thought and glanced at her phone. No response to her last message to Sam. She sighed, then blocked Sam's number again. Then unblocked it.

She had deeply considered what it would be like to freeze to death. She hadn't really pondered what it would be like to get caught up in some weather war. Was this China? Or Russia? People speculated about the storm on Twitter and Reddit — many also thought it was a weather attack. Others said that was impossible because to seed snow clouds you needed to fire rockets or lasers into clouds or fly planes through them, and surely people would have seen the planes or rockets. It all made her head spin.

Leave it up to men to figure out how to shoot lasers into clouds, she thought.

When she learned that the US had first used weather attacks in the Vietnam war, via planes loaded with silver iodine, to cause severe flooding and block enemy routes, she put her phone down. It was too depressing.

The stream of complainers continued and after about the 10th, like the reception scene, her role of frustrated-woman-waiting-in-the-lobby would also be recast; she relinquished her spot on the sofa to another lady and rode the elevator to her room.

Her roommates stared at her like she'd arrived from outer space. The mother's eyes, red and drained, fixed themselves on the open window, the endless falling snow. The father focused on the screen of his phone. The TV blared annoying cartoons. With the extra bed, you could barely walk through the suite. The younger of the kids sneezed and the mom coughed. Gretchen asked the child to tell his mother to wear a mask, but the woman either didn't understand or didn't care because she kept coughing into only her hand.

Tense, Gretchen slipped to the bathroom and checked her facial blisters in the mirror. The only good thing about the family was that the mom kept cleaning their bathroom, probably for stress relief away from her shitty husband. Still, it was nice, and she probably wouldn't have done it herself. Without access to a real doctor, she'd consulted a medical Ai and followed a strict schedule of warm water compresses, gentle soap, no alcohol, and regular doses of Advil, plus a moisturizing routine on the surrounding skin. It had paid off, no more blisters, all healed.

And now, she thought, it's time for a freaking drink.

She called the only person she knew in the hotel: some guy named Vybes.

Chapter Twenty-Nine

VYBES VYBRATING

He waded to the hallway with his phone, leaving the talking frog behind. Liquid steps.

"Hey, what's up?" It was the cute girl from the cafeteria on the phone.

Yes, he would meet her. Where? She explained, but it was kind of unclear. The breezeway. Okay, he'd find it.

He didn't invite Candi or Franck, nor did he go back to the room to explain. He couldn't be in a small room right now. His hands beamed blue lights from his nails. The floor puddled like swampland. A few deep breaths. The bar. No, the breezeway. Meet the girl. Thoughts like clouds. Drinks would be good. Drinks would slow down this shit show. Ripples on the river. He found a wind. It glowed with hanging strings, a work of art.

He searched for the breezeway. He wanted to go outside, to touch the snow, but he knew better. It was too cold. He'd seen what the cold had done to Candi's toes. A window would have to do. It would work, or it wouldn't work. On the waves of current he floated, avoiding the eyes of all who passed. More graceful than a jet, more buoyant than a bird flying south. Carried by color and light, he found the breezeway and waited, watching the setting sun turn the snow from white to fire to blue night. Then all the real light got lost in the cotton mouth of the atmosphere, somewhere behind these ghostly clouds, on the other side of the spinning earth, so connected that they made one heavy blanket, and the electric, artificial light switched on, and in the shimmer of falling snow like smashed crystals, beyond the glass he noticed something else. He traced it with his eyes. It was a being, a single thing, but he knew it was a thing, a creature, a real, breathing or maybe not exactly breathing, but something alive. Sentient. It moved in a million particles.

Vybes backed away from the window.

Fear replaced wonder, gripping his gut and chest. His bowels churned.

Was he in the right place?

Where was the girl? Shouldn't she be here by now?

He wanted to run, but his eyes were like insects caught in a spider's web.

Then he heard it again, the frog's voice, but there was no frog, only the snow and the string thing.

Relax, it said.

Just relax. We see you. You are okay with us.

Us?

Who are you? Vybes asked. He took deep breaths. He watched the thing sway, taller than the tallest tree. It had no head, no eyes, only a collective of synchronized lines, a pattern too complex to fully realize.

We are here again, it said. In time, you will understand. Do not be afraid. You can see us and we can see you. The time will come soon.

Now watch.

Watch what?

Close your eyes.

And he did.

There was a Christmas tree and a Rastafarian man carrying a sack. He was with Candi. The Black man lit a fire. Vybes put the green book in his sack.

This is your job, the frog voice said.

What time?

THE time.

The time for what?

For time to turn from a line to a circle. For the arrow to orbit.

Vybes rubbed his unblinking eyes. "I've gone mad," he whispered.

You have not, it replied. Relax. Look again at your phone.

The girl was calling. He was in the wrong place. Fuck.

"Okay," she said, "just come to the hotel lobby, by the Christmas tree."

Wonder returned. The voice spoke again. It told him more things. Though they were hard to remember, like a foreign language he only partially understood. Then it showed him the way.

He obeyed and as if there was an open window, a breeze of cold touched his cheeks, his neck, the skin of his arms. The web released him. It said goodbye.

In the lobby, he waited by the Christmas tree, which he hadn't noticed before. Had it been here the whole time? It sparkled with bulbs and light and green and gold garlands. It was lovely but absent of life. He studied it and let it connect him to the past, the past of everyone who'd made the tree, the past of everyone who believed in Christmas. A series of faces emerged like a dream to him. All were men. There was a blond one with blue eyes, a Black man, an Asian man, and then he saw his own face— a brown man, then another man, and another, and another. He lost count. Each man looked different. Why?

No answer.

Then the first woman appeared. Then more women. All were young, beautiful women, in their late teens or early twenties. He snapped his eyes open. The last one was the journalist, Gretchen. She stood beside him.

Strange.

Another realization struck him: I saw angels. Real angels. Giant angels. Snow angels. He laughed out loud at the discovery.

"Hey, what's so funny?"

He looked down at Gretchen. "Just had a funny thought. It's hard to explain."

"Well, I'm glad someone's laughing, cause I'm not. Let's get a drink. It's been a day."

By some miracle, the airport bar remained open, and they took the last high-top table. He wanted to be near, as it was hard to hear with the other patrons talking and the acid coursing through his veins. He moved his chair by hers, first asking if it was okay. Of course, she said yes. Most girls liked him, and he liked most girls. Her hair smelled like coconut lotion. Vybes giggled and did his best to follow Gretchen's words. Though he still wished, desperately wished, that he could go outside. The crowded bar felt so confining. He wanted to taste the snow on his tongue, to pick it up in his hands and sense its changing texture, see its intricate, natural art, listen to it crunch under his hind, but he knew he shouldn't, not now, and possibly not for a very long time.

The snow wasn't for him. It was them.

And before he knew it, his hands were on Gretchen's thighs and her warm lips kissed his.

Wake up, he thought he heard her whisper, or maybe it was *them*.

Then, he realized he was imagining things. He drank more beer. They weren't kissing. But had they?

The journalist kept talking.

He tried hard to focus.

"I heard about a tunnel," she said. "We should look for it."

Chapter Thirty

CANDI CREEPER

Buzzing like a beehive from all the wine, Candi studied Franck. He was shorter than Vybes, closer in height to Jasper, but more hulkling, with broad shoulders, a barrel chest, wide hips, and thick thighs that pressed the edges of his sweatpants. Whereas her Jasper was lanky, Franck was tanky.

He rubbed his stubble-covered chin. She could feel her eyes sparkling from the Merlot and Bordeaux. Jasper could barely grow a beard.

"I preferred the first red." Franck said.

She thought they were both great; anything was preferable to bad coffee and crackers, or room-temperature, rubbery pancakes, and overly sweetened orange juice. She hadn't eaten anything since breakfast.

"Vybes must have gone somewhere to talk on the phone," she said.

"Great, let him talk to someone who wants to listen."

She almost spit out her wine, "That's mean."

He shrugged, "You haven't spent several days with him."

Soon, they sat on her kingsize bed together, laughing, opening the third bottle of wine. Franck told her about growing up with his immigrant Indian parents in London, then moving to the

Netherlands for university, where he'd studied finance, then worked on a vineyard in France, flirted with the French girls, married a Tunisian woman, and finally settled in Belgium, but they'd divorced after she'd had an abortion without his knowledge or consent.

Candi's voice softened, how sad. "Did you really want kids?"

"Yes, and I really wanted an honest spouse."

She thought about confessing her own troubles, but decided against it as it would entail explaining that she wasn't married. Shit. For a moment, she'd forgotten about the 100-year blizzard, forgotten she was stuck in Canada, forgotten about death. Remembered how to have fun and she didn't want to stop. Candi drank more wine.

"Are you seeing anyone now?" She asked Franck, trying not to hold his eye contact, aware that they sat a little too close on the bed.

"There is a woman, a neighbor. We met during the pandemic. We have, what do you call it? A situationship."

Candi giggled.

"I'm not interested in getting married again, but you know, we all have physical needs." He trailed off then his expression widened to a sly grin. "I probably shouldn't be telling you any of this."

"Your secret situationship is safe with me."

Franck tilted towards her and raised his plastic cup. She toasted him.

"What about you?" He asked. "How did you meet your husband?"

"We met on an elevator in college, in Vegas."

"Was Elvis there?"

She made a weird face.

"Elvis impersonators—I thought they were all over Vegas?" Franck caught her in his tipsy eyes which twinkled with a naughty delight.

"That's only at weddings."

"What does he do? Your husband."

"He's a professor," she said, on autopilot, as if he wasn't dead, but poised at the lectern.

"So, still at school, and what does he teach?"

"Philosophy."

"Ahh... You like the thinking types."

"You could say that."

"And are you happy with him?"

The last question was a spitball through a straw. Suddenly, Candi wanted to cry. She stood up from the bed. Was she happy with him? She was unhappy without him. That was the answer. Only a European would ask such personal stuff. "Yes. We're very happy," she lied.

"That's good," Franck leaned back and crossed his bulging legs, "A good relationship is a good life."

She stood awkwardly by the bed. "Actually, studies show that single women are happier and live longer than married ones, but men live longer when they're married."

"'Cause men are babies and women do all the work," Franck also stood up and touched her arm. "Should I crack the third bottle of red? Or we could see what's for dinner."

Her body tingled where he touched her. He was kind of handsome. Maybe she shouldn't have lied about still being married to Jasper, but no, this wasn't what she wanted either. Where had Vybes gone? She wondered. Shouldn't he be back by now?

Franck removed yet another bottle from his carry-on. How did he fit so much in it?

"Maybe we should conserve the wine? I think I'm drunk."

"Okay, dinner then? If only I could take you somewhere nice," he raised his eyebrows.

She blushed and looked away. Vybes needed to come back, and soon.

Chapter Thirty-One

GRETCHEN'S TUNNEL

Gretchen grinned over her good luck. Of all the guys in this fiasco, despite her plus-sized figure, she'd bagged a hot one. I should never be insecure about my body, she thought; everyone has their own taste. Lots of guys like bigger girls. They were definitely going to smash. She could tell. No way he would be getting so close otherwise. His gaze lingered on her curves, tracing the contours of her body with an intensity that made her feel both seen and stimulated, checking out her chest and even her crotch. Hey, why not? Everyone in the hotel was probably horny from being cooped up, and not like she had a girlfriend anymore. They were both single as a slice of pie.

The image she'd snapped during the mayor's slideshow of the airport property, included an outline of the tunnel beyond the south fence of the property, but no indication of its entry point.

"I'll follow you. Lead the way," he said, and he did, like a gigantic puppy lopping along beside her. Two teenagers necked in a corner. Vybes and Gretchen exchanged bemused looks as they passed the young lovers unnoticed. Since forced to move in with the Portuguese-speaking family, not wanting to stay in the room, she'd already searched the unrestricted parts of Terminal One. She led him to Terminal Two, then down the escalator to the ground level. He maintained his permagrin. What a happy guy, she thought, again marveling at her luck, and maybe the cutest one she was ever going to bang, but where? Not her room or his. Plus, the way his white chick friend eyed her earlier, that girl probably had the hots for him too. Maybe a bathroom would have to do. At least the tunnel search served as the perfect excuse to scour the building for a private spot.

On the lowest floor, in the dim, reduced-wattage fluorescent lighting, with all the windows completely packed in with snow, a spooky liminal atmosphere cloaked the baggage claim. Her breath caught in her throat, and she halted. "Is it me, or it's fucking creepy down here?"

"I wish we could go outside."

"Oh no, it's way too cold."

"I know. I just wish..." he put his arm around her. "But hey, don't be scared. Everything will be fine."

Did she appear scared? Wow, he was perceptive and deluded, but his embrace switched on her lady parts. Their bodies rotated together like two kids at a middle school dance, eyes on eyes, her hands went to his hips, his to her shoulders. Their heights differed by at least a foot. She licked her lips and inhaled, ready to be kissed. This was going to be so, so good.

But he didn't kiss her, not yet.

"The tunnel," she said.

Chapter Thirty-Two

CANDI COVERS

They ate trays again from the cafeteria—meatloaf with cold mashed potatoes, unappetizing, but she finished her whole plate, hoping the food would absorb all the alcohol in her system. Vybes still hadn't returned, and she wondered where he'd gone without telling them.

Franck switched off the overhead hotel lights and turned on the bedside lamps. He played music for her on his laptop, things he thought she'd like. A song she loved from her teen years came on, a solo female singer crooning about being a naughty girl. "Ooh yassss." She swayed to the music with her drink, then dropped her booty low and gave a tiny twerk. Franck's face was a smirk. "This is way better than my old room."

High on wine and a blizzard that was feeling more like an apocalypse, she kept dancing. He watched her from the bed. As the song ended, he lowered the music a click. "Did you hear something?"

Candi shook her head, but then she heard it. Someone was banging on the door.

They stared at each other and froze.

"Oh," she said, "It must be Vybes."

Franck opened the door, but instead of the young man, an

older white woman burst into the room. She had stringy gray hair and a grim expression. "Can you all please keep it down?"

The playlist rotated to the jam "No Diggity."

Candi reached to lower the music, embarrassed.

"Sorry, just blowing off steam," Franck said.

"This isn't the time to be partying," the lady snapped. "Don't you all realize what's happening? We're being attacked!" The woman waved a finger at them. "You think this is normal? I've lived in Canada my whole life. I've never seen snow like this."

"Would you like a drink?" Franck asked.

"Absolutely not. I'm trying to go to bed!" The woman sputtered, flabbergasted.

"Well, have a good night," Franck ushered her to the door.

"I'm calling security if that music keeps up!"

Franck shut the door and put the dead bolt on, then turned up the music.

"No," Candi said, "Really?"

Then the two of them fell onto the bed and burst out laughing. The song "Bitter Sweet Symphony" played and it seemed all too appropriate.

"God, I haven't heard this song in ages," Franck said.

"We should probably turn it down though, like keep the peace."

"Nonsense. It isn't even very loud."

"Too loud for the Karen," Candi giggled, drunk now and feeling emboldened a little by Franck's no-nonsense attitude. He was kind of like Chad, always on top of everything. She respected that.

"Karen Von Party Pooper—always a critic, never a dancer."

"If the world ends tomorrow, we won't care because we're all going to feel like shit." She giggled.

"Speak for yourself. Here, drink more water."

"Okay, dad." She followed his advice and drank water, then more wine. They finished the bottle. Vybes still hadn't returned.

Had he met up with that journalist? "Maybe we should call Vybes, see if he's okay?" she suggested.

Franck gave her a dubious look, "He's a big boy."

"But does he have a key?"

"Doubtful, but we can't leave it unlocked, we'd have to leave the whole door open." Franck raised his eyebrows, "Perhaps, he'll find somewhere else to sleep."

"Or one of us will have to wake up. I should call him."

He didn't answer.

By midnight, worn from stress and booze, her body wanted to power down. Were they really going to share a bed? She wished Vybes would come back. The situation didn't feel right, though something in her lower stomach stirred at the thought of sharing a bed with Franck, a little too low for her taste. It must be the wine.

Franck turned off the music and they ran through their bathroom routines. She crawled under the covers in her tank top and satin pajama shorts. As she snuggled under the duvet, Franck also slipped under it. Her body stiffened. He wasn't sleeping on top of the sheets like they'd agreed. Had he forgotten? Should she say something?

He rolled away from her, reached over, and turned off the bedside lamp.

It would be fine, she decided. It was a king size bed after all, plenty of room. Darkness enclosed them and she shut her eyes, expecting to fall asleep immediately, but with all the wine in her system, the room spun. She opened her eyes to stop the unpleasant, spiraling feeling.

"Goodnight," Franck whispered.

"Goodnight."

Motionless, she could feel him, sense him. He smelled like toothpaste and men's aftershave. It reminded her of being beside Jasper. She hadn't slept with another person since his death. Jasper. She wished he was here.

Go to sleep. Go to sleep. She told herself. But it was hard to relax beside Franck. She squeezed her eyes shut, fighting the spins, willing herself into slumber, but after several minutes, tossing and turning, she opened her eyes again and there he was, his pupils catching in the moonlight, his black hair on the pillow; he faced her, watching her—not Jasper, but Franck.

Chapter Thirty-Three

NIGHT VYBES

Vybes wanted to kiss the Black American girl, what was her name? He couldn't remember at the moment. Her image blended and fluctuated with the lights, the room, his imagination. Could he land his lips in the correct spot?

"Let's test interior doors," she said.

"I want to enter your inner door."

She laughed and her skin glimmered, alive, colors in motion. He really needed to sit down. Everything shuddered. Was this the acid peak? Just touching her shoulders was enough electricity to make his head explode.

He led her by the hand to a row of seats in between a luggage carousel and the street exit. Could he really do this? He wanted to.

Seated, he pulled her onto his lap, right there in the baggage claim. She complied, straddling his wide thighs with hers. God, her weight on him felt great. He pulled her closer, feeling her breath and body heat against his chest, her breasts. He kissed her neck and squeezed her round ass and a million sensations splintered and roamed his veins. Images. Ideas. Sounds. Geometry. A merging.

"We should go someplace," she whispered, leaning back from his lips, looking around. "This is crazy."

But they were alone and he didn't want to walk.

"It's cool here," he pressed her lips to his, entered her with his tongue. With each motion, colors became crystal snowflakes and rotated, twirled, danced, and intertwined. This is like the book of acid, he thought, as he kissed her. He wondered if he'd be able to get hard while tripping.

She moved her hand to his crotch. The answer was yes.

They stayed clothed and he rubbed her crotch on his dick until she came, moaning hot sounds in his ear. Then they went to the bathroom and she blew him.

"Good God, you're big," she choked between sucks.

But he couldn't cum. Was this really happening? It felt good, but also weird, like he was detached from his own body.

He closed his eyes and floated through all the stars, all the clouds, the snow, maybe God. They sat on the floor, backs against the wall of the baggage claim for the equivalent of apocalyptic pillow talk. Things simmered down. The night grew late. He held her hand. She lay her head on his shoulder, his lap. Kissed him more. The acid wore off. Both yawning, out of other things to say, they said goodbye; he promised to call. She apologized for not successfully finishing him off. He said it wasn't her; it was him and apologized for not finding the tunnel and kissed her again and again, grasping both of her full breasts in his hands before they parted ways.

Chapter Thirty-Four

GRETCHEN'S NOSE FOR NEWS

With the sun already up, Gretchen scuttled to her room, panties damp, body buttery and tired, relaxed, but excited, drained, but tingling. What a night. In gray, velvet-lined leggings, and the Arizona hoodie, before she reached the door, she called her family for an update on Kevin. Her mom and Kendra didn't answer. Finally, her dad picked up his phone. "Hello?" His voice was gruff.

"Hey, are you with mom?"

"No, she's in bed asleep."

It was five AM there; she'd forgotten about the time difference.

"How are you doing up there in all that snow? Your mother and I've been watching the weather channel."

She rarely spoke to her dad on the phone, and it felt odd. "I'm fine," her voice cracked a little, "I'm—I'm just worried about Kevin and I'm ready to be home."

"Well, you're better off staying up there, with this variant I wouldn't be getting on a plane."

Her mood dropped like a snowball in water. She hated that her parents couldn't enjoy their retirement and had to worry about the pandemic yet again.

"They moved Kevin to a cardiac ward."

She let out an exhale, "Oh thank God."

"I don't know if it's really any better." Her dad sounded tired.

"Are they letting Kendra at least stay with him?"

"Your mom didn't tell you?"

"Tell me what?

"Kendra's in quarantine in a different part of the hospital. She's also positive and they're taking all precautions."

Gretchen swallowed, hard. "But if she's positive, what about the kids?"

"So far so good."

"You guys should wear masks in the house with them."

"We are."

This year was proving to be the worst Christmas of all time. "What else are they saying about Kevin? Is he improving?"

"He may need a heart graft or something. They've got him on all kinds of drugs and blood thinners."

Gretchen's hand moved to her chest. "What? Like surgery? What kind of graft?"

"I don't know."

How could her parents not ask these important questions? She wondered.

"But Kevin's not out of the woods yet."

Gretchen slumped against the wall. Her face smelled like Vybes' dick and bodily scent. Warm tears hovered in her eyes. Don't upset your dad, she thought. Be positive. "Please stay safe. I miss you guys. I'm trying to get home however I can."

"Well, don't do anything foolish in that blizzard, and don't worry about us. I'm going back to sleep."

They ended the call and she shuffled to the door of her room with dread, deciding she would pack up her things and leave, find somewhere else to sleep. She couldn't face another day of Portuguese shouting or kid's cartoons, but the family was gone—or maybe out to breakfast.

Her body instantly relaxed a notch, knowing she was alone,

and she donned a black eye mask, stuffed her ears with orange foam earplugs, put on her satin headwrap, and secured the bed covers over her head, struggling to remember the last time she'd cum so hard or stayed out so late, literally all night long. Despite the bad news about Kevin, a half-smile lifted the corners of her lips. Sex was still good, even when everything else was shit.

Chapter Thirty-Five

CANDI SEES THE LIGHT

Candi and Franck locked eyes for a moment, two strangers in a strange bed, and not quickly enough, she turned away. Wet with wine, she buried herself in the sheets. When she finally awoke, that's what she remembered first, Franck's piercing gaze, but now everything in her field of vision confused her. Like a clock after a power outage, she'd missed something. Instead of Franck, a young man with a shadow of a beard, a thin nose, and black tendrils of hair, snored gently on top of the covers beside her.

Vybes... Vybes had finally come back.

I am a curse, was her next thought.

She remembered it all now. She was in Toronto, in a blizzard. The plane had crashed. Adrienne had died. Jasper had died. PumpkinChai had died. Would there be a funeral for Adrienne? Who would organize it? She'd left a comment on Adrienne's social media account, expressing her condolences, but she didn't know Adrienne's parents. Will they even contact me if there was a funeral? She wondered.

A tear threatened to drip from her short-circuiting retina; her head felt stuffed with nails. Bright snow drifted beyond the window. At least the sun shone brighter today, giving the room more natural light than she'd seen in a week, or did it only seem brighter because she was so hungover?

As her eyes swung around the room, trying to grip onto reality, a lump caught her attention and she instinctively put her hand over her mouth; Vybes' crotch bulged in his sweatpants. The peak in his pants projected out like a microphone pointing at her; did she have something to say? Her green eyes widened. Holy shit. He has morning wood. Massive morning wood. Of all the things to see. Candi slid out of bed. Her feet remained asleep. She covered her mouth, not to stifle her reaction, but because she was about to throw up.

Like a plate thrown against the wall, she hurried to the bathroom, slumped onto the toilet and held her head in both hands, trying to put herself back together while she emptied her fiery bowels.

God, why did I drink so much wine? Her head hurt so bad. The sounds of her rumbling diarrhea filled the cream-colored, tile room. It stunk like a dead raccoon. With a throbbing forehead and a dry, corpse-tasting mouth, she chugged water straight from the sink, splashing it all over her face and neck. There was Advil in her toiletry bag and trying not to gag on them, she swallowed two pills, then brushed her teeth. Soon, she would run out of her travel-sized toothpaste and mouthwash, a terrible realization.

The chances of getting home for Jasper's ceremony now appeared as slim as a pin. Jasper's mother wouldn't be happy. Puffy and red, she wanted to crawl into the bathtub like a junkie girl in the movies and just bawl. But tears don't bring back dead lovers, she knew that already.

Still nauseous, she ran the shower. Maybe a cold shower will wake me up, she thought, but to her delight, the water was hot. Candi almost clapped at the heat on her hand as she ran her fingers through the steaming stream.

She shampooed and conditioned her hair, washed her armpits and crotch, then looked around to identify what objects she might insert into her vagina. She needed a break. A release, anything to quash her misery while she waited for the Advil to kick in. As she maintained fairly long nails, she'd never liked fingering herself, and preferred using objects for pleasure. At home she had a palm-sized silicone dildo, something she purchased after losing access to Jasper's penis on demand, but her choices appeared to be the top of a bottle of conditioner or the handle of her hairbrush. Not great options, but she picked the hairbrush, since the conditioner might squirt.

On some level, she understood she was using fantasy to distract herself from the current emotional state, but like a drug addict looking for drugs—she didn't care about the why, only the when. She wanted to feel better right now, even if only a brief interlude.

Reclined in the tub, she swirled the base of the brush around her vulva while the hot shower pelted her legs. Jasper's naked body came to mind, his erection thick in a nest of dark pubic hair, but despite her efforts at fantasy, a tormenting thought intruded: Chad's chiseled body frozen under 10 feet of snow.

Ugh. Stop. She thought and pushed the brush in harder, but it wasn't working. She couldn't fully relax or focus and her head still pounded.

Despite the long shower, she returned to the room to find Vybes still asleep. She curled up in the swivel chair and glanced at his erection, expecting it to have gone down, but it persisted. Crazy. Returning to bed didn't seem appropriate, not with the campground constructed in his pants. Did adult men still get wet dreams? Or was that only a teenage boy thing? She remembered that Jasper used to wake up with a raging erection, and they would make morning love, but she couldn't recall him ever jizzing in his sleep.

Franck must be working somewhere else or at yoga. He probably wasn't hung over at all. He seemed like that type, and she cursed him for it. Though maybe he'd get updates about the mining plane.

Not wanting to wake Vybes, she passed more time by looking

at pictures of the blizzard on her phone. The connection ran slower than usual, but she read that Toronto had an underground city, called The Path, a giant indoor shopping mall connected to subway stations. A few restaurants and bars in the Path had been able to stay open and people from condos connected to The Path congregated there nightly, throwing parties, playing music, and dancing in the tunnels.

Aside from The Path parties, the news was grim. Over 100 people had died between the US and Canada, mostly elderly, from heart attacks, likely caused by too much physical labor, as with the extra heavy snow; shoveling was tantamount to pushing rocks. Roofs all over Toronto collapsed under the weight of snow. People moved in with friends or family, or into shelters. In a hotel downtown, a riot broke out because there'd been no water for over two days; the pipes had frozen. It was discovered that the hotel's manager had hoarded all the bottled water, claiming them all for himself and a woman he'd shacked up with in the penthouse suite. The other residents beat him to death, then redistributed the water. So far, no one was under arrest for the incident because law enforcement was consumed with saving people from the blizzard. As the snow reached higher, those on low floors of apartment buildings consolidated upwards with neighbors. Adventurous folk attempted to walk towards families in other parts of Canada and New York state, but the authorities warned against it, because with the ongoing snow and wind chill, the risk of freezing to death was high.

Left with a chill from the horrible stories, she shivered and prayed for the blizzard to end. Hadn't the world been through enough? First the pandemic, then the war with Russia and Ukraine, and now this? Why couldn't the world just be nice?

After another hour, Vybes finally stirred. "Hey," he mumbled, "Good morning."

"Good afternoon, you mean," she avoided looking at his lower half.

He sat up in bed and realized the situation. "Oh, oops." He

laughed and grabbed a pillow to cover his erection. "Just the ole' alarm cock going off; time to get a girlfriend."

Candi almost fell out of her swivel chair. Alarm cock. She tried to think of a witty response, but failed. Instead she giggled which made her head hurt again.

He stretched his muscular arms, revealing a bicep tattoo, though she couldn't make out what it was. A flag maybe.

"You were out late," she said.

"Yeah, I met up with that reporter and we looked for a tunnel. Didn't find it though. We're gonna try again. You should come next time. Sorry I didn't invite you guys. I just..." He hesitated.

"Oh, I get it. You and Franck have been together a lot."

"Yeah, I. I don't know." He kept the pillow over his crotch.

"Did you see Franck this morning?"

"Nah. My head hurts though. Do you have any pain killers?" He rubbed his forehead.

She brought him the Advil and a cup of water, sitting by his bedside.

"You're like, still my flight attendant," Vybes grinned. "Or my nurse."

"Right. Sorry, this is so weird."

"Not at all. Thank you, Snow White."

Her cheeks flushed with heat. Why would he call her that? "Snow White has black hair," she said. "And you're hardly a dwarf."

He swallowed her pills. "Maybe I'm a prince," he laughed.

Was he flirting with her again? She couldn't tell. "Hey, at least the hot water is back on."

"You're freaking kidding me. In that case, I'm going to take a shower right now before it randomly goes off again."

She could only imagine what he was going to do in the shower with that boner. "Well, um. I think I'll go down to the lobby and see if they have any more coffee. I'm pretty hungover."

Hopefully, he'd have more success than her in the shower, but he made no move to get up and instead flopped back down on the pillow and closed his eyes again.

People packed the first elevator that arrived, so Candi waited for another. When it came and went full of parents and their kids; she gave up. Maybe doing some steps would help the hangover.

Cigarette butts littered the stairwell, and she recoiled at the smell of stale tobacco mixed with urine. Guess it was too cold for the smokers to go outside. She almost stepped in a pile of dried-up dog poo on the next floor's landing, and the stenches made her want to vomit yet again.

In the lobby, no one was at the reception desk. A cluster of hotel guests and staff gathered by the front windows, checking out the view, or lack thereof. Candi squinted and wondered what they were all looking at. The only view came from a tunnel-like path, the only exit, dug by the hotel staff through high walls of snow, but she couldn't see much. It was like looking from inside an igloo.

The people by the door pointed up at something.

"What's going on?" she asked a woman nearby.

"There's a strange light."

"A strange light?"

The woman nodded, "Up in the sky."

Candi's shoulders clenched.

Probably more military planes, someone said, coming to blow snow off the roof again.

The dystopian scene depressed her and her stomach rumbled, she glanced back at the unoccupied front desk. Maybe she could sneak behind and see if there was any coffee for their in-room machine, or better yet, extra toothpaste, or snacks.

As more people gathered to look up at the sky, Candi backed out of the crowd. Peaking over the reception desk, she only saw toilet paper and office supplies. She grabbed two rolls and stuffed them into her deep coat pockets, then hiked back up the nasty steps. On her floor, she found a supply closet, but it was locked.

Inside the room, Franck typed on his laptop at the small desk.

Vybes came out of the bathroom in a towel, fresh from the shower. "Did you find any coffee?" A thin stream of black hair dripped down to his navel over defined abs.

"Sadly, no, just toilet paper." Candi turned and put the two rolls on their TV stand, but not without first noticing Vybe's well-defined pecs.

"Hey, put on some clothes, kid," Franck said. "This isn't your Only Fans."

Vybes threw his head back and laughed, shaking water from his black curls onto his bare, broad shoulders like a dog, bouncing his pectoral muscles, jiggling his dark nipples. She could see his bicep tattoo now; it wasn't a flag, but a seal of some sort, like the kind of badge that would be on a coat of arms or an ancient shield.

"Sorry, I forgot my shirt."

Candi tried not to stare at his body. He was more ripped than she'd imagined.

Vybes went to his duffel bag. "For total strangers sharing a small hotel room, we're doing pretty well."

"Yeah, great roommates." Franck said, "Now get dressed before Candi chokes on a fly."

Both men laughed, but she wasn't laughing and her mouth wasn't hanging open anymore because of Vybes. Her entire body had frozen in place. Through the open window there was something.

"Oh shit," Vybes said, "What the fuck is that?" he pointed at what Candi's eyes had already found, a curved rod of light in the sky.

Franck stood. "*Mon dieu.*"

"Bloody hell. It's like an upside-down rainbow."

Beyond the glass, an enormous, glowing U floated in the air, shining through the heavy snow like a neon smile on a dental office sign.

Candi couldn't breathe or move. This wasn't real. This couldn't be real.

"It's massive," Franck said.

The surreal object floated in the clouds of snow, seemingly attached to nothing.

Vybes snapped a picture of it with his phone.

"There must be a logical explanation," Franck said.

Goosebumps raised on her arms. The desire to run crossed her mind, but the sight outside kept her immobile. Was it the government testing some new technique to end the storm? She wondered. The light contained a warmer sheen than pure white, like the gold haze of an angel's halo.

"Guys, I'm seeing something really crazy right now," Vybes said to his phone, live streaming a video of the thing outside. She watched Vybes zoom in on the shape with two fingers. "I think it's moving. Could be drones, but it looks solid. Can y'all see this?"

The arc rotated 180 degrees then flattened into a straight, thick line.

Candi's lips began to work again, "Guys, I have a bad feeling about this." Her eyes locked onto the incandescent U. What if this was the attack?

Franck stepped away from the window. "I... I think we should go to the ground floor."

The beam grew brighter. Fear pooled in her limbs and the muscles in her thighs tightened, readying her to run.

"Maybe it's the military doing some trick to stop the storm, CIA or some shit," Vybes continued narrating to his phone.

"I'm getting out of here," Franck said.

The flat line broke like a severed bridge, with a loud sizzle and snap, into two lines, side by side. They pulsed then rotated from horizontal to vertical and extended their beams to the ground. As they entered the snow, a flash of light burst from the beams.

Blinding light filled the room. The floor vibrated and shocks of electricity surged through her skin. Candi stumbled backwards. Her bladder loosened and before she could stop herself, she was on the carpet, peeing her pants.

Candi screamed and clutched at the rug with her fists. Her body tossed and jostled with volts of energy, like she was a flopping fish on a boat. Vybes crashed down beside her. A deafening crack like a whip split the air.

Covered in pee, she screamed and reached out her hand.

Vybes grabbed her arm and they shook together. Pain. Intense pain. Every nerve scraped open with a knife. She gyrated like a wind-up doll and pushed away from Vybes. He jolted up and his towel slipped off his waist.

The last thing she saw was his penis before another cracking shot of electricity shot up her legs and short circuited her brain.

Part Three

DEPARTURES

Teddy's Hymn for Help

Oh, the weather outside is frightful
    But the airport is not delightful
    But since we've all got places to go,
    let me know, let me know, let me know —
    Were you a good kiddo this year?
    No? Well, that's too bad to hear.
    A lump of coal for you my dear!
    Don't blow your candles out, cause your wish ain't comin' true!
    Life is like what's trapped under the snow; we don't exactly know.

The change of the climate
    They say is so real
    The end of the planet
    They say is so near
    They say they want power
    They have so many ideas
    So many fears
    They want to change nature
    Like God, or some angels

I'd be saying, please!!
Resolve our tangles.
Let my people live!
I'm not a denier, but seriously
can't we admit that we don't control fire,
Or tornados, or snow?
I just wish I could take the train home, but it isn't running, just people running
from their past.
The climate of change, they say, is so real.

The mayor even came, and surveyed the scene, waved his hands and smiled grimly.

But now he'll retreat, like a Bridal Path King.

He'll kick this frozen turd on down the road, to the provincial government. Then to the PM and his pretty face, smile, and sweet speeches, thick hair. Oh how the ladies love him. But when a man makes a plan either for himself or his clan, he forgets that he's just one element in a swirl of bedlam.

They're sending us away now, shops gotta close, no more coffee, no more TimBits, no more hot grease.

At least I have my pen. At least I have this poetry.

We're here like shepherds without sheep, and I'm without a manger to rest my weary dreads. When oh when will I see my bed again, and why oh why didn't I go home when I had the chance?

The rest of this story isn't as sweet as Boston cream, and my uniform is as stiff as a snowman's frozen carrot nose. If I had rocks for eyes I might be less wise, less worried, but alas I can still see.

Oh Nature, oh Nature
How we loath and adore thee.

The ferris wheel of life, like a Buddhist mandala, it destroys thee.

Well, time to clean up and gather my things, back to our delusional patience, the magical thinking that help will suddenly appear, that the government knows exactly what to prepare.

Chapter Thirty-Six

VYBE QUAKE

When he awoke on the floor, the sounds, surges, and vibrations had stopped, but the smells had multiplied. He could taste blood in his mouth like he'd chewed on a penny. Candi lay beside him, limp. Oh no, was she dead? He grabbed her wrist. Thankfully, her pulse was still there. Her body felt hot and he could smell her hair, her urine, and something else, a rotting aroma like old meat.

He tried to stir her. "It's okay. We're okay."

She coughed, but didn't wake up. Outside, the lines still hovered beyond the window, filling the space with alien light. Still wearing nothing but a towel, he scanned himself for signs of damage. He'd felt like for sure his skin was burning right off, but there were no burns, though he felt a bit achy in his joints. With stiff muscles he got up and put on a -shirt and sweatpants and cleaned the rug as best he could using soap and water, checking periodically to make sure Candi still had a pulse.

Franck wasn't there and Vybes wondered if he'd made it to the lobby or if he was in the hallway, passed out, but he didn't want to leave Candi to check. Instead, he shook her shoulders, very lightly, nudging her to wake. "Candi, are you there? Wake up. Hey, Snow White, please wake up."

When she finally came too, the first thing she did was lean over and puke on the rug. The smell of vomit filled the room, and he wanted to gag, but stifled the urge, knowing his reaction would only make things worse. "Hey, hey, are you okay?" He put his hand on her back. "Hold on, I'll get you some water."

She didn't speak, but let him wipe her mouth with a wet washcloth. She didn't want to drink the water though.

"You're okay," Vybes repeated, kneeling beside her, rubbing her back again.

But he could tell she wasn't. Not at all. She didn't look well to him. Her face was very red and something was amiss. He realized it was her eyebrows, or rather lack thereof. The blasts had burned the hair off her face. Her eyelashes too. His hand moved to his own forehead, but his eyebrows were there. He exhaled. His hair was still there too, as was hers. But he didn't tell her. Not now. There was too much going on. I should tell her about the acid too, he thought. When she calmed down he would tell her, because he'd seen things. He *needed* to tell her.

"How are you feeling?" he asked instead, to which she only groaned and crawled to his lap, curling herself in a fetal position with her head on his thigh.

"We're all gonna die," she finally whispered. "We're all going to fucking die."

And before he could reply, before he could reassure her in the slightest, the lightbulbs in the bedside lamps exploded.

Candi went rigid against him and her hands flew to her eyes, covering them like she could stop whatever was happening by not seeing it, but then she shrieked, no doubt realizing her eyebrows were gone. She clawed at her own face.

The other lights in the room flickered and flashed as he turned his head to the window. The glowing bars shifted to onyx, and streaks of blue and black light shot through them, racing up like they were sucking fluorescent oil or something out of the snow. Sizzling, slapping sounds ricocheted around the room, echoing over them.

Vybes leaned over and held Candi, as if to shield her from a storm, like his body was enough to stop death himself from coming through the window. She clenched her arms around his back, squeezing him, gasping, hyperventilating, shaking, and he watched the scene outside. Was it the government trying to stop the storm? But surely no government could do this? What even was this? Part of him wished he had his phone, he would've tried to video this again, but he didn't want to let Candi go to get it.

He braced his body for another electrical shock, but it didn't happen again.

The sound ended.

The lines faded into the snowstorm.

Everything was changing.

Did they know the truth? The things he'd seen.

This was crazy. So crazy. So surreal that awe replaced his fear. What on earth had they just lived through?

The pretty, red-headed flight attendant hung onto him like a small child, and he could feel every micromovement of her body–her quivering muscles, her breath, her heartbeat. He wanted to stay as close to her as possible, and he did. They held one another for a solid minute, maybe five, then ten, until the moment grew too long; it transformed into the kind of time that slips out of normal life and becomes like the star on top of a Christmas tree, not just another ornament, but the centerpiece. She finally sat up and looked at him. Tears filled her light, eyelash-less hazel eyes. Her chapped lips quivered.

"Hey, hey, don't cry," he pulled her to his chest. "Come on. It's okay now. Let's get you cleaned up. Let's put on our pajamas and get in bed."

He couldn't leave her alone. She was too fragile. He had to try and keep her safe. "Where's Franck?" Candi's voice quivered and "We should look for him too. Make sure he's okay."

Vybes nodded and remembered the journalist too. He should also check on her. Had she experienced the same shock waves?

But he figured she was probably fine; she was tough. Candi, on the other hand, she needed him.

Chapter Thirty-Seven

GRETCHEN'S GLOW STICK

The TV still worked, but not the internet. Gretchen stuffed her backpack with clothes. No way would she lay around in this room like a trapped mouse in someone's sadistic blizzard lab. She called Sam's cop friend Daniel Ford twenty times, but he didn't pick up. How typical. Why am I even surprised—the police only show up when you don't want them to, she thought. For all she knew, he was already dead.

Her family of roommates hadn't returned, but she wouldn't stay, not after what had happened.

Fast asleep, she'd woken up shaking, electrocuted. Her limbs still tingled, and her hair smelled burnt. At first, she thought it was a dream, but when she saw the parallel lines beyond the window, she knew. The U.S. Consulate had also known something. They must have.

As she gathered her things, the TV shared news clips from social media and buzzed with speculation and shared tweets of people calling the glowing beams different names—the snow arch, the electric horseshoe, the SnowBow, The SnowU, and even Santa's Evil Grin, but a comedian named it The Glow Stick and that stuck, though it was hardly a stick, more like two rods. The reporter estimated that it was bigger than the CN Tower. Jokes commenced on every platform about snow raves and aliens on MDMA, but Gretchen wasn't laughing, not one bit.

Conversely, the government officially claimed The Glow Stick, which they called "unusual weather phenomenon," was a natural, albeit rare occurrence, called "Thundersnow," which was like lightning during a blizzard, and no cause for alarm. Wow, Gretchen thought, they have absolutely no shame telling lies.

The news channel posted a phone number and invited people to call in, to share what they'd seen. One caller believed it was the work of God. The end was nigh, they said. Another woman called in hysterical, sobbing. The shocks had triggered a seizure in her child and they wouldn't wake up now.

Gretchen zipped her bag and laced her boots. Nope. Screw this. This wasn't thundersnow, or lightning, or Northern Lights, or any other type of natural phenomenon. At best, it was some kind of electronic military device to stop the storm. At worst... She didn't want to think about it. She'd find the tunnel and leave or die trying. Whatever was going on, whoever the hell had made the stupid Glow Stick, she was surely safer underground.

The news switched to another story—another Covid variant going around, now identified in five states, sending the U.S. economy once again into a freefall. A chill ran through her. The variant was spreading. A pediatrician in San Francisco had died. This strain caused sudden strokes and cardiac arrest, according to the news. Shit, Kevin. Please, let him make it, she thought and headed for her door.

"Also, this just in: it is snowing in LA," the reporter announced.

What? Gretchen stopped and turned up the TV's volume. Snowing in LA? What the fuck?

Three inches so far. Clips rolled of a white Venice beach with heavy snow flakes falling. Goosebumps raised on her arms. She recognized those clouds, those unusually large flakes. No. No.

California was way too close to where her parents and brother were.

Her phone buzzed. It was a text from Vybes— "Are you okay?"

She replied, "I guess..." and sent an alien emoji.

Chapter Thirty-Eight

CANDI CRUSH

For the second time in her life, Candi prepared to die. Vybes cleaned up her mess and she curled in a fetal position, near paralyzed, still shaking, crying. They didn't say much to one another. Then, he turned on the TV and she crawled under the covers of their bed. Friends she hadn't heard from in ages texted her videos of The Glow Stick, as if she hadn't seen it live. Her mother believed the government's explanation and sent texts telling her to, "hang tight, honey."

Alerts went off on their phones, messages that said military helicopters would be dropping packets of non-perishable food onto every residential street. Citizens were advised to bundle up, go outside, collect one food bag per family member, boil snow if they needed water, to shelter in place and await further instructions.

For many, The Glow Stick had appeared in the northern hemisphere, an indication that it had reached higher than the atmosphere. Despite the low visibility and bad weather, millions saw it, and many stayed by their windows, clutching their cellphones, hoping to film it if it reappeared, or, for the even braver, wandering in ski pants and boots into open fields, lugging tripods and cameras, with GoPros strapped to their heads, unafraid of the shocks, because they hadn't felt them, but she had. She knew; next time, it would kill them.

All she could do was try not to cry and even that was hard.

Franck finally returned around dusk, sauntering into the room as if nothing unusual had transpired, as if they weren't in the middle of some supernatural electric terrorist attack.

"Good news," he said and dropped into the swivel chair, "We have a ride."

Candi sat up. "Really?" Her heart fluttered like a trapped fly. "With the mining lady?"

"Yes."

She leaned forward. "When are we leaving?"

"Not today, and not tomorrow, but the following morning."

"What? That's too long." Her expression collapsed. "Why not today? Or at least tomorrow?"

"That's the best they can manage. It's been hard for them to find a pilot who would actually fly in. Everyone's afraid. I've bought us two seats." He glanced at Vybes, "Sorry, man, I tried to get three, but it wasn't possible."

Air sucked through her pursed lips. Poor Vybes, but she needed to get out of here, away from the evil thing outside.

Vybes shrugged, "I'm happy for you guys. I'm sure I'll be fine."

Candi stared at him. He was clearly delusional, but what could she do? Overwhelmed with joy at the prospect of departure, Candi got up and hugged him. "Thank you. Thank you so much."

"Yes, it's time to go," he said with a grave tone.

"Where will we fly to?"

"To a regional airport, then to Myrtle Beach to refuel, and then to West Palm Beach and then from there we're on our own."

But despite the good news, her fear of The Glow Stick's return remained, and she felt like a rabbit dropped into a snake's cage. In the suspended state of emergency, they drank vodka, said little, and fell asleep with the TV on, this time with Vybes beside her.

In the morning, her ankles felt swollen, but she ignored the sensation. She'd change the bandages later, after coffee. Instead, she focused on the hope of leaving. Only one more day to go. Just get through today.

The three of them waited for their breakfast trays in silence. A young girl ahead in line coughed repeatedly—loud, wet, and congested hacking from behind a cloth face mask. Many wore face masks now, as if a thin cloth could protect their entire lives from whatever was outside, from whatever they couldn't understand.

She yawned, having struggled to fall asleep, consumed with worry, wondering the truth, fearing the answer. When she'd finally fallen asleep, it was riddled by troubling dreams. She was in a Japanese restaurant with Jasper, but when she looked up from her menu, he was gone. She'd searched the restaurant, the bathroom. She'd wandered around Vegas looking for him, calling his name, but instead of finding him, she'd found Franck outside a casino. They'd gone up to his hotel room and kissed again. It felt nice, too nice. She'd woken up brimming with guilt, wondering how her brain could possibly conjure sexual fantasies in a time like this.

The girl in line kept hacking and coughing. Everyone looked weary, depressed, and fearful. Eyes darted around the room or studied the carpet.

"She sounds really sick," Vybes whispered.

"Let's get our food and get out of here," Franck added in a low tone.

A military officer approached and spoke to the girl and her mother. The pair, as well as a man and another child left the line and followed the officer out of the makeshift cafeteria. Candi wished she had a mask, the last thing she wanted was to get sick on top of all of this. The line inched forward, but she didn't move, leaving a gap. People bunched behind her. "I think I need to lie down," she said.

Vybes looked concerned, "Are you sure?"

"Will you grab me a tray?"

"I can come with you," Franck offered.

"No, I'll be fine, I just hardly slept last night," and she hurried out.

Back in their room, it smelled like an older house inhabited by too many people, like they needed air freshener. She closed the curtains and stretched onto the bed, shutting her eyes in search of a more ordered world. She imagined her wedding day, remembered the taste of her vanilla cake and Champagne, Jasper licking the butter cream frosting from her ringed finger. There was a time when she looked forward to things, now she only looked backwards.

Her phone rang; it was Jasper's mother.

Candi took a very deep breath.

"Hello dear. How are you?" His mother's tone was as casual as a Sunday.

"I'm okay," she lied.

"When could we get together? I could sure use your help with everything."

Did her mother-in-law not realize where she was? Had she not seen the news? "I'm still in Toronto, stuck in the blizzard at the airport."

"What a month," his mom continued. "You know Francis is supposed to come with her kids for Jasper's event?" Francis was Jasper's aunt from Maine.

Candi wanted to hang up. The way his mother said "event" made it sound like Jasper would be there, like it was an art opening or something. She swallowed and sucked in more air, reading herself mentally for the conversation to follow, then said, "I think we should postpone it."

"What? No, we can't. It's all been paid for and arranged, and we've waited long enough. Bill and I need this closure." His mom's tone changed abruptly from cheery to gruff. "And you need closure too, I'm sure. No, absolutely not. We are not postponing it."

"Only because of the storm," Candi corrected the course of the conversation. "I don't want you to have to do everything yourself." Though this was only half true. All she wanted to do was sleep, for like a year, if she could even make it home.

"Surely it has to stop. We still have time. I can't believe you'd even suggest canceling it," his mother continued. "I'm disappointed to hear you say such a thing."

The room's door cracked open. Vybes and Franck were back with breakfast.

"Sorry, I don't know," she backpedaled, wanting to end the conversation, "The blizzard has been stressful. That's all. Anyway, I've got to go."

"Well, wait. I have some questions for you."

"Sorry. Something's going on here. I'll call you later."

"Candi, now wait a minute."

Somewhat numb, she hung up on Jasper's mom.

"Everything okay?" Vybes asked.

"Oh yeah, everything's great," she waved her hands around the room, like see, isn't this glorious?

"Well, here's your food." Franck handed her a paper bag. "They ran out of trays and they really didn't want to give it to us. We had to say you'd sprained your ankle."

Vybes didn't press her for more details about the phone call. Nor did they talk about The Glow Stick. What was there to say? They sat against the bed's headboard and ate the hotel's cold and floppy eggs on toast. He nudged her, "Hey, do you want to try some of that acid today? That will wake us up and pass the time until your ride."

She scrunched her face. The idea sounded terrible.

They settled instead on watching a gritty crime drama

centered on an occult murder in the Deep South. Candi's thoughts wandered. What would Jasper's mom think if she knew Candi was sharing a room with two guys? She wants me to move on and find closure… Here you go, mom.

But, when her phone buzzed again with a call from Jasper's mom, she didn't answer.

"Well, I'd give that three stars," Vybes said when the movie ended.

"Or two. What should we do now?" Franck asked.

Candi had no answer to that question.

"I'd say the gym, but I don't want to get my clothes even more gross than they already are," Franck sighed and turned the TV to the news.

A nefarious gang of men in black now roamed the city on snowmobiles digging into buildings and looting abandoned stores and homes. Food was becoming a major issue with grocery stores closed. The military used tanks to supply emergency meals to shelters. More and more people froze to death and many resorted to trapping and eating rats and raccoons.

She shuddered, feeling the most concern for the children with bad parents, or with no heat. "Maybe we shouldn't watch this. I'm going to have nightmares."

Franck switched off the TV. "They say we're only four missed meals between peace and total anarchy."

"Then let's hope this storm ends soon," Vybes said.

Franck's phone rang and he answered. "Okay," he said somberly. "Well, keep me posted."

Candi would have furrowed her brow if her muscles weren't frozen with Botox. It had to be the mining lady, and it was.

"Delayed another day," Franck said after hanging up, shaking his head. "The pilot backed out."

She couldn't even speak. Instead, a tear slid down her cheek.

Vybes put his large hand on top of her palm, which was resting on her thigh, "We're going to be okay."

His unexpected touch sent a torrent through her limbs. She tensed up, surprised by the sensations.

That night, they all drank vodka again. What else was there to do? After two drinks, Vybes announced he was going to meet Gretchen to look for the tunnel, did they want to come too? Candi considered, but said no. Her ankles still hurt, and she needed to change her bandages, she'd procrastinated on doing it all day.

After Vybes left, Franck sprawled on the bed beside her. "I bet he's hooking up with that journalist."

She took a sip of vodka; it stung her tongue.

"But he can't bring her back here." Franck added. Candi barely listened, but he kept talking. "My colleague said they've got a variant outbreak in Belgium," Franck told her. "They're seeing new cases."

"It never ends."

He swirled the vodka in his cup, swallowed it, then poured himself another. "Just like this shit weather. Your family must be worried about you."

"Not really," she mumbled. "They don't follow the news much."

"Neither does my mother. She's too busy with her goats."

"Her goats?"

"Yes, she lives outside Brussels, on a goat cheese farm with her new wife."

"Oh," Candi couldn't help but register surprise.

"Yes, they met after my parents separated. She's a very good cook and I think my mother was honestly so tired of cooking for men that she became a lesbian."

The vodka buzz trickled into her extremities and Candi had to giggle at the idea. Maybe that's what she would do after this, become a lesbian goatherder; if there was anything after this, but then again, women didn't interest her sexually.

"Wish I was on their farm right now." Franck said, "You would love it." He scooted closer to her on the bed.

She took another big gulp of vodka. He was her only chance out.

Franck watched her. He looked like he wanted to say something. His stare was more intense than usual.

"What?" she asked.

"You just look pretty. Really pretty." He put his hand on her thigh. "What happens in Toronto stays in Toronto?"

She stiffened. She'd told him she was married. Why did he keep harping on this? She wondered. Now was really not the time. Life as a lesbian would be much easier. She moved his hand. "I can't. I'm sorry."

He leaned on the bed's headboard and crossed his arms. "I know you aren't married."

Her green eyes sprung open. Oh no.

"I found you online. You're a widow. Your husband died. You can stop lying."

She swung off the bed, then winced as pain ran up her legs, vodka still in hand; blood rushed to her head.

"You could have just been honest," he scowled and switched on the news again, but it was only static. "You're kidding me," he unplugged and plugged in the TV. Same result. All the channels were digital snow. "Is this the beginning of another ice age, or what?" he asked.

The idea made her whole body weak. "I'm sorry I lied," she said.

Franck rubbed his temples with both hands, "Why does this seem like the beginning of the end?"

She realized he hadn't heard her. He was talking to himself. Her lips puckered. She wanted to scream at him and hit him, maybe suffocate him with a pillow, but instead she murmured "I'm sorry."

"It's whatever," he fiddled more with the TV.

She locked herself in the bathroom, her only refuge, chugged the rest of her cup of vodka, then called Jasper. "Hey babe" she said to his voice mail, "I miss you. I really fucking miss you. I'll never stop missing you. I'll never stop loving you, no matter what."

After a few deep breaths and a concerted effort to stop her tears, she returned to the room and to Franck, swallowed another vodka shot, and cleared all the thoughts from her mind. She created a thin smile on her tired face and went and put her arm around the only man in a position to save her. "I'm sorry I lied," she whispered in his ear, close, so he could feel her breath, her body, her breasts against him. "That was fucked up. I should have told you the truth. I didn't think any of this was going to happen."

He softened his shoulders, turned his head, and kissed her on the lips.

She didn't want to feel anything from his kiss, but she did. Her body heat rose and she froze, surprised, but also transfixed by the soft feeling of his lips and the smell of his skin, his cologne. He brought her body closer on the bed, kissing her deeply. He tried to press his tongue between her lips. She stiffened her shoulders and pulled her head back, but he only strengthened his grip on her sides, bringing her lips again to his. His other hand ran along the curve of her hips and around to her bottom. Relaxing her resistance, she let his tongue fill her mouth, then found herself on top of him, straddling him. Drunk, her physical sensations took over and she rocked her hips gently against him. He moaned and ran his hands through her hair, kissing her faster and harder, sucking on her neck.

Separate from her thoughts, the space between her legs tingled and warmed, opened, lubricated itself. Her breasts rose and fell against Franck's chest, and he rubbed his erection between the gap in her thighs. He's turned me on, she realized, somewhat amazed. Everything moved on a delay. He pressed himself between her legs, firm and warm. His fingers traced her shoulder blades, the indent in her spine; they lingered at her hips. No, this wasn't right. Candi pulled away again, but he rose to meet her. I don't really want this, she thought, but yet she kissed him, squeezed his skin between her fingers, smelled his hair, felt the stubble of his beard against her cheeks.

He's my only ride, she told herself, as his hands applied pressure through her pajamas, making small circles with his thumbs, massaging her flesh.

"No. We have to stop," she moaned.

But he didn't stop.

Vodka and pleasure swam through her as he rubbed her harder, kissed her harder. Oh God, it felt good. She melted into him, getting wetter and wetter. Her body wanted this. She couldn't stop herself or him.

Chapter Thirty-Nine

HUNGRY VYBES

Feeling cold despite his puffy red jacket, Vybes took the stairs two at a time, down, down, down to the ground floor. The restaurant-turned-makeshift cafeteria's door was locked, and the lights were off. That's odd, he thought. They should still be serving dinner. His stomach grumbled. He'd planned to bring Gretchen food as well. Likewise, at the lobby entrance, two army guys blocked the way. Beyond them, medics in hazmat suits moved sofas to make room for folding tables.

"You can't be here," one said and waved him off. "Go back to your room."

He stood on his tip toes, though he barely needed to, peering over their heads. Hanging plastic sheets taped to the ceiling blocked off half the lobby area. Two people in dark teal hazmat suits pushed a rolling cart. They disappeared through a slit in the plastic. Was it a stretcher? He couldn't tell, but from his jacket pocket he fished out his minimally compliant mask and slipped it over his mouth.

With his empty stomach still rumbling, he went to Gretchen's room, but she didn't answer his knock. Weird, she'd asked him to come only twenty minutes ago. He called her. The phone went straight to voicemail. What the hell? He knocked harder on her door. "Gretchen," he called. "Are you there?"

It didn't make sense. She'd just told him to come. The hallway was quiet and empty. An uneasy feeling reached into his empty stomach and his shoulders tensed. He headed to the conference room where the overflow guests slept. Maybe they'd moved her there for some reason.

But Gretchen wasn't there either. An older woman coughed on a cot and another man in the back also hacked and sneezed. Everyone in the packed room stared at him like hungry dogs. Vybes hurried out and went to the gym; it was also dark and locked.

Returning to his own door, he slipped off his mask before he went inside, but Franck immediately asked him what was wrong, like it was obvious from his face, and Candi looked pink and flustered like she'd been crying or jogging. He sensed a stiff, anxious tension in the air. "You guys okay?" He furrowed his brows.

"Fine, but you certainly weren't gone long," Franck crossed his arms. "I've heard of a quickie, but..."

"Very funny. Gretchen wasn't in her room or in the conference room." He considered telling them about the hazmat crew and the lobby, but decided against it for now given Candi's fragile state. "Do you mind if I check the news on the TV?"

"Don't bother, all the channels are down and the internet's down."

No data. Crap. No wonder Gretchen didn't answer.

"I'm going to check on Emily, see if she has any update," Franck announced and stood up, smoothing out his t-shirt and sweatpants.

"That's the helicopter lady?" Candi asked.

"Yes. We can't be too proactive in these situations." Franck slipped on a sweater and left.

Candi went to the bathroom for a long time and Vybes watched the snow sift like flour falling into a mixing bowl, like it would never stop. When she returned, she came and stood beside him, facing the window. How did she still smell so good, even in dirty pajamas? He wanted to wrap his arms around her shoulders, but settled for inching closer to her. "When I was a kid in Kampala," he said, "we didn't get any TV channels, but sometimes a man would bring us tapes of Bollywood or American movies, and we'd watch those."

She kept her eyes fixed on the endlessly growing snow. "What was your favorite movie as a kid?"

"I always loved Star Wars." He touched his hand to the window, feeling a chill through it that traveled from his fingers and into his chest. "And Grease."

"Grease? Like the musical?" She slurred her words.

"Yeah, I loved all the cars."

"Not Olivia Newton John's leather pants?"

He grinned, "You're right, it was Sandra Dee's pants. Olivia Newton John was hot."

"That's funny. I played Sandra Dee in our high school's musical."

"Shut up! What? You're kidding me! You also sing?"

"I wasn't good, but there wasn't much competition at my high school."

"I'd love to hear you sing." He hoped it didn't sound like he was coming onto her. It wasn't his intention to make things awkward.

"I was into the boy who sang Beauty School Dropout in our school production. That was the only reason I tried out for the show."

He angled his torso towards her. He wanted to say something witty, but maybe it was too inappropriate. Though life was short, and maybe this was the apocalypse for real. She was really hot. He debated running his fingertip down her arm but didn't. Adrenaline stirred through him. Nah, I'm going there, he thought, and then he let himself go. "And tell me Sandra Dee, when did you lose your virginity?" The words went from his lips, hot, breathy, into her ear.

She didn't flinch, but she looked at him. Her green eyes sparkling in the daylight like Christmas ornaments. "I lost it in 11th grade," she said, "To a boy named Ryan Simmons."

"What a lucky guy." He studied her lips. He wanted to kiss them, but did she feel the same way? He was almost 100% sure that she didn't, but the slight possibility was enough to make him think he had a chance. Blood rushed to his limbs.

"What about you? How did you lose your virginity?"

"I was 17. The girl was an older friend of my cousins. She was in college, and she seduced me."

"Seduced you?" Candi raised her eyebrows ever so slightly.

"Well, it wasn't too hard." I should stop flirting, he thought. She's really drunk. But he couldn't take his gaze off her.

"I bet it wasn't." She turned back to the window.

He wanted to rub his hands over every round shape under her clothes, to feel her nipples between his fingers, to chew on her soft, plump lips like they were gumdrops, but it probably wasn't a good idea, at least not yet. He'd been mentally ready to hit it with Gretchen again, and that energy lingered. Plus, if he was being honest, he'd wanted to also hit it with Candi, basically from the moment he'd first seen her on the plane, though now maybe it was from the stress, because he'd been feeling unusually wound up, ready to burst. He couldn't turn that part of himself off, not even in an alien weather attack, or whatever this was. And where was Gretchen? He took a deep breath, and left Candi standing by the window.

Trying to clear his head, he ran the shower water. Yes, hot again. Thank you, universe. Under the steaming flow, he stroked himself. It didn't take much these days to make him hard, not after sleeping next to Candi. He imagined her on her knees, licking the tip of his dick. He tapped it on her nose like he was sprinkling pixie dust, and she grabbed him in her fist. His eyes closed. Up and down the shaft; she rocked him between her cupid lips. He grew bigger in his own hand and fucked her mouth harder in his imagination, making her green eyes water. Yes, yes, yes. In his mind, he squeezed her tiny pink nipples between his fingers as he came into the spray of water.

Chapter Forty

NOT GRETCHEN'S KNIGHT

Just when she'd given up on leaving, when she'd booty called Vybes, deciding to make the best of her seemingly now-empty room, Sam's old cop friend Daniel Ford's call finally came through.

"I've found a way for you to go to the Armed Forces College," he explained. She was to meet another man, James Rededfer, a U.S. Marine stationed at the college on an exchange. He was bringing supplies to the U.S. customs chief who lived near the Toronto airport and on his way back to the college's base, he would pick her up. All she had to do was go to the hotel lobby and wait by the front door. The marine would arrive within thirty minutes, and this would probably be her only chance for at least a week. She'd be much safer at the base, Ford said, and maybe when they airlifted the American officers, she could negotiate a ride south. They were allowing her to come because Ford's friend had somehow convinced his superiors for an American reporter to document the rescue and return home of the stranded U.S. troops and government employees in Canada.

She thanked Ford profusely, and without wasting a moment, bolted to the lobby. She'd text Vybes later and explain.

Almost out of breath, she reached the lobby entrance, but guards in hazmat suits blocked her path.

Gretchen slowed down, and a wave of fear washed over her. "Excuse me, I'm meeting a military exit," she said.

"Not here. This space is under quarantine," the man explained.

"No, I really need to meet my ride."

"Trust me," he said, "You don't want to go through there."

She blinked. "Quarantined from what?" and though the guard wouldn't tell her, she already knew the answer.

Speed-walking to the stairwell, she called Ford again but got a busy tone. She'd use the fire exit, but she needed to tell the Marine. Going from the side of the building to the front might be impossible for her with all the snow. She looked at her phone. No cell bars.

"Fuck," she growled and picked up her pace. She'd have to walk around. This was her only chance.

In the stairway, she sped down one flight of steps to an emergency exit door, slightly below the lobby level, but try as she might, pushing and shoving, kicking and screaming, the door would not budge. It wasn't that it was locked, she realized—the knob turned—but it was entirely, impenetrably blocked by snow.

Chapter Forty-One

CANDI'S CHANCE

The private plane was back on. They found a willing pilot, Franck explained to Candi as the sun set on another day of endless snow, now inching up to the third floor of the hotel. First a helicopter would pick them up, then they'd take a short flight to a cleared, private airstrip, then depart in a different plane, fly to Myrtle Beach, and be on their way home.

"Get yourself together and pack your things," he told her, moving in close to her body, his words warm on her face. She took a step back. After this, she told herself, you won't see him again. Just get through this. Though would she want to see him again? Her body buzzed with anxious energy.

"We're finally going home."

"Wait. Are you sure?" She didn't want to get too excited again, what if the pilot didn't show up. She felt drunk but nodded.

"Yes, so bundle up. We're going to have to walk outside to the adjacent terminal."

Panic rose in her chest. "What? No. We can't be outside long. I don't have boots."

"This is the only way. Put on every pair of socks you own. We will move as fast as we can."

Her heart pounded. The thought of going outside filled her with dread, but so did the idea of staying in the hotel. She nodded and switched her vodka to water. At least it was almost time for bed anyway. He's right. I need to get my shit together, she thought, as she struggled to unwind the ball of anxiety wrapped around her core. And what about Vybes? She felt guilty for leaving him. "I'll try to get help for you once I'm home," she told him.

Vybes was sprawled on the bed in his pajamas with his eyes unfocused, like he was trying not to see them. "Yeah, I'm happy for you guys."

"At least you'll get the entire room to yourself," Franck offered, though his grin didn't look sincere to Candi.

Her heart welled with affection for the young, tall man. Yet, he seemed like a dream she would soon forget as the plane lifted off and she was homeward bound.

Franck put his arm unexpectedly around her shoulder, "This will all be over soon."

Not soon enough, she thought.

After she'd finished organizing her things and figuring out what she was going to wear, Candi removed the last bottle of wine from her shopping bag, an Ontario ice wine meant as a gift for her parents, and gave it to Vybes along with the book of LSD.

"Are you sure it wouldn't be safer for you to stay here?" He whispered. "I have a bad feeling about this."

She hadn't really considered the safety of the chopper. Surely it would be fine if the rich guy would risk it for his wife; pilots didn't fly when it was too risky. "I'm going to miss you. I hope we can meet again one day," she whispered back, surprising even herself, because it was true.

His concerned expression softened, "Me too."

But Franck was watching them again. Candi exhaled; she couldn't wait to have privacy.

"Take the book and eat one of those tabs for me," she said, ignoring Franck, "if you're still here on Christmas Eve, which I sincerely hope you won't be."

Vybes agreed, "I will. Pick out a page for me."

They sat on the bed, and she selected an image from the fourth page, of a psychedelic princess floating on an astral plane, holding a torch high in the air like the Statue of Liberty. Vybes stuck a piece of the hotel's stationary in the book to mark the page.

Franck announced that he was going to see Emily, the mining wife, one more time, to confirm that Candi would join the group.

"Should I go with you?" she asked.

"No, no need. I won't be long."

And he wasn't. When he returned, instead of taking his turn in bed with her again, he offered the spot to Vybes.

"Are you sure man? I don't mind the floor."

Franck waved his hand, "No, no. This is the least I can do. After all, I'll be sleeping in a real bed very soon."

They all set their phone's alarm clocks for 6 AM, to give them plenty of time to reach the designated rendezvous spot by 8 AM. They would go with Emily who would meet them in the lobby at 7:45 AM.

Candi wondered just how much Franck had paid for her flight, though she didn't ask, probably more than she could ever afford to pay him back. Yawning, with way too much vodka still in her system, she drank a full cup of water.

Would the helicopter make it? She wondered.

Snowing in LA? That's what the news had said before the TV went off, but how could that be?

She lay in bed beside Vybes, tossing and turning.

They needed to mitigate the time spent in the elements before the plane's departure; the subarctic temperature could kill them. Candi could hear Vybes breathing. She felt the urge to hug him again. It was, after all, their last night, and who knows if she'd ever see him again. Something deep inside her swelled with affection for the young man. Despite her initial misgivings, he'd been so kind to her this whole time, a blessing in fact. Adrienne would have loved spending time with him and he'd really grown on her. She wasn't lying when she said she'd miss him.

Turning, she touched his shoulder, and he rotated toward her in the dim light. She motioned for him to get under the covers, and he obliged. They both hesitated, making eye contact. Then she hugged him and he cuddled her into his extra-large arms like she was his stuffed teddy bear. They stayed like that, breathing together, not making any unnecessary sounds. I need this human comfort, Candi realized, hoping she didn't reek of booze. She was so grateful for him, this overgrown British-Ugandan boy who was really a man. He'd maybe saved her from sleeping with Franck too, which she still couldn't believe had almost happened. Thankfully, they hadn't gotten that far. Vybes had returned to the room at exactly the right time. That was probably the real reason Franck had given him the bed, to avoid a possible awkward rejection from her now that she'd sobered up a bit.

Vybes hugged her closer, his lips near her ears, warm on her jawline, her cheek, so tender, not kissing her, but almost touching her skin and she squeezed him back. She prayed Franck wouldn't wake up and find them cuddling. She'd forgotten about this feeling, the joy of being cared for, of being supported by a man. She wished, but she didn't speak; instead, the warmth of his body lulled her towards sleep and calmed her anxiety.

In the warmth of Vybes' arms, she slipped fully into darkness, and without the awareness of a beginning, entered a dream.

The tall young man walked beside her through a snowy, empty city, with tall buildings and narrow streets. She realized it was Las Vegas, only with snow everywhere. The lights of the casinos were turned off. They went into a restaurant and sat at a table. A waiter brought them roasted duck and dumplings. The food was cold; she wanted to send it back, but all the waiters were gone, so they left.

Outside, a large military truck drove by, black with a camouflage and green canvas top. Scientists rode in the back in white winter jackets with fox-fur lined rims. They hopped in. A blast of cold air struck her through her clothes. She realized she'd forgotten her coat in the restaurant. "Hey, I need to go back," she told one of the scientists, but they only responded in a foreign language that sounded German, or Norwegian.

"I forgot my jacket. I need to get out," she repeated. Her hands turned red. "I'm really cold," she told a scientist. They ignored her and the truck kept driving. "Please," Candi pleaded, almost crying. "I'm going to freeze to death." Vybes was no longer in the truck with her. "Please stop and let me out. I've got to get my jacket."

And the truck stopped, but when she got out, she was alone in a winter landscape, like a desert of ice. She looked at her hands. Her gloves were gone and so were her fingers. Only black stumps remained.

Candi screamed.

Chapter Forty-Two

GRETCHEN'S RUN

For what felt like the tenth time, Gretchen went around the airport as fast as she could, huffing, looking for any viable exit. Every door wouldn't open. She ran, then jogged, then speed-walked, then trotted, searched and scoured. After an hour, she slumped into a seat and moped for twenty minutes, gritting her teeth. Fuck. Now she couldn't even call to check on Kevin. Nor could she reach Daniel Ford, her only viable way out of here. The weight of so many questions, of fears, pressed and crushed on her chest. It made her angry, then afraid, then mad again. I better at least lose some weight from this shit, she thought as her emotions cycled and churned in rapid succession.

Finally, after trying every door she could find once more, she gave up and let herself cry. That was it. She was stuck here until the phones started working again. Whatever tunnel was here, she couldn't find it, nor could she get outside. Did everyone else realize just how trapped they were? Why wasn't everyone freaking out?

Airport staff and stranded passengers taking walks passed by, but no one stopped to ask what was wrong. Of course, they all knew. Outside was what was wrong. Well, at least I still have a bed to return to and hopefully an empty room, she told herself, trying to lift her own mood. All is not lost.

With her shoulders slumped, carrying her bookbag, she returned to the hotel, but on her floor, to the left of the elevator every room was blocked off with police tape and an officer in a hazmat suit informed her that they'd just put the wing under total quarantine.

"But my room is just down there. I can go quarantine inside."

"That won't be possible. This floor is now closed. No one can re-enter. You shouldn't even be here. I'll have someone come escort you to the conference room. Trust me, you don't want to risk infection."

Her lip quivered, as her hope hollowed out like the last bite of oatmeal in a bowl. No. Dammit. She wanted her own bed. This wasn't fair.

He raised his walkie-talkie to call another officer.

"Hey, it's okay, thank you. I'll just go then," she mumbled, but he insisted on the escort. He took her temperature while they waited. Normal. Okay, she could go. The second army officer deposited her in the conference room where another checked her in, gave her a blanket, and assigned her a cot. The last cot, he said. She was lucky, but she could barely nod. No one here is lucky, she thought, not a single one of us.

Chapter Forty-Three

FRANCK'S CUT

In his socks and wearing two layers of clothes, Franck listened from his blanket on the floor for the sounds of snoring. He knew for certain they both snored. It took a while, quite a bit of tossing and turning before the unmistakable, nasal rumbling began; first Candi's lighter, higher-pitched sounds, then Vybes' deeper snore. Peas in a pod, he thought, snoring each other to sleep. He waited longer to be sure; then as the pair settled fully into their rhythmic, annoying guttural snore patterns, Franck removed his blankets, taking great care not to make a sound, picked up his two bags and his shoes, and headed for the door.

Still, as he tiptoed past the bed, he couldn't help but glance at Candi. He stopped. Vybes was under the cover with his arm draped over her, spooning her. Well, this makes things easier, Franck thought. Fuck her. A wave of heat, anger, and jealousy rushed through him. Until that afternoon, she'd resisted all his advances, but she was willing with Vybes? What a slut, probably playing them both this whole time. Now, he knew he was making the right decision.

With a bitter taste in his mouth, he shut the door, slipped on his boots, and rode the elevator up to the 15th floor.

Emily Villeneuve answered the penthouse suite's door fully dressed. They spoke in French. "My daughter is asleep," Emily said, "But I'll wake her soon. It's almost time."

"Thank you again," Franck said. "From the bottom of my heart."

Emily sunk into one of the living room chairs and rubbed her eyes. "I just hope it works. I'm afraid."

"Of course. Everything will work." Franck lowered himself on the opulent, penthouse sofa, hot, dressed in every item of clothing from his suitcase, and gazed out the windows toward the city of Toronto, but where now there was nothing but darkness and snow and the dying or the dead. "We're getting out just in time."

"Just in time would have been before this," Emily said, brushing a stray strand of her wispy blond hair from her face. Her forehead and the corners of her blue eyes wrinkled with worry.

"Things will get worse, much worse."

Franck had told her what his younger brother, who worked for the UK government, had reported to him concerning the storm. He'd shown her the satellite images, the new pictures he hadn't shown Vybes and Candi. The storm wasn't ending; it was intensifying, and The Glow Stick hadn't gone away—it was only hovering higher over the clouds, beyond the sight of the civilians and reporters. No one knew what it was. The U.S. government wanted to shoot missiles at it and the Canadian government wanted to study it with drones. His brother thought it might be the Chinese at best, or at worst, extra-terrestrial.

The other mother and daughter joining them on the chopper arrived, French Canadian like Emily, and they all waited for the call from the pilot. Unlike their room, Emily had a landline and unlike Franck, Vybes, and Candi, whose foreign, roaming phones no longer worked, Emily's penthouse suite landline could still make and receive outside calls. Their ride, a helicopter specially designed to withstand storms, that her husband had managed to rent from a Russian mining mogul contact would soon attempt to land on the roof of the hotel, having deemed that evening that it was too dangerous for them to travel on foot to the adjacent landing pad in the frigid conditions. Then it would take them to a private airstrip nearby, supposedly cleared enough for planes to land. There they'd transfer to a private plane and carry on to Myrtle Beach, that part was all true.

With a twinge of guilt, he thought about Candi for a moment as he readied himself mentally for the cold of the roof. He had wanted to bring her. It wasn't his plan to lie, but at the last minute, Emily had changed her mind and given the extra seat to the other mother and daughter pair. The chopper was already too crowded and despite his offer to pay triple, she'd said no to Candi. Maybe he should have just told her, but then again, she'd lied to him and was probably sleeping with Vybes, so fine. She could stay here with that flamboyant teenager she was always hugging and looking at with googly eyes, anyway, and cuddle her lying heart away while the world froze.

It was time to go. He prayed in his mind to Allah, asking for safe passage, for protection from harm.

The helicopter lifted into the snowy, lightless sky and Franck held his breath. They flew across the dark, blustery sky, with falling snow like glittering stars in the helicopter lights. In his mind, he thanked Allah, his mother, and his father, and his brother, this woman, and her husband, and all the people he worked with. He thanked his ex for getting him into yoga. He thanked the men who had founded the bank, the men who built planes and mines, and the women who birthed them, but most of all, he thanked himself, for striving to ensure his financial success, because without money, a lot of money, if he'd just stayed in the airport and waited, wouldn't he die?

At least with money, he had a chance.

Then again, a helicopter in a blizzard wasn't the greatest plan either, but it was worth a try.

The metal bird careened and shrieked in the wind, shaking him in his seat, passing through the worst turbulence he'd ever known. Franck gripped his arm rests and didn't stop praying. His heart thumped faster and faster the higher they rose. Come on, old boy, he thought. Calm down. Don't die from a stroke before you even land.

Chapter Forty-Four

CANDI FREAK

Candi awoke in the dim, but familiar room. Her fingers were still there. It was just a bad dream. She shivered; the room was really freezing. Vybes snored and her alarm hadn't gone off yet, but as she got out of bed to put on her extra sweater she noticed that Franck was not on the floor. Even his duvet was gone. Knocking on the bathroom door, she whispered, "Franck, are you in there?"

No answer.

She swung open the door. Empty. Blood rushed to her brain. Where the fuck was Franck? Her eyes scanned the dark room again like he was hiding in a crack. She opened the closet. His coat and luggage were missing.

Candi grabbed her bag from the closet, threw on her jacket, and frantically shoved her bandaged feet into three pairs of socks, slid on her boots, wincing as pain arched up her legs, and remembering that she'd once again, probably due to the vodka, forgotten to change her bandages.

Vybes woke up, "What's going on?"

"Franck left me."

"What?"

She grabbed her purse and turned back to Vybes, "Take care."

"Hey, wait," he called, but she sprinted down the hall. She couldn't miss this chance.

She raced down seven flights of steps to the lobby, their original meeting point, but it was blocked off with heavy plastic sheeting and a security guard. Gasping for breath, she rode the elevator to the penthouse floor. Maybe they were still in Emily's room, but it was locked. "Hello, is anyone there? Franck? Emily?" She pounded on the door with her fist.

No response.

She tried calling him, but her phone didn't work. It wasn't their scheduled departure time yet; maybe she could still make it to the air strip or catch them on their way. God, why had he left her. That bastard, she cursed in her head as she ran as fast as she could, back down the steps, through the breezeway to the airport, then out the airport door when the snowstorm smacked her in the face. She stopped. Fear gripped her chest. She stepped back inside the building. Only one thin path from one exterior door to the road was cleared. Even through the window, she could feel the wind nip at her skin. But this might be her only chance. She thought of Jasper, his ceremony, his mother, her mother, she didn't want to let them down, but most of all, she didn't want to stay trapped in this arctic hell hole. She took a deep breath, pulled up her sweater, wrapped her jacket hood around her face, and using her hotel towel like a burka to cover her cheeks, she went outside again.

Snow piled high around like a tunnel as she moved in the direction Franck had described, but she couldn't run. The snow was too deep. She sank almost to her knees with every step. She knew she was probably higher than the ground level. What if she fell through? The most recent layer of precipitation hadn't compacted like the older snow, but right below it, the older snow felt firm to her feet.

She scanned the sky. The way Franck explained the directions, the chopper would land to the north of the airport. Out of breath, she wished she had better boots. Why the fuck did he go without me? She wondered and cursed herself for falling asleep. Had this been his plan all along? To never take her?

It was dark still, early morning, and the sky glowed a weird gray. She waded forward, teary, thighs burning. She had to get out of the snow, or she'd get frostbite again. The wind chafed her nose and cheeks. Around her snowdrifts towered ten, twelve, maybe even fifteen feet high. Did they cover buildings? Cars? Everything looked unfamiliar and she could no longer see the hotel behind her. She reached what she thought was the airport parking lot, with rows of light poles sticking out of the high snow, barely visible. Yes, she'd made it. She knew where she was. The main road in front of the terminal was the only area they still bothered to clear with plows. She slid down a snowy slope onto the thinner coating of snow at the street level. She screamed Franck's name. No one answered.

She needed to find the plane fast or go back inside. She trod in the direction she thought was north. Keep going. Get to the plane. Get out of here. Get home.

As tiny flying pieces of ice stung her eyes, she saw it, the next terminal, where their ride would be, in the distance, the familiar outline of the Canadian red maple leaf. She could make it. Then she could smack Franck and yell at him for leaving her. He'd probably be surprised to see her. That rat bastard.

Feeling a burst of energy and a swell of hope, she forced her tired, frozen legs faster through the snow. A rumbling sound erupted over her head and the wind intensified. No, fuck, not now, she thought and shielded her eyes to look up. A military helicopter zoomed across the sky, then disappeared.

"Franck," she screamed. Was it him? Or someone else? Through wet eyelashes she squinted at the sky, but the chopper was gone, swallowed by the blizzard's abyss along with her hopes of getting home for Christmas.

Hands shaking, she screamed for help.

An engine rumbled to life. Then another, and suddenly the sky filled with lights, headlights, and the flicker of planes... no drones. Or... A flash blinded her and she dropped to her knees. The blazing lights illuminated everything around her now, turning day to night.

"Candi," she heard someone scream her name.

"Help," she screamed. "Franck!"

"I'm coming," a man's voice shouted, but it wasn't Franck; it was Vybes, a red figure in the distance.

"Vybes," she screamed and, rising, staggered towards the sound of his yells. High in the sky—The Glow Stick rose again, a glowing, upside-down white horseshoe lowering from the clouds. It generated a bright, but cold, intense force as it flattened into a line.

With a surge of fear, she bolted towards him.

All went blindingly white. The Glow Stick shot out an ear-piercing sound and the force of the storm accelerated. Heavy snowflakes flew like giant balls of hail and pummeled her body. She screamed as the ground churned and sprayed up powder. The snow deepened and deepened around her, threatening to drown her, freeze her alive. There was nowhere to run, nowhere safe. Heaps of white moved fast in quivering mountains, grinding and sliding across the landscape, swaying her body and knocking her backwards. A quaking, frozen mass toppled off the roof of the airport, crashing down in thunderous chunks like exploding drywall. Like facing an oncoming tsunami, she watched in horror as an avalanche hurled in her direction.

"Candi!" Vybes reached her and lifted her in his arms. He flung her on his back like a sack and lurched through the storm, running out of the way with her just quickly enough to evade the cascade of rushing snow that would have buried them both alive.

She held on tight, wrapping her legs around his waist like a scarf, moaning, "He left me, he left me. Franck left me."

They reached the hotel's revolving door just as The Glow Stick's rods lowered to the ground. Everything vibrated again, and like the first time, shocks of current raged through her body. She screamed in pain. Vybes kept moving. He barged past plastic sheets, stretchers, and medics, humans convulsing and collapsing, men with guns screaming and wriggling like worms. The earth spasmed like a dead bird and knocked everyone to the floor, including the two of them. She clung to his torso as The Glow Stick electrocuted them again and again. They curled together in a fetal position on the hotel's carpet and seethed in unrelenting waves of pain. The taste of burning hair and skin filled her mouth. She went limp and prayed that the thing would finally kill her.

Chapter Forty-Five

GRETCHEN'S BOOK

The crowded conference room smelled like shit and piss and vomit and sweat. Kids and adults sobbed and hugged one another. Stories often contained half-truths, like the stories the government made up. Someone knew more about The Glow Stick, Gretchen believed, and they weren't saying. Or maybe they were, but without a working phone or TV, how would she know? Lying on her cot, she blocked out the room's noise with her own thoughts. What she knew was that she wanted to go home, and not to a home without her brother. His kids needed a dad. After this, she'd move home permanently, stop traveling so much. What was the point of gallivanting around the globe at her age anyway, with no partner, no kids, and her parents in their seventies?

The man beside her coughed. She glanced at him, and he said, "allergies." Around the room, no one looked well. Hell, I probably don't look great either, she thought. But was there safety in numbers? Or would she be better off alone? This situation no longer felt like an unpleasant inconvenience; it felt like life or death. What hope was there now, with The Glow Stick outside, besides the tunnel? She couldn't give up on it. Not yet.

As the room attendant helped an older woman, she took her

bag and slipped out. Her legs felt like cinder blocks, but she focused on Kevin, and this kept her moving. Despite their differences, he was the one she called when she needed advice. He never made her feel like a failure or a black sheep. He appreciated her relentless, probing intellect. Without him, family gatherings would be empty, sad. No, he had to live, and she had to get home.

If The Glow Stick sent out shocks again, the terminal might be safer than the hotel; it was wider, more industrial, and maybe it had thicker walls. She rationalized that staying in the middle, away from windows, might be safer. The shocks seemed airborne, so perhaps underground would be safest. She hadn't tried crawling through the baggage claim shoots. She'd do that tomorrow, after she got some rest.

First, though, she wanted to find Vybes. Not because he could help, but because she needed a friend for the end of the world, someone to process this crazy shit with, to talk to. Otherwise, she'd go insane—that seemed like a real possibility, not just for her, but for anyone. Plus, he had booze and drugs, maybe snacks.

His floor was either six, seven, or eight. She couldn't remember the number. Systematically, she knocked on every door. Strangers of all races, ages, and genders answered, but they all had the same prey-like look in their eyes—darting pupils, corners contracted, skittish, weary. No, he wasn't there, they said. No, they hadn't seen anyone matching that description. Finally, an older man remembered seeing his flamboyant style, but wasn't sure of his room.

Gretchen grew tired. Talking to this many strangers would have worn her out on any day, let alone today. She'd look for Vybes again tomorrow. Guess I'm riding this train from hell solo, at least for tonight, she thought and headed to the terminal to find a safe place to sleep.

The airport was more packed than before. As she descended to the lowest level, a few single men, a couple, and another lone woman walked by. No one made eye contact. Everyone kept to themselves.

Next to a baggage carousel, a Black man around her age, with dreadlocks and a slight pot belly, relaxed against the wall, writing in a notebook and eating what appeared to be a cinnamon raisin bagel with cream cheese. God, would she love to have a bagel. On one side of him was a stack of paperback books, and on the other, a large black trash bag. He'd either broken into the airport bookstore or had worked there. She almost stopped to ask if he had another bagel, but he didn't look up from his notebook, and she kept walking.

Open suitcases lay strewn about the dirty floor, no doubt already scoured for leftover food. Dang, society broke down fast, she thought, and found an empty bench. Lying down, she pulled her toboggan over her ears.

Eyes closed, her mind drifted. She imagined the end of the tunnel; the U.S. Army would ferry her across the frozen Lake Ontario and return her to the States. The only hitch in her plan was that she actually didn't know where the tunnel ended. On the map, it looked like it connected to a food depot, the entry and inspection point for groceries and produce imported from the U.S. into Canada. If she was designing an emergency escape, surely she'd design it to go somewhere safe, and what better place than a warehouse full of food? At the thought, her stomach grumbled. She hadn't eaten much, though from watching several seasons of the reality show, *Alone*, which took place in the Canadian wilderness, she knew her excess body weight could tide her over for days, maybe even a month. On the show, the person who lasted the longest alone in the wild won a large sum of money, and usually, the heaviest person won. Being chunky was a best-case scenario for an apocalypse. Yep, I'll outlast all these skinny bitches. Even if I have to hide in the tunnel for weeks, I'll be okay with just water.

But where the hell was it? She hadn't searched inside the locked airline offices, though it seemed unlikely that an emergency tunnel would be in a private office. Then again, it would make sense for it to be in the airport director's office. Where was that?

Maybe she could find one of those emergency glass boxes with an ax and use it to break the locked doors. Would anyone stop her? Did those boxes even exist? She also wondered if her editor had published her latest piece, put together in haste with her cell phone photos of The Glow Stick, which she'd snapped right before it shocked the shit out of her the first time.

They probably published it. People might be tweeting it right now. It could be going viral. If I survive this, she thought, I'll write a book, obvi. Of course, the biggest story of my life and I can't even see the reaction. At the same time, who cared about some stupid internet article? Nature certainly did not.

Chapter Forty-Six

CANDI CRY

When the vibrating finally stopped, Vybes carried her like a child to their room and tried to dry her jacket and pants off with towels. She couldn't stop crying. Her body rattled like an old truck. This isn't climate change, she thought. This has to be an attack. It has to be.

"You've got to get out of your wet clothes and boots," Vybes said. "We've got to get you warmed up."

She studied the ceiling, numb to his touch, while he removed her boots, socks, and jacket.

"Do you have dry pants? Where are your extra bandages? I'll change them for you."

She didn't respond but continued wondering how Franck, that motherfucker, could have left her.

Vybes opened the curtains, but she wished he wouldn't. She couldn't help but stare at the scene beyond the ice-edged glass; there floated The Glow Stick, a radiating u-shaped rod at present, but it could split at any time and shock them. Why was it still there? She hugged herself and tried to stop shaking. Her teeth clattered. No longer caring if he saw her body, she removed her pants and teetered into the bed.

Her whole body felt slightly asleep. He wrapped her shaking

frame in the extra duvet from Franck's bed on the floor and rubbed her arms and legs under the cover, saying he was trying to help her blood circulate. "Please, let me change your bandages. They're wet."

But she rolled face down into her pillow. After Jasper, she kept wondering if she'd ever run out of tears, but it hadn't happened yet.

Vybes waited beside her and held his warm hands on her trembling calves.

Chapter Forty-Seven

GRETCHEN'S GUMPTION

Gretchen's growling stomach roused her from the bench. Though exhausted, she returned to the middle level of the airport, hoping to find an emergency meal distribution area like in the hotel.

Upstairs, airport staff and army officers arranged folding cots. Amongst the staff were two men in police uniforms. She recognized one of them and slowed her steps. It was the guy who'd been a dick to her outside when she found the dead body. Good lord, that already seemed like a hundred years ago.

Approaching one of the airport staff, in an extra sweet, almost Southern voice, she said, "Hi, excuse me, sir. Sorry to bother you, but what's going on? Are these for anyone to sleep here?"

"They're for the officers and staff," he cocked his head, "but if you head down there, they have them for anyone." He pointed behind her, then went back to arranging the makeshift beds. Gretchen's heart rate picked up. This wasn't a good sign. If they couldn't even get people home that lived by the airport, what hope did she have? But a cot would be better than that cold bench for the night, even if it wasn't on the lower level. She made her way to the public cots, picked one out, and dragged it to the center of the terminal, away from the windows.

As the sun set, single adults and couples trickled in and claimed beds. A few stayed up talking in groups, but most kept quiet. This is so weird, Gretchen thought. We're trying to act normal, like everything's fine, like this isn't totally insane. It was like the pandemic had trained people to accept whatever. She exhaled and shook her head, glowering. It all made her angry.

An older couple with a tiny gray lap dog on a thin leash arrived carrying bags. "Are these taken?" The woman asked, pointing to two empty cots near Gretchen's.

"No, go ahead. Cute pup."

"That's Foxy," the man said.

The couple settled in with their small dog. Under her blanket, still fully dressed, with nothing better to do, she half-listened to them talk.

"I'm exhausted," the man said.

"Lie down. I'm going to brush my teeth and fill the water bottles." The woman handed him the leash and the little gray dog jumped onto the man's cot.

Gretchen closed her eyes. As a child, when she couldn't sleep, her father told her to imagine walking in white snow, the soft crunch, a forest, to visualize about each step until she fell asleep, a substitute for counting sheep, to count steps, but now, that seemed like a nightmare.

He must be worried about me now, she thought, but as she tried to picture sheep, cats, unicorns, anything except snow, the man near her screamed.

Gretchen shot upright on her cot.

"My chest, my chest." He clutched himself. "Help. Help me. It hurts. Something's wrong with me." The man reached one arm out and clutched his breast with the other. His wife wasn't there. The dog went nuts, barking.

Gretchen ran over and yelled for help, but it was too late. The man collapsed onto his back, seizing and shaking.

She backed away from the cot. A heart attack, he's having a heart attack. "Help! Someone help," she yelled. Other people saw them, but no one moved. The man's wife reappeared and ran to his side, screaming for help. The dog barked and barked and the military swooped in and rolled the man away. The wife trailed after them, trying to keep up, sobbing, and the little dog ran with her, barking.

Gretchen realized she should probably leave too, in case they tried to quarantine her with the sick people, but was it even too late? If they were infected, was she?

The little gray dog returned and sniffed around her feet. She put her hand to her heart and tried to slow her breath. Calm down. Think. But that's what had happened to Kevin. That's the pain Kevin must have felt. A tear trickled down her cheek. It had happened so fast, as fast as the plane crash—one-minute chaos, the next an empty space.

The dog walked in circles, sniffing the ground where the cot once was.

"Come here, boy," she said.

It ignored her.

"Foxy," she added, remembering its name. The pup glanced at her with skeptical eyes, then sat on its haunches, waiting for its master to return, but she gathered up her things and left.

Chapter Forty-Eight

VYBE CHECK

He let her cry it out. Despite the pain The Glow Stick inflicted, as he watched its bizarre currents of light flickering through the snow beyond their window, he only felt awe. He contemplated eating another tab of the LSD, but maybe this time only a half tab, to see if he could repeat his experience, but with more control of reality.

"Candi," he said as he rubbed her back, "I want to tell you about something else that happened whenever you're ready to talk."

She moaned into her pillow in response.

Maybe he could even get her to eat some. It would take her mind off things.

She rolled over and faced him with the saddest expression he'd ever seen.

"He left me here," she said. "He left me here to die."

"You might be safer here. We don't know what happened to him and we may never know. Maybe the helicopter never took off, or they already crashed. He might walk in the door any minute. We can't dwell on it, though. It's already in the past."

She rubbed her beautiful green eyes, still pinkish around the edges and puffy underneath, but it didn't deter from her looks.

Even without eyebrows, she was still beautiful. He saw an innocence in her, a lonely refinement, like a porcelain doll.

"I deserve this," she said. "This is my karma."

"What?" He moved closer to her. "No one deserves this. Nothing you did caused this."

She shook her head and her lip trembled. "No, you don't understand. I'm a bad person."

"Come on, let's get your new bandages on." He put his hand gently on her shoulder. "Please, I don't want you to cry like this."

"I let my husband die."

He withdrew his hand. "What?" He'd seen her call him just yesterday. "Your husband died?"

"I could have prevented it, but I didn't."

She must be confused, he thought. The shock of the cold, the volts from The Glow Stick—it must have rattled her brain. "No, sweetie, your husband isn't dead. You called him yesterday. You're in shock. We need to get you cozy and dry."

"No," she sat up and grabbed his hand. "I lied. My husband is dead. I've been calling his voice mail because I'm a fucked up, sad person. And I'll get what I deserve." Tears streaked her cheeks.

He didn't know what to say.

"I'm a widow and a liar."

"Candi, I'm so sorry, but whatever happened to your husband, I'm sure it wasn't your fault. What are you saying? That you murdered your husband? I find that hard to believe."

She shivered and shook her head, squeezing her arms around herself and rocking. More tears streamed from her reddened eyes.

"Hey, hey. Whatever it is, you'll feel better if you let it out. Let it out."

"He was murdered, and it was partly my fault." Her voice wavered and cracked. "When things reopened from the lockdowns, my husband, Jasper, his name was Jasper. He—he wanted to support the small restaurants, the ones struggling from the pandemic. He made a list of them for us to try, and we went once a week to a new place. But one week, he picked a place on the edge of an area called Naked City, but I didn't want to go. I knew we shouldn't go, but I didn't listen to myself. I told him we shouldn't go. That's a bad part of town." She closed her eyes. "But he said the rougher areas were the places that needed the most support from people like us. I let him convince me. So we went to this Hakka Chinese place, and it was all okay until the end. The food wasn't bad, and we were happy. We drank some beers, ate, but then..." she shook her head and looked down. Her sobs grew in volume. "Then—then on the way back to the car, two guys in black masks stood us up with a gun. I screamed, and they told me to shut up, but I couldn't. I-I was so scared, and Jasper..." she choked up.

"Hey, hey, it's okay. You can tell me. Let it out."

"Jasper, he stepped in front of me to shield me, but they thought he was moving in on them and they shot him. It was so fast. He fell, and they took my purse." She kept her eyes lowered and continued the story through jagged gasps for air and sobs. "One put his gun in my mouth while the other took Jasper's wallet out of his pants, while he was just lying there, face down, bleeding." She covered her eyes with her hands and rocked.

Vybes couldn't take it any longer. He put his arms around her again. "Candi, Oh my god. I'm so sorry." He hugged and rocked her, letting her cry into his chest. No wonder she'd been so depressed, he realized, it wasn't only the storm; she was grieving, a feeling he knew all too well, and worse, traumatized. She probably had PTSD. Anyone would. "That wasn't your fault," he whispered, struggling to keep his own eyes dry. I'll tell her about Nakimuli, too, he thought. That's the least I can do.

She pulled away and wiped her face, calming down, but visibly shivering. "We made it to the hospital with him barely alive and I thought he would make it, but he didn't. And he died. He fucking died." She again pressed herself to Vybes' chest, and he squeezed her tighter.

"There. There. Thank you for telling me." Like a sticker from paper, he peeled her body from his sweater. "I'm so sorry that happened to you, and I wouldn't tell a bunch of strange guys I was forced to share a hotel room with, either. I totally understand why you didn't tell us."

This comment brought her the slightest respite, and she stopped sobbing. "I'm sorry."

"No, don't be."

"I'm still in denial, I think. Like, it can't be real. He can't really be gone. That's why I call him."

"Listen, I get it." He put his hand on her shoulder. "Not that it is the same at all, but well, I can relate a bit because my little sister died also, tragically, and I blamed myself. It was awful. I beat myself up about it for years."

She straightened up and wiped her eyes. "Really? Why did you blame yourself?"

"It's a long story, but the good news is that eventually you will forgive yourself. You will heal. I'm living proof of it. But it takes time."

"How did she die?"

He raised his eyebrows. "I'll tell you the whole story, and I want to tell you about something else too, but first, let's get those wet bandages off. I don't want you to get hypothermia or more frostbite."

She took a deep breath, then nodded. He hugged her one more time, wishing he could kiss her, wanting to kiss her, but knowing it wasn't the right time. Maybe that moment would come, or maybe it wouldn't. But he needed to take care of her for now, make her comfortable, make sure nothing worse happened.

Another thought nagged at him as well; am I really over Naki's death? Or did I just say that? He thought about his mom and sister as he dug through Candi's packed bag to find the gauze at the bottom.

Chapter Forty-Nine

CANDI FEET

Despite her predicament, sharing the details of Jasper's death was like a heartworm releasing its grip on her chest. The act of finally telling someone other than the police let loose something intangible, something she hadn't even realized was constricting her so tightly, not shame or guilt, that persisted, but the secret itself. *Jasper wouldn't have wanted me to keep everything plugged up like a constipated pomeranian, anyway,* she realized.

Now, someone else had heard the true details, and they still accepted her. All of a sudden, she cared about everything a little less.

"Thank you for helping me," she said. "And thank you for listening."

Vybes flashed her a charismatic smile, "I'll listen to you anytime. You can tell me everything. I mean, what else do we have to do?"

As he prepared to unwrap her bandages, she took another deep breath, and it filled her in a new way, entering fresh, cleared space. She felt hollowed out, emptied a little of her grief.

He spread a towel under her feet and told her about his childhood in Uganda and his younger sister. "Her name was Nakimuli, which means flower, and when she was a little kid she was so sweet, like one of those babies that always laughs and never cries, never whines and always makes everyone happy, a really smart girl. Everyone loved her the best, you know."

"That's like Jasper, too," Candi said, feeling a swell of warm fondness rise in her chest. "His mom said he rarely cried as a baby. He was everyone's favorite kid."

"Yeah, so it was sad, like really sad." He paused. "My mother was heartbroken especially, because Naki died of malaria when she was only nine, and my parents had money; they could have prevented her death, but it happened really fast, and they'd been busy with me. I was five years older, and I'd gotten into trouble. They had to pick me up from the police station. It was this whole thing. So, it was late when we got home, and my mother waited until the morning to take Naki to the doctor, but by then, well, it was too late. I guess she'd had it for a day or two already and hadn't complained. No one acted fast enough to save her." He closed his eyes. His pain from the memory was still present, but he could manage it. He could hold it and the happy memories of Naki in his heart at the same time.

She put her hand on his shoulder. He really can relate, she thought. "That must have been awful as a kid, and awful for your mother. I'm so sorry."

"Completely tragic." He cast his eyes at her still-bandaged feet. "Cerebral malaria. Not so common in Uganda, but very difficult for anyone to survive once it advances."

"I'm so sorry," she repeated. They had more in common than she thought, and she could understand his guilt, too.

"My mother was never really the same." He looked back up and a darkness flashed in his cinnamon eyes; she recognized it as regret.

"That's terrible, but also not your fault. Teenagers all get into trouble, and you didn't cause her malaria."

"Yeah. I know. It was just dumb kid stuff, out joyriding, being stupid, drinking, but I blamed myself for years, and my mother hated me for a while. She felt like God had taken her good kid and left her with the bad apple. She grieved for years, didn't even want to look at me, same with my grandmother."

Candi folded her lips like an unsent letter and thought of Jasper's own mother. She'd lost her favorite son, too. She must be as devastated as Candi was, yet they never spoke about it other than to futz over plans for the ceremony, as if shopping for groceries. They were closer before his death. She could hardly shoulder her own pain, much less anyone else's. Guilt nibbled at her for ignoring so many of his mother's calls, and she vowed to do better when this was all over. "I'm sure they didn't hate you," she told Vybes.

"Oh, they did, and it made me never want to have kids. It's just too damn sad if they die. But I got my act together after that. I worked harder, focused on moving abroad, all of that. Anyway..." he trailed off and unwrapped her old gauze. He was gentle, but he needn't be; she felt nothing but numbness below her calf.

"I always wanted kids," she muttered, "like before Jasper died we were trying, but now, after everything, I'm glad we didn't. Like, what kind of world is this?"

"It's a lot," Vybes replied. "This world..." He stopped. His hands froze mid-air, holding a strip of gauze. His jaw hung open.

Before she could ask what was wrong, she saw it. She gasped.

Her entire foot was as black as a burnt pizza.

Chapter Fifty

DOCTOR VYBES

Candi thrashed and screamed on the bed. "My feet!" she shrieked.

Not knowing what else to do but wanting her to stop screaming and flinging around her limbs, Vybes climbed onto the bed and held her to the mattress, pinning her arms with his hands. "Please, you need to calm down." He held her as she cried out, wiggled, and writhed.

"Let me bandage you." He gritted his teeth. "Please relax."

She wailed and kicked the air like a toddler.

"It isn't that bad." But he knew he was lying. It was very bad. The sight of them made him want to throw up.

Fear filled her face. "No, no."

"Candi, please, you've got to get a hold of yourself."

"I can't do this. I can't do this." She was frantic, beyond hysterical, convulsing with emotion.

He didn't want to hurt her, but her unhinged reaction was making him panic, too. He held her more firmly, almost laying on her, but trying to avoid her feet. This was wrong, so wrong. He felt like he'd swallowed lead, but he maintained his firm expression. "Let's go downstairs. I'll take you to a doctor. There are medics in the lobby."

She let out a ripping scream and kicked and swung her legs at him. He released her to gyrate on the bed, not knowing what else to do, when from behind him came a pounding knock on the door.

Another knock, louder.

Candi must have heard it too because her mouth shut and she froze, wide eyed, black feet in the air. He turned his head to the door, then back to her. The pounding continued.

She bit her lip and tears streamed from her jade eyes. She grabbed onto his forearms, digging her nails into his skin, terrified. "Don't answer it. I don't want to see anyone," she whispered.

Another forceful knock.

"What if it's something about Franck?"

She let go and his heart double pumped. "Who's there?" He called. The knock was aggressive. Whoever was on the other side of that door, he hoped it was good news, but it didn't sound like it.

"Open up," said a woman's voice.

Maybe it's someone from the hotel, he thought. And though she was shaking her head no, he covered Candi's legs with the blanket and left her to open the door. As he did, his tension lowered a notch: it was an older woman with gray hair dressed in jeans and a black ski jacket.

"Can I help you?"

The woman stepped inside and eyed him with suspicion. "Is everything alright? I heard screaming."

"My friend was just upset about something, but she's okay now."

The woman brushed past him.

"Um, we're actually kind of in the middle of something," he said.

"Are you alright? Do you need help?" she looked at Candi and back to Vybes, her eyes narrowing.

Candi shook her head and blinked rapidly.

"She has frostbite, but we're fine," Vybes said.

"I think she can answer for herself."

"It's okay, she's the neighbor next door," Candi murmured. "But yes. I was—I was just scared about my feet. Sorry." She cast her eyes down to the blanket covering her legs.

The woman frowned at Vybes, then shifted her attention again to Candi. "You're sure you're safe here?"

Bloody hell, Vybes realized, this lady thought he'd been abusing Candi or something. "Um," he glanced back at Candi. "We're actually...it's been a stressful time." As he spoke, tendrils of anger crept into his brain. He'd never hurt a woman; he was trying to help. This lady had to go.

"Okay, well, I wanted to make sure everyone was safe."

"It's not safe for anyone here," Candi snapped.

The lady pursed her lips. "You think I don't know that?" She leaned forward, her eyes narrowing. "My sister got infected, and they took her away. She's probably going to die."

"What? Then you *really* need to leave." Candi shook her head with vigor.

"Well, forgive me for being concerned," the woman crossed her arms. "It sounded like someone was being murdered in here."

"Please go, now." Candi said.

Emotion strained the older woman's reddening face. "This isn't how you treat people."

"We're all going to die," Candi repeated in an ice-cold tone. "Aliens are attacking us."

The neighbor furrowed her brow, and opened and closed her mouth, perhaps trying to conjure an appropriate response.

"Well, thank you so much, and sorry about your sister." Vybes said as he ushered the neighbor out, latching the deadbolt before she could say anything more.

Candi reached for him when he returned, and he took her outstretched hand and patted it. "Let me re-bandage your feet, and I'll take you downstairs to find a doctor."

"There's probably no point, but I guess." She stiffened her jaw and squeezed her eyes shut as he applied the cream from the medics and redid the bandages in silence, trying not to look at her blackened, disfigured toes, which resembled burnt sausages.

"I can't believe this is happening." She put her hand on his arm, as if to steady herself.

He finished.

"Thank you. I'm sorry I freaked out. I just..."

"You don't need to apologize. This isn't something any human should ever have to go through."

She wiped her eyes and nodded.

They put on more layers, and he wheeled her to the elevator to look for a medic.

Chapter Fifty-One

GRETCHEN'S PRAYER

As Gretchen walked once again through the main floor of the terminal, she considered going back to find the man with the bagel and the paperback books, to try and make him her friend for the end of the world, but if she was infected from her interaction with the couple, she'd only be hurting a stranger.

Outside, darkness settled on the airport and the snow accumulation crept to the edge of the tall building's glass windows. God, would it ever stop snowing? Was this really the cold, bitter end? She kept checking her phone for a signal, but no bars appeared. At least she still had power.

Without a cot, she returned to the same bench near a baggage carousel and bed down for the night using her winter jacket as a pillow. It smelled like wet exhaust, but it was better than putting her face on the dirty metal bench. Though she hadn't previously believed in aliens, she whole-heartedly believed in the stupidity of men. All the weapons—men made them. And they had probably made The Glow Stick too. Probably the variant too. All the mistakes that impacted everyone— men made them, and this thing had Silicon Valley written all over it, she thought. Some overgrown, star-wars loving, rocket-building troll with lots of money was responsible for this.

Though that didn't make any difference, whoever had concocted The Glow Stick, and for whatever reason, they either had a plan for it, or they'd lost control of the thing. Either way, she wasn't going to let it intimidate her or turn her into a trembling, meek sheep. No. She planned to survive. With her hand on her heart, she counted its beats and hoped for sleep. She prayed the snow would end. She begged for God or Jesus or anyone, Allah, Krishna, Beyoncé, whoever was left out there, to help. "Please," she whispered, "Please, let there be a way out."

Chapter Fifty-Two

CANDI GUARD

The main floor of the hotel was as quiet as a church on Tuesday. Wet stains covered the rug. Garbage bags leaned beside walls, and the odor of old food permeated the chilly air. They made their way to the lobby's entrance, which now resembled some combination of a military base and a hospital emergency room. Though Candi no longer cried for her feet, the image of her squat black toes held steady in her mind's eye. They reminded her of a gorilla's hands and she felt like a dying animal. She tried not to cry as Vybes pushed her towards the men.

Four Canadian army officers guarded the lobby's blocked-off entrance. They wore gray and white camouflage uniforms, heavy winter boots, black gloves, and what appeared to be gas masks. Handguns rested on each man's hips in black leather holsters. They looked like video game characters to her.

"You should be in your rooms," one man said, his voice muffled by his mask.

"She's got bad frostbite and urgently needs a doctor," Vybes said.

"That won't be possible. This area is no longer open."

"Please, could you ask a doctor or nurse to come have a look?"

"Everyone who isn't sick nust shelter in place." His face was stern, his tone aggressive. "And no one should be trying to go outside."

Candi's eyes widened. Were that many people sick? She wondered.

"Please, can you ask?"

The man motioned to another officer. "Escort them to their rooms."

"It's really not necessary," Vybes said. "We'll go straight back. We didn't know."

The second soldier nodded. "I'll take you, let's go."

As he led them to the now-disgusting elevator, despite her best efforts, Candi started to cry again.

Vybes squeezed her shoulder as he gave the soldier their room number. "Do you know what's going on with the heat? It's gotten really cold in our room."

"They're working on it."

Candi's own hands felt frozen to the bone, like half-defrosted chicken breasts. She kept them in her coat pockets.

"And what were all those planes earlier?" Vybes asked.

"They evacuated some military personnel."

Candi, tense already, tensed further.

"Wait. The military is leaving? What about everyone else?" Vybes stopped walking.

"Don't leave your room again unless you're told to. Come on." The officer returned them to their door.

"Please," Vybes said again, "If you see any doctors, please give them our room number and ask them to come here. Her feet are in bad shape. She needs medical help."

The officer hesitated, then tipped his helmet forward. "I will, but I don't want to give you false hope; they won't come. The only doctor and the nurses here are in quarantine themselves, tending to the patients there."

Inside the room, Candi slid onto the bed, almost ill with fatigue.

"Well, that was intense. Guess now we just wait. I still have battery on my laptop. We could watch a movie."

But she didn't want to. She wanted to sleep, to make everything go away, if only for a few hours.

He agreed and turned off the lights. They lay in bed together, not touching, not talking, but she couldn't sleep. Her body, full of anxiety and fear, stayed unreasonably alert and despite all her layers, her limbs ached with an inner chill, like floating in a frigid lake. This is the worst day of my life, she thought, and wondered why she hadn't tried harder to leave after the plane had crashed. She could have rented a car, or maybe found someone else working for the airline and gotten on a different plane before they grounded flights. Now her toes were black. Now there were no doctors. Now there was a strange, evil machine floating in the sky. God, what have I done? She wondered. Did I sabotage my chances of going home just to avoid Jasper's ceremony?

Vybes faced her. "I can't sleep."

"I can't either."

"Tomorrow is Christmas Eve. Do you know what that means?"

"That we might freeze to death?"

"Guess again."

"That we're going to make a gingerbread house and watch Miracle of 34th Street?"

Vybes chuckled, "I wish."

"That we've been wearing the same dirty clothes for days?"

"Well, yes, but all things considered, you still smell pretty good to me."

She half-smiled. There are worse people to be stuck with, she thought. "So what does it mean?"

"Christmas Eve is the day for LSD."

"You want this situation to get even crazier? No thanks."

"To pass the time while we wait for the storm to end."

"It's never going to end."

"All things end."

A shiver passed through her chest despite all the blankets. He was a lunatic. "If it gets any colder, we'll have to set the furniture on fire."

"It might be warmer if we got under the covers with fewer clothes and put our jackets on top of the blankets. That's what they say to do if you're camping in the cold with a sleeping bag."

She raised the skin where her eyebrows should have been. "You want us to get naked?" It sounded like a terrible idea.

"No, silly, not naked. Leave like one layer. Let's see if it helps."

They did and Candi noticed a subtle difference, but the cold air still hurt to breathe. The temperature in the room felt like it was below zero, and she wondered if her frostbite was making it feel even colder. Her stomach rumbled audibly.

"If we take a little LSD, it will also help with the hunger. It reduces your appetite," Vybes said.

"You must be hungry, too."

"I am, but we're out of food, or at least I am."

"I'm out too. We only have alcohol." She shivered.

He moved closer to her and whispered. "Can we cuddle? For body heat?"

Agreeing without words, she slipped into his embrace. Soon, sleep transported her to another place. She bathed in a hot bath in an opulent spa of marble floors, maroon curtains, and crystal chandeliers. Franck was there, too, and he approached her in nothing but a towel, grinning.

"Candi," he said, "I'm so glad you came."

She stood up in the water and realized she was naked. He removed his towel, revealing his own unclothed body, and stepped into the pool with her. They embraced, kissing passionately, but after a few moments, he grabbed her by the hair and turned her away from him. Vybes rose from the water before her, his tall, broad body also wet, warm, and naked from the hot jacuzzi. Franck pushed her to the young man like a sacrifice and Vybes kissed her lips while Franck held her hair and sucked on the back of her neck. She moaned and Vybes pressed his long, erect penis into her stomach, making her quake with desire. The two men worked on her pale, damp body, touching her, squeezing her like an orange in their fists. In the bubbling water, Vybes lowered onto a stone bench, and she straddled him, but as she did, Franck pulled her hair again, twisting her to him. Then he shoved her head underwater. Without fighting it, she sank below the surface, then swam to a deep, dark world, alone, to nothingness.

She awoke with a sticky feeling in her underwear, with her legs wedged between Vybes' thighs. He breathed beside her, and a soft pulse of desire expanded and contracted in her pelvis, then throbbed. For a moment, things felt normal, even nice. She marveled at her own reproductive system's attempts to function, even in situations of destruction, calamity, and despair. She considered pulling away from the young man to combat the sensations, but instead she snuggled closer to him, letting her arousal rise, letting it warm her from the inside.

Outside, night had fallen. The room was dark.

With her cheek to his enormous chest, listening to his heartbeat, she forgot about her charred feet and thought about one of the last things her friend Adrienne had said, that no woman could resist a handsome, tall man.

Chapter Fifty-Three

GRETCHEN'S CHRISTMAS CARD

As if in answer to her prayers, the snow stopped. At the window, Gretchen studied the white landscape. She gazed at the desolate landscape in disbelief, her jaw slack. Snow. Nothing but snow as far as she could see. She blinked. Am I dreaming? She wondered for a second. But she wasn't. Snow also covered the entire crashed airplane, a new peninsula, like a glacier attached to the terminal.

Despite the sudden cessation in snow, a sense of foreboding still lingered in her thoughts like frost on a windshield. She took a few deep breaths as she studied the silent, crystalized landscape. Her neck and back ached. Sleeping on the floor wasn't doing her spine any favors. She rotated her head, working out a kink, and her bone cracked. This doesn't feel right, she thought. Is this like the eye of the storm or something? Around her, the airport buzzed. People chatted, arranged their things, even laughed. The halt of snow heralded a new mood—one she'd almost given up on: hope. Yet she couldn't shake her sense of dread.

Also, where were the snowmobiles? She wondered. Shouldn't they be seizing this chance? The only response she received was a rumble in her tummy, now as empty as a discarded pack of cigarettes.

Stashing her few belongings under the bench, hoping no one would take them, she set off again, heading to the area where she'd seen the man with all the books. He looked like her people, and right now, she needed her people. Also, maybe he had more food and maybe she could borrow a book to take on her journey. It was almost better to have friends in times of hope than in despair, she thought, trying to feel more excited about the change in weather. Plus, she didn't have a temperature or a sore throat or any sign of being sick, and it was possible that the older gentleman beside her had randomly had a heart problem without it being related to the variant. People had strokes all the time at that age, especially when stressed.

When she reached the circle of stacked books, however, the man wasn't there. She waited a bit. Maybe he'd gone to the bathroom. Seated cross-legged on the floor, she opened one of the paperbacks, a thriller by an author she'd never heard of and read the first page, an intro describing a girl who'd lost her parents and inherited their old house which contained a vault with mysterious paintings. It didn't grab her.

As she picked up another book, author John le Carré's memoir, a glint of something shiny caught her eye. A square of plastic and silver peeked from under the man's blanket. She lifted the fabric and there was his mug shot on an airport ID badge. Blood rushed to her brain and then to her hand and she snatched the ID, stuffed it in her sweatpants pocket, lanyard and all. He was an employee, after all, with an access card. With the Carré book under her arm, she turned to leave, but instead almost bumped against the owner of the card in her pocket.

"Hello, there." He said as her heart jumped to her throat.

"Hi, sorry, I was just looking at your books."

"Ah, a fellow reader. And I see you picked one." He pointed to the novel in her hand.

More blood rushed to her cheeks. "I hope that's okay? Sorry, I didn't see anyone here."

"It's more than okay." He stretched out his hand. "I'm Teddy."

Chapter Fifty-Four

TRIPPING VYBES

Vybes waited in the swivel chair, sipping warm coffee, grinning, fidgeting, turning from the window to Candi and back to the window. He couldn't wait to show her the good news, that the snow had stopped. He almost wanted to wake her just to tell her, but she looked too peaceful, too blissfully somewhere else.

"Good morning, sleeping beauty," he said when she finally awoke.

She sat up in bed and stretched.

"While you were still sleeping, I went downstairs to look for food and, lo-and-behold, they had coffee." He passed her a cup.

"Maybe the world isn't ending after all," she mumbled, sipped, and sighed. "Impressive."

"Not just that. The heat is on again too. There is warm air coming out of our vent, and look at this," he pointed to the window.

Her mouth opened and her eyes widened.

"I—I can hardly believe it." She rose from the bed, but then stumbled and winced. He pulled her chair around and she sat down for him to push her to the window.

"I couldn't believe it either, but it hasn't snowed a single flake for at least two hours, as long as I've been up."

"Oh my God. Thank God. Finally."

"Without the blizzard, they'll get this cleared and we can all leave." He bent down and hugged her in the wheelchair. A wave of happiness washed over him. They were going to be okay.

"There is nothing I want more on earth, no offense." She leaned back from him. "By the way, I had a dream about you last night."

He gazed into her green, now-hopeful eyes and even noticed a hint of mirth in her expression. "I hope it was dirty," he said without thinking. Then put his hand over his mouth. "Oops, forget I said that."

She giggled, making dimples in her rosy cheeks.

He kneeled beside her wheelchair, feeling more excited than he had in days. "Hey, listen, I don't want to hide anything from you. I wanted to tell you about something yesterday, but things were too crazy, and we were too tired."

"Tell me what?" A look of apprehension clouded her gaze.

"No, don't worry, it isn't bad."

"Okay, what is it then?"

"I took the LSD."

She cocked her head. "Really? But when?"

"The first time we saw The Glow Stick. I got scared and thought it was the end, so I took two tabs."

Her lips parted like she was about to speak, but she didn't. He couldn't tell if she was upset or surprised, but he explained all that had transpired, though he left out hooking up with Gretchen, which he felt a tad guilty about, but he'd been fucked up, *really* fucked up. Plus, he rationalized, it was private between him and Gretchen and wasn't pertinent information for Candi. If she knew, it might make things awkward, especially if they ran into Gretchen again, wherever she was. So, I know we're going to be okay," he finished. "It's all connected, and I saw you in my vision during the trip."

"You don't know that," she said. "But I guess we know it's really LSD."

"Exactly, and I think it has a protective quality, because I never got shocked as badly as you and I still have my eyebrows."

"You're totally insane." She sipped her coffee.

"So, I think maybe we should take some, but a lower dose. Plus, it's Christmas Eve. No way we're leaving yet, and it will pass the time, and like I said, it's an appetite suppressant. We can play music, trip, and chill out."

"I can't even feel my feet."

"Maybe it will help get your blood circulating. I think it does that. Anyway, something in my gut is telling me today is the day. Acid Christmas. This is what needs to happen."

"I think I need to lie down."

He wheeled her back to the bed, and she slid in. They sat against the bed's headboard, sipping their lattes.

"I also want you to see these creatures I saw."

"What makes you so sure you'll see them again? Couldn't it just have been a one-off thing?"

"I can't explain, but I just know." He turned to her with a serious expression. "Candi, trust me. Look outside. Things are getting better and we're going to be fine. We can even have a lovely Christmas." As he said the words, he believed them even more than before. Things were turning a corner. He sensed it. "This book is meant for you and me."

But she didn't look outside. She held his gaze. Did she want him to kiss her? Was now the right time? "We're stuck here," he added, "We should make the best of things." He leaned in closer.

"I'm not the type of person who does this."

He moved a stray piece of red hair from her cheek and tucked it behind her ear. "Then, do it for me. Do it for Jasper and for Nakimuli, who never got to enjoy such things." Part of him wondered why he wanted this so so much, why he couldn't leave it alone. He finished the rest of his coffee in one swig and said, "Listen, I don't know why I'm pressuring you, or why I want to do it today, but I want it more than anything else. It's all I've been able to think about since I woke up. It feels right. It feels necessary even. We're meant to do this together. It has to be both of us, and today. I can't really explain it, but I know it's true." He took a deep breath, then exhaled. "I hope you'll say yes."

Her lips parted, and, to his surprise, she agreed with him.

"Really?" He raised his eyebrows. Well, he had laid it on really thick, bringing up the dead and all, but she wouldn't be sorry—he knew that for sure.

"If you really want me to, then I guess I will. I mean, you seem really convinced and there isn't anything better to do. If we end up dying, we may as well be high."

"That's the spirit, only no one is dying."

"Except maybe Franck, who totally deserves it."

"Correct." He laughed.

Afraid she would change her mind; he didn't waste time, but got out the green book and flipped through the pages. His eyes darted from image to image. Maybe the rest of his time in Toronto would be spent tripping and making love with this gorgeous flight attendant? Then the whole storm would almost be worth it.

He settled on tabs from a page with a painting of a cabin on a lake surrounded by pine trees, falling snow, shooting stars, and floating, glowing luminous purple balls of string. A fireplace glowed orange through its window. Two shadowy men stood outside; their arms raised to the hovering fibers.

"Are you ready?"

"No."

"Don't worry. It will be beautiful, and I'll be right here the whole time. We don't have to leave the bed. When you can't go outside; go inside."

Candi eyed the tab with suspicion, but opened her mouth.

"Here we go. Merry Christmas." And with the little stamp looking so tiny on his long, brown finger, he placed the acid like a sacrament on her outstretched, salmon-colored tongue.

Chapter Fifty-Five

CANDI TRIPPING JINGLE BALLS

Who cares anymore, Candi thought and held her lips shut, but despite her attempts at nihilism and apathy, within seconds, she considered spitting the tab back out. It felt like a bug in her mouth.Why did I agree to such an insane idea? She wondered. The end of the blizzard, the coffee, Vybes' excitement, it had all somehow gone to her head, making her forget the true gravity of their situation. This was possibly a terrible mistake, and it wasn't too late to stop it. If she removed the tab now, she might not trip.

"This is going to be the best part of this entire experience. You're going to feel so amazing." Vybes said.

"I think I've lost my mind."

"Let's set an intention for our trip."

"Don't answer the door again, no matter what."

"I won't, but I mean a more spiritual intention. I'm setting the intention for us to have a peaceful, euphoric journey, to feel a deep connection to the universe and to the earth."

Candi again considered removing the tab. Vybes was waiting for her to share her intention, but nothing came to her. "I intend to feel happy," she said finally.

"That's a great intention. I love that." With enthusiasm, he hugged her.

This must be our hundredth hug, she thought. Why did I agree to this? Though he was right. They were stuck. There was nothing else to do. Also, she didn't want to think too much anymore. Not only was she tired of the hotel room; she was tired of her own brain. It would be an escape from present circumstances. Nothing seems real anymore, so why not hallucinate? For Jasper, she thought, and she held onto the idea like a tow rope. "How long will it take to kick in?"

"It's pretty fast, maybe fifteen, twenty minutes." Vybes reclined in the chair beside the window. "The last time I took acid before this book was on my 24th birthday. I was dating this woman from Norway, and we went to a resort in Goa. We were out on the beach and this hippie hobo type offered us LSD. I didn't even think about it, I just put it on my tongue. My girlfriend was mortified. She refused to take it and went back to our room all in a huff. So, I spent the day wandering up and down the beach, tripping my balls off. It was amazing."

"You're lucky you didn't get sunburnt," Candi said. "I would literally die in that scenario; I'd come out a boiled lobster."

Vybes laughed and scooted his chair closer. "I'm glad I have a willing partner in crime this time."

Their eyes met, and a sensation like she was about to step off a 10-story building fizzled in her limbs. "Barely willing and extremely nervous."

"We should get festive." He put on some old school holiday music and swayed his towering body to the tune.

"I'll be home for Christmas," Bing Crosby crooned from the computer's speakers.

"I can't believe you have this music downloaded to your laptop."

"Prepared for any kind of party." The young man laughed and threw up his hands, dancing around the room.

He had such a genuine smile, and with his size, he seemed to her almost like a different species. Was he feeling the acid already? Was she? She took a deep breath. "I... I just can't believe..." The air around Vybes bubbled and undulated. Fizzy sensations buzzed all over her body. It was a pleasant feeling, like the revival of new molecules, the shifting of normality to bliss. He stood by the bed for a minute, taking deep breaths, seeming to reconnect with himself. Prisms of color danced from her chipped fingernail polish.

"I'm so glad you're here with me." He touched her leg, and it made her feel electric, hot even. She took off her sweater. "I think I'm tripping."

"Good." He leaned over and kissed her on the lips.

It felt surprising, but incredible, warm, and it sent the same fizzing feelings straight to her brain. When he pulled away, she gasped, not from disgust, but from euphoria.

"Sorry, I've been wanting to do it since you woke up. I hope that was okay."

"Really?" She felt more curious than confused and she couldn't help but smile, which made her face feel weird, like her lips wouldn't stop, like the corners of her mouth might touch the ceiling.

He kissed her again, but on the cheek, like they were kids, and he was just testing it out.

Her body swam with a feeling like swirls of warm yellow light, and he returned to dancing. The solid walls around her converted to complex patterns. Under her skin, it felt like repair men working on her internal parts. Vybes' black hair shined, and he looked older and wiser to her, like a shaman. She sat on the edge of the bed and gazed out the window, which was now full of geometric crystals.

He came behind her and draped his arms over her shoulders. "Are you happy?"

She could only nod.

Beyond the glass, forms materialized, giant creatures with glass limbs, marching tubular shapes, all connected to one another by tendrils of translucent matter. "Oh my god," she breathed. "Do you see them?"

"Yes. I saw them before, too."

"They're everywhere" She gazed at the beings with wonder. Were they always there? Or were they a figment of her mind? But how could Vybes see them too? They breathed like lungs in the snowscape. Each contained intricate patterns resembling Aztec art. Or was it Aztec? It was something she recognized but couldn't place. She sensed the beings had been on earth for many years, like hidden trees, another species, an invisible forest.

"They could be Gods," Vybes said. "Or alien machines."

But they didn't look like machines to her. "I need to lie down," she said, suddenly overwhelmed by everything, by her body, the acid, the idea that she'd been living in this universe of unseen creatures her entire life.

She closed her eyes. Each music note became an exploding world. Time parted like blowing powder.

Vybes snuggled beside her.

"Thank you," she whispered.

They lay together in bed, listening to the music, no longer wondering what would happen next. He became her world. The room expanded and contracted. She felt his consciousness and her own and sensed she could read his mind. The universe was big and small and alive and dead at the same time.

She opened her eyes and saw he contained many colors, and his face was changing so much that she couldn't keep up with it. She saw every pore, every hair, every line, every particle of his skin, all alive.

He kissed her again on her lips, then on her cheek, sparklers going off against her skin.

"I love this, but I think I want to leave the room," he said. "I want to find a bigger window."

"I don't know." She couldn't imagine moving.

"I'll wheel you. It'll be nice. Then we'll come back here."

Beyond words, she didn't agree or disagree, but let him put her jacket on her, her boots. He lifted her and put her in the chair. She marveled at his ability to still function.

As they rode down the elevator, the LSD kicked in harder, and the carpeted chamber bulged around her. "I want to go back," she said, grabbing his hand. "Sorry."

"It's okay." He pushed her back to their room, through a world of silk, the empty hallway, and she felt again at peace.

"You know, in the early 70s there were groups that took acid and studied the Bible," Vybes said.

She giggled. "How could they read anything?"

His laugh echoed like a penny in a small pot. "Who knows? But they said there were giants in the Bible times."

"I've never heard that before."

The return to their room felt like home, no longer like a prison, but like they were two college kids on a date, returning to their dorm.

They took off their jackets and shoes and he held her in bed as they drifted together through fields of warm sensation, geometrical shapes, Christmas music, the laughter of elves, and rainbows, ideas, emotions like blooming flowers.

She burrowed into his arms, and he touched the side of her face with his large hand, traced her lips with his finger. She studied his brown eyes and saw a microcosm of life. They kissed again, and it sent sensations like popcorn popping to her mind.

"Woah," he said. "Do you feel that? You're so warm now."

"I feel it."

"I like you, Candi. I really do."

She pressed her mouth against his, feeling complete joy in his taste. It was better than kissing Franck. Much, much better. God, this acid was fucking amazing. He folded around her like soft blankets, then parted her lips, their tongues touched for a second, but she couldn't handle it. Her body burst with unfelt sensations. Everything released, and she slipped into another dimension.

A flash—the image of him and her floating in snow— behind a window—running together. A Christmas tree aglow with lights. In a sunset, streams of eclectic reds, strings of green, a landscape of white and gold.

Time elapsed. The sun moved. Sounds progressed. The earth spun. Stars died. Plans evolved.

Outside, The Glow Stick returned to the sky. Vybes noticed it first, but it had transformed from dangerous to beautiful. They watched the luminous strings sing and connect around it like a maypole.

"Do you think it's still shocking people?" She lay with her head on his chest, her pupils wide, her green eyes fixed on the window.

"I don't feel anything bad."

Then the room filled with them, the stringed beams, and they touched her. She absorbed their words, their breath, meanings she couldn't fully interpret. They had to leave—her and Vybes. That was the message. But how? she asked. Where? The strings of air vibrated, emitting arpeggios like a harp. They flitted about her skin like insect wings.

Not yet, but soon.

She touched them, held them in her hand, pulled on one from the air and put it in her mouth. It was hot and tasted like melted plastic. She recoiled and spat it out. Her bowls rumbled. "I —I've got to go to the bathroom," she said. Vybes helped her, but the bathroom was another world—harsh lights and undulating wallpaper. Her gut felt like Satan himself had reached up and rung her out. Her whole body shook. Then, everything flooded into the toilet, and she felt better. Steadying herself on the wall, she tried to walk. It worked.

With socks covering her black feet, which she'd forgotten about anyway, she returned to bed. Vybes didn't speak. He was wrapped in strings. They wound around him like transparent snakes, almost like Christmas lights on a tree. She wondered if she should tell him, but she knew that was far beyond her means.

Not yet, but soon. It's almost time.

She heard it again.

Chapter Fifty-Six

GRETCHEN'S FRIEND FOR THE END

Gretchen and Teddy leaned against the wall of the baggage claim area, surrounded by stacks of novels, both munching on a week old bagel.

"Sorry it's so stale," Teddy said.

"Are you kidding me? I was prepared to not eat again for a month."

After brief intros, Gretchen discovered that Teddy didn't work in the bookstore, he worked at the Tim Horton's, and was also a writer, like her, but an aspiring poet. He held up his notebook, "As bad as this situation is, it's given me so much new material."

"Lucky you, I've been too stressed to write much of anything, and I was sharing a room with a bunch of kids, and a family, so it was hard to concentrate."

"Well, who knows if it's any good." Teddy shrugged, "But it's been helping me to write. Takes my mind off things. I want to start doing slam poetry too if we ever get out of here. Always thought about it, never did it, but life is too short. Ya know?" He raised his eyebrows.

"Tell me about it. And all these books? I thought maybe you worked at the bookstore."

He chuckled and explained that while searching through discarded baggage, in an effort to find a blanket and pillow for himself, he'd found what's known as an M-bag, a cargo bag containing stacks of printed matter destined for a foreign country. It was full of the novels that now surrounded them. "I'll return them if this all ends," he concluded.

"When it ends."

He shrugged. "I'm not sure this isn't the beginning of something much longer."

"I was just upstairs. The end has already begun. It stopped snowing."

"Really? I wasn't expecting that."

Gretchen glanced at him and he looked genuinely puzzled. "I mean, I assume it hasn't restarted. I should probably go upstairs again and see."

He rubbed his graying beard. "I stopped going upstairs. The shocks are worse up there."

So we're on the same wavelength, Gretchen thought. He looked a little older than her, and he was taller, but they were about the same size, weight-wise, and the same skin tone. He could have passed for her brother. In fact, he looked more like her than Kevin did. Kevin would also never wear his hair in dreads. "My brother is pretty sick," she said, "So, I keep going to check the cell service. I really want to get in touch with my family."

He studied her. "You're not Canadian, are you?"

"No. I'm American."

"I thought so."

"How can you tell?" She tilted her head.

"Canadians aren't so friendly."

"I thought Canadians were supposed to be so nice and open-minded."

"Not what I see. They keep to themselves."

"Hey, you worked here. Did you ever hear anything about a tunnel in the airport? Like an emergency underground exit."

Teddy nodded.

She leaned in closer. "Any idea where it is?"

He paused for a second, then closed his eyes, as if trying to remember the details. "I remember seeing a construction notice about it, but I don't know exactly where it was. Funny you brought it up though, because I was just looking for it myself."

A jittery feeling bloomed in her abdomen. "Really?"

"Yeah, I've been looking for it for a few days now."

Gretchen couldn't believe her ears. She'd clearly found her friend for the end of the world, or at least for the end of the blizzard, and though he smelled like coffee and unwashed underarms, she didn't mind. She probably didn't smell so great herself. They shared where they'd both searched so far.

"My only thought is that maybe it isn't in the commercial terminals."

"Where else could it be?"

"There are three cargo buildings separate from the terminals. No way to get to them now, not with the snow, though. So, we might be stuck here together." The corners of his brown eyes crinkled.

He's flirting with me, she realized. However, it would be quite awkward if they went looking for the tunnel and he needed his badge, which was still in her pocket. Now that they were on the same mission, or so it seemed, she planned to return the ID when he wasn't looking. "Do you know where the tunnel leads?"

He didn't.

"Though anyplace would be preferable to here," she said.

"We don't know about that."

She finished her bagel and they sat in silence for a while. Teddy picked up the book he'd been reading. She noted that it was non-fiction, one of those how to stop giving a fuck books. Well, that's appropriate, she thought. She considered slipping the ID back under the blanket, but she was afraid he might look up. Maybe it was better to hold on to it for a bit. The bagel had renewed her energy, though, and she wasn't in the mood to read.

"Will you be here for a while? I'm thinking I'll move my bag here. I left it under a bench."

"Of course, please do. I'd love the company."

"And I want to check upstairs to see if they've resumed clearing the snow."

She moved her few belongings beside Teddy, then hiked the broken escalator. Before reaching even halfway, the screams began. She couldn't see The Glow Stick, but felt it on her skin. The shocks attacked her core, her hands, her brain. She grabbed onto the escalator's railing, trying not to fall, shaking, grinding her teeth, accidentally biting her tongue, tasting blood and smelling her own hair burn.

This is what it must be like, she thought for a split second, to be a prisoner on death row, to be executed in an electric chair with a flip of a switch. This is it. I'm going to die now. She shrieked in pain and her vision, like an innocent man gasping his last breath, sputtered, then went out. Departure.

She lost her grip and fell backwards.

Chapter Fifty-Seven

VYBES DROP

His perception shifted, and as if he'd time traveled, everything was different again. Both now naked under the covers, he reached between her legs and touched Candi's soft, light red pubic hair. She made cooing sounds and her hand wound around his erect penis, long and thick now. She let out a gasp.

Vybes leaned back. "What's wrong?"

"It's so big," she whispered.

He laughed and rolled her to his side, stroking the edge of bare stomach. He could feel the acid coming down. They were on the other side of the peak. His control over his surroundings increased. This had been the best day, his best idea. Exactly what he'd wanted. "I'm going to put on a condom," he said.

"Don't bother."

He put one on anyway. "Are you sure about this?"

"I'm sure." She kissed him, pulling him to her. A moment could have been a minute and or an hour. He entered her and it felt like bursting into a dream.

She made a loud sound, what they called a *kosikina*—a sex scream—back in Uganda.

"Are you okay?"

"Don't stop."

After only a few minutes of slow, shallow thrusts, she orgasmed. Or at least he thought she did. It was hard to tell. Had she? Maybe not. She said again that she didn't want him to stop. She convulsed and moaned, and he kept sliding on top of her, sweating now, telling her that he was about to make her cum again. Pleasure expanded in his core. He closed his eyes and moved on her, holding her, kissing her neck. He heard a sound like the sky ripping open, like jets and brakes and earthquakes rushing through his ears. She felt so, so good. Her nails dug into his back. A boom. He went in deeper. He was about to cum. Lights flashed behind his closed eyes.

Then he came like a spray of hot water, but as he did, a gust of cold air blew across his backside. He sunk into her breasts, and she held him, hugging him. His dick quaked and sputtered. He tried to catch his breath and felt the cold air again. It felt surreal, like he was in a movie, but in a good way. It was only after he pulled out that he realized their hotel room's window had shattered. The cold wind he'd felt wasn't some weird dream or odd sensation from the acid; it was fucking real. Most of the window was gone. The heavy drapes swayed slightly back and forth. He blinked. He even rubbed his eyes. The room sputtered and fear spiked in him like a pole vaulter.

"Vybes," she said. "The window. The window's broken."

He couldn't speak. He gaped at the jagged glass hole, almost trying to will it to reassemble. Again, his timeline jumped. Suddenly, he was playing an entirely different video game.

And then he saw the snow. Not only was it falling again, it was blowing into their room.

Chapter Fifty-Eight

CANDI SLIPPING

An icy feeling, like swallowing frozen knives, filled her throat. Another strange sound, like an amber alert, filled the room. She covered her ears. Was it coming from The Glow Stick?

"Candi," he grabbed her arm, "Get dressed. Get your things. We can't stay here. There's glass everywhere. We have to leave."

"How—how did it break?"

It felt like she was waking up from a dream. The Christmas music was still going and Diana Ross was singing. They had slept together. I finally slept with someone, she thought. I did it. But she couldn't linger on the situation. He was right. It was freezing.

Vybes pulled the extra duvet off the bed and wrapped it around her shoulders like a cape, and wrapped Franck's blanket around his shoulders over it. He again looked like a shaman to her. I'm still really fucked up, she thought and closed her eyes for a moment. The darkness turned into rocks, then steps, then a tower she climbed. There was a goat made of blankets. There was snow on her arms. She needed to pee and maybe drink some water, and she was so cold.

"Candi?" Vybes snapped her out of her trance.

"I'm coming." They both put on their clothes and boots.

He turned and went to the door.

"Hey, wait for me at least."

But he wasn't leaving without her. The neighbor had returned.

"I've been banging on your door. I heard your music still on. We've all got to go to the airport," the woman yelled over the Christmas songs. She waved her hands at him, "Hey, are you deaf? Didn't you hear the alarm? The thing blew out the window. Look at your window!"

Vybes turned off the music, but they both just stared at the women.

"Hey, wait a second. Are you guys on drugs? Hello?"

"We're leaving," Vybes said. "Right now. We'll come with you."

The woman grimaced. She opened her mouth as if to respond, but her eyes widened and her expression turned to one of panic. The neighbor's body first went rigid, then vibrated and shook in place. Candi watched in shock as smoke rose from the lady's flurrying hands and yellow pulses of light shot out from her ears and neck. The woman lurched, screamed, and tumbled backwards. Her booted feet went out from under her and her head whacked the edge of their TV stand. She slid to the carpet, convulsing.

Vybes dropped down to help, but Candi turned to the window, her eyes following waves of light that raced from The Glow Stick into their room. Sounds again ripped through the air, but this time Candi felt nothing, no shocks, no pain.

The woman made guttural, gurgling sounds and writhed on the floor. Vybes wasn't getting shocked either, she saw. Has the acid done something to us? She wondered. Was it because they'd seen the string beings? Were they somehow protected from the shocks?

The woman lost her bowels, shrieked one last time, stiffened like a log, then went silent, her blank eyes fixed to the ceiling. Blood oozed from every opening in her face.

Candi's hand flew to her mouth.

The smell of excrement and burning skin permeated the room. Vybes held two fingers to the woman's neck, then to her heart. He lifted up the woman's hand to feel for a pulse. Her fingers had turned black, charred. He dropped her hand and got up from the floor, backing away from the body. More snow blew in, covering the carpet by the window in white dust.

"Why didn't we get shocked?" she asked.

"I don't know, but let's get out of here."

They took the blankets and sheets, even their pillows, shoving them into Vybes' black duffel bag. He left behind anything he had that wasn't clothes.

"Hey wait, where's the book?

She didn't know, couldn't remember. She was still seeing strange things, but reality was returning like grass in spring, only it wasn't good.

He managed to find it along with his gloves. She got into the wheelchair and he rolled her out.

The woman's body stayed on the floor; its color draining like a fading photo.

Part Four

LOST AND FOUND

Interlude: Teddy's Terminal Conditions

After Gretchen left, Teddy opened his notebook and resumed working on a poem he'd written earlier that week.

Trees grow in graveyards
Ergot from rot
Does the blue spruce dream?
Does nature ever stop?

"*Everybody has a heartache,*" I sing in the bathroom, rubbing brown disposable paper towels under my stinking armpits, trying to stay clean in a world so filthy we need a galaxy-sized washing machine.

Last night, I had a bad dream too.
And it scared me a lot.

I was on my way to a party in Scarborough and when I got there, I climbed the house's steps, but they cut off before the door. To reach my family, I had to traverse a set of metal monkey bars. Hands cold and feet numb, I swung one aching, burning limb and then another. But the bars began to bite. I screamed and screamed. The way grew longer, my grip too tight. The teeth sharper. Their lashes like a knife.

Finally, I reached the door and I went inside. In tears, I showed my bloody, black skin to my kin. Turning purple and spreading red, my arms grew infested.

So, I called my doctor. "Hello. I need help!"

But it was only an answering service in the Philippines.

So, I died.

Yes, when all isn't calm, when all isn't bright,
That's when everyone freezes at night.

I'm in the terminal again wondering if conditions are terminal.

I'm holding onto a bag of stale bagels and toast. Hope they can keep me, but I fear they won't.

I fear that I'll soon settle in for an indefinite winter's nap...

These poems are all I'll leave behind...

But at least I found a friend, a friend for the end, Lady Gretchen. He added, but after reading the whole thing again, he thought the last lines sounded a little too corny. Maybe he'd delete that part. He turned to another page and started writing again.

Chapter Fifty-Nine

DISCONNECTED CANDI

As Vybes and Candi rushed to the elevator, a voice came over the loudspeaker. "A full transfer of hotel guests to the airport will begin in the next hour. An officer will come to your door and let you know when to depart. If you have face masks or facial coverings, please wear them." The voice overhead then reassured the guests that everything would be fine. Evacuation from the airport would begin as soon as possible. This was a temporary, but necessary step for the safety of the guests, sorry for the inconvenience and blah blah blah.

Vybes pressed the elevator, but the light didn't come on. They waited. Nothing happened. "I think it's out," he said.

"I can walk, but can you carry my chair?"

He agreed and they began the long descent down the stairwell. Candi gripped the railing, still tripping. She wasn't in pain anymore, but it was weird to walk on numb feet. She feared she might fall.

The stairwell smelled like urine and old wine. They stopped on a landing and Vybes passed her his refillable water bottle. She let the cold liquid drip down her throat.

"We should take another tab," he said. "This one is wearing

down and if it's really somehow protecting us from the shocks, we should take more."

"I thought it's because those strings touched us."

"We don't know. Taking more seems worth the risk."

He was right, she realized. It wasn't just the risk of being shocked or frozen. That woman had died from The Glow Stick's last round. He ripped out two tabs. She took a deep breath and put one on her tongue.

Chapter Sixty

GRETCHEN WON'T BE STOPPED

The first thing Gretchen saw when she opened her eyes was a Black Santa Clause. She blinked. What? Where am I?

"You're awake? Gretchen?"

A man leaned over her. It wasn't actually Santa, but Teddy. She tried to look around and yelped. Fiery pain shot up her neck. Her back ached. "What? What happened?" She murmured.

"You fell. The thing in the sky is back. You got shocked. Can you sit up? Try and drink." He helped her into his lap, and brought a water bottle to her lips. She swallowed but couldn't seem to catch her breath. Pain radiated through her limbs with her every move and exhaustion made her want to shut her eyes and sleep.

"You're lucky to be alive," Teddy said. "I thought you were dead at first."

She couldn't remember. "I feel so tired."

"You're in shock. Maybe you have a concussion. But we can't stay here. I'm going to carry you now." He slid a blanket kind of under her and lifted her like a baby. How long was I knocked out? She wondered. She couldn't turn her head. It hurt too much and her elbow hurt, and her thigh.

Teddy moved her through the terminal and she could hear people in all directions talking and crying. She heard her name, but couldn't keep her eyes open.

"Gretchen," a voice called. Her body lowered to the ground. Something cold on her face. She opened her eyes. "Gretchen." It was Teddy leaning over her again. "Wake up. You can't sleep."

"Shit, I fell asleep?" she murmured. She hadn't even realized she was sleeping.

He pulled her up to her feet. "Can you walk? Try to walk. You've got to keep yourself awake."

She willed her eyes to stay open. She took a step. Everything hurt, but nothing was actually broken. Sprained, yes, but not broken. She could still move.

"Do not sit down. Do not close your eyes. Do not lie down, not even for a second. Okay?"

"Yes."

"Let's find this tunnel."

"Wait." It suddenly came to her like the fall had shaken loose the memory. "There is another place I didn't look. The gate where the plane crashed. I never went past where they had it blocked off." The damaged lounge wasn't far from the conference room where she'd listened to the Mayor's presentation. She remembered now. She'd prioritized looking on the bottom level, but there could easily be a stairwell leading down from the main floor. She should have thought of it before. Maybe the mayor had visited the tunnel after the meeting. Maybe it was in the so-called classified area. That would make perfect sense. After all, expensive escape routes weren't for the masses. They were for the important people, the ones with power. Her head pounded harder. I probably shouldn't think too much, she thought. Though at this point, a concussion was perhaps the least of her worries.

Teddy came eye to eye with her. "You smart American girl. Now that you say it, I didn't look there either. Let's go." He picked up his bag of leftover baked goods and guided her, limping, back up the escalators.

Chapter Sixty-One

CANDI TO THE DEATH LOUNGE

The breezeway flickered and twinkled. Snowflakes littered the glass walls and reflected like blinking crystals in the interior lights. "Let's stay here," she said. "It's pretty. Dystopian, but..."

"I don't think that's a good idea."

"This glass didn't break. Maybe it's safer."

Accumulated snow half covered the breezeway's tubular windows. Some people walked to the terminal and others ran. Outside the glass tube, their own inverted snow globe, the sky giants still roamed, reflecting in the airport's external lights which illuminated their designs amidst the drifting snow.

"I can see them again." She pointed to the glass to their left, in the direction of America, or where she thought America was.

"Hey," Vybes nudged her, "Army guys are coming."

She looked around, dazed. "Really?"

But he didn't answer. He was already pushing her to the side, closer to the glass wall. The officer led a line of people like a rack of black winter jackets.

They followed the crowd and as the breezeway opened into the departure area, more soldiers appeared. The carpet swirled below her wheelchair in peppermint candy pinwheels. Candi clutched her purse, which she'd almost forgotten she had. Will I ever need my phone or wallet again? She wondered.

"This way," an officer said, and gestured for them to get in line. Vybes hesitated, but the officer repeated the order, and he complied.

Overwhelmed by all the people, she kept her focus on the moving patterns below her boots. They reached a checkpoint leading into the airport's entrance, and another officer ushered them to gate D29. He pointed towards a cluster of stranded travelers in the distance.

Candi's body felt heavy in the chair, like she was attached to a bag of ice. Is my second dose kicking in? She wondered. They entered a fluorescent space. The overhead lights were way too bright. She shielded her browless eyes with one hand. Many people cried. Some kneeled beside bodies. It felt biblical to her, like an exodus, like the start of a bad trip. She tugged Vybes' red sleeve, but he didn't register it and kept walking.

"Vybes," she hissed. "We should go back."

"They won't let us."

She tugged his jacket again. "There are too many people here."

"Children of Men," he said, but she didn't know what that meant.

She closed her eyes. Colors danced. The second dose welled in her system. She opened them again. People everywhere. Patterns moving everywhere. God, how did it all come to this? She squeezed Vybes' hand for reassurance and he squeezed her back.

At another more open area with displaced passengers lying on cots, men in army uniforms organized lines for beds. Someone behind them shouted for help. Candi turned her head. A man in the distance writhed on the ground. Another yelled beside him. She looked to the window for The Glow Stick, but couldn't see it. The strings weren't there either. No one else was convulsing. A family with children ran past.

Vybes sharply pivoted out of the crowd and bolted, pushing

her in the chair, running through the rest of the D gates and into F. They passed a closed Tim Hortons. After many gates and a long corridor with no windows, with Vybes sprinting and her holding onto the chair, the stranded travelers thinned out. He slowed their pace. The airport opened to a shopping area. They'd reached the other terminal, the one with the plane crash. The stores and kiosks were closed, and the space was chillier, but in the center stood a giant, three-story Christmas tree with its colorful light bulbs still glowing.

"I need to sit down for a minute," Vybes said, breathing heavy. "I'm really fucked up." He wheeled her to an empty bench near the tree. Its decorations gave the space a festive glow, and for a moment, she almost lost herself in the image, expanded and made more complex, more awe-inspiring by the psychedelic drugs.

"We could stay and watch the sunset here," Vybes said.

"The sunset? It's nighttime." She attempted to wrangle her mind from the grips of the acid. "Didn't the sun already set?"

He pointed to the window. "It's there, to the left of the plane."

Only then did she realize they faced the crash. Then she saw what he meant, but it wasn't the sunset; a white hollow ring glowed in the sky, a different formation of The Glow Stick, a Glow Circle. Surrounding the ring, the clear giants loomed, geometric and wavy outlines in falling, icy dust, illuminated by the circle which floated over the mountains of snow like a halo.

Vybes took out the green book. "I remember seeing a picture in here like this."

Candi glanced around. A few other people were in the area. "We should maybe put that away."

"It's okay. Everyone's busy with their own problems." He flipped through the pages. "Have you wondered who made it?"

"I'd imagine some guy in his parent's basement."

Vybes chuckled. "It must all be connected. They must have left it on purpose, because how could they leave this by mistake?"

Together, they looked at the art. In some corner of her mind, she remained aware of the seriousness of their environment, but she didn't know what else to do, other than to stay in this moment. There was nowhere else to go.

In the book, the designs were bright and full of movement and light. It's truly a work of great art, she thought. They examined each page, and she slipped deeper into the acid's grip.

"What do you think is inside the circle in the sky?" she breathed.

"In there? Only God, the aliens, and the inter-dimensional giants can know."

"What about the psychic cats? Or Santa on his sleigh with Rudolph?"

He laughed. "Yes, of course, and the elephants who never forget."

"I hope all the zoo animals will survive."

She made him laugh again, and he brought her closer to him, "That might be what they're saying about us, if they haven't all frozen to death."

"Or maybe the aliens are just shaking our cages right now, to check if we're still alive?" Candi offered, the idea oddly comforting.

"They're in their pet shop and sprinkling stuff into all the different galaxy tanks on the shelf."

"Maybe we're just like germs in an alien's belly."

"And they've got a tummy ache."

"From eating too many Christmas cookies," she giggled and watched through the window as the creatures sifted out snowflakes like the earth was a bowl of pasta and they were parmesan cheese graters. While on some level, she knew she was out of her mind on drugs, what did it really matter? "Or we're just lost people in an airport and it's the end of the world," she said, "And we're too high to feel cold or sad anymore."

"I'm not convinced this is the end."

"Well, it's at least the end of my feet."

"That very well may be. You're taking it well though."

She leaned back into his side, under his arm, pressing her cheek to his ribs, to his red, puffy coat.

Another couple came and sat on the bench beside them. Vybes said hello to them. Then he suddenly stood up and went to them, holding the book in one hand. He said something to them that she couldn't hear, then opened the book, tore out an entire page, and handed it to them. Candi's eyes reacted like she'd seen a moose.

"You gave them the LSD?" she whispered in an accusatory tone as he sat back down.

"To save them."

"What about us?"

"There's enough."

Her head swam. The couple waved and their hands moved lights and colors through the air. They looked like melting Christmas sweaters.

Vybes waved back and grinned. "I knew they'd appreciate it." He held her chin in his hand and kissed her. "'Tis the season of giving."

To save them, she thought, like Jasper had tried to save me, but now I'm here, worried, scared, and I'll probably die, anyway. Her lip quivered. Tears welled in her eyes. The LSD wasn't enough to keep her emotions at bay. Her mood felt like an agitated bird, trapped in an attic, flying around, slamming into old things.

"Hey, hey, don't cry. We're going to be fine." Vybes cuddled her to his chest.

Like a plunged toilet, she came unclogged. She buried her face in his jacket and released her tears. She cried for them, for the dead woman in the hotel, for Adrienne, for Chad, for Jasper, and for the world.

A series of images played rapidly in her mind. Holding hands with Jasper outside the restaurant. The men. The ambulance. She tried to push them away, but they persisted. The hospital. The gunshots. The blood. His mother's face. Her alone on their bed, without him, crying. The sequence repeated, with all its pain, all its heartbreak, but the second time, he appeared in the bedroom with her, alive, smiling, without his shirt on.

Something warm touched the back of her neck and slithered into her red hair. Her body tensed. It wrapped itself around her forehead. It constricted against her skin, gentle, but firm.

Let go. You've done nothing wrong. It's almost time, it said.

A withered, ice-encrusted blue rose cracked open and rebloomed in her mind, a bright yellow flower sprouting in the snow. Her limbs warmed and her sadness shifted to gratitude.

Jasper sat beside her on their bed back home in Vegas. It was spring outside. Her little dog PumpkinChai climbed into her lap. They pet the dog's soft apricot-colored fur together. Jasper gazed at her with loving, mahogany eyes. "I'm just as much here as I am in the ambulance," he said. "And I'm no longer in either place. Neither of them are real, now. I'm no longer hurt. I'm no longer being shot. I'm no longer in the hospital. You can stop going back there. I'm not there. It's over, and you are right here, only right here."

The rope thing slipped off her, and her consciousness returned to the bench.

They were still alive; Vybes was right. They could make it through this alive. Look at how much we've already survived, she thought. Jasper would be proud of me. He would want me to be happy. He would even like Vybes.

She faced the young man, her best friend now. Here right now. A little dog sat on his lap.

"This guy hopped right up," he said, petting the gray and white furry creature.

Candi petted the dog too and it came onto her lap. "Hey, I've seen this dog before. This dog was on our plane." She couldn't be totally sure, it looked like the same dog. She looked around but didn't see his owners. Maybe it was lost, but recognized her smell. "Don't bite me this time," she told the animal.

"And don't fear the tears," Vybes declared. "It's your Christmas party and you can cry if you want to."

"You think this is a party?"

They broke into giggles and a feeling of peace, of absolute joy, blossomed in her chest, despite everything.

"Thank you," she whispered to him.

"For what?"

"For this moment."

And they rested in each other's arms, cradling and stroking the tiny schnauzer on her lap, watching the kaleidoscope world, forgetting their pasts and their futures.

Chapter Sixty-Two

GRETCHEN CONNECTIN'

With her blanket draped over her shoulders, and her neck, shoulder, back, and legs in pain, Gretchen moved like a hunchback through the main terminal, gripping Teddy's arm. People scattered in all directions. They reminded her of bugs sprayed with Raid, confused, looking to escape, but not knowing how to flee. Unlike them, however, she and Teddy had a plan.

"This way," Teddy said, and led her into a crowded area with a massive Christmas tree.

As they worked through the crowds, Gretchen noticed the space was brighter than the rest of the terminal. Was it the lights on the tree?

"Gretchen," A man yelled.

She halted in her tracks. Teddy stopped as well.

"Gretchen!"

She heard it again and scanned the mob of women and crying children.

A red jacket, and a red-headed woman moved towards them.

"Oh my God, Vybes," she yelled.

"Gretchen!" He waved and made his way with the woman

through the crowd. As he was about to hug her she said, "Wait, no stop. I'm injured. I fell. My back's all messed up."

"I'm so happy to see you." The young man stuck his hand out to Teddy. "I'm Vybes."

"I'm Teddy."

The other woman, who Gretchen recognized from the hotel, caught up to them. She was also limping and holding a small dog. Both she and the animal looked terrified, wide-eyed, manic almost, though Gretchen could hardly blame her.

"Hey, I know that dog," Gretchen said. "His owners got taken away by the army. His name is Foxy."

"We know him too," the red-head woman said, her voice sounding odd, almost distant, vague and dreamy. Weird, Gretchen thought, but didn't question it further. She had other priorities that didn't involve a lost dog.

"What happened to you? I got to your room and you were gone," Vybes said. He towered over her and Teddy, his black pupils the size of quarters. The girl grabbed onto his arm again and Vybes moved her thin body closer to his side. Gretchen registered that they were a couple now, but the situation was too crazy for her to care. He was just a random hookup anyway. "Long ass story," she said. "But we've got to move. This is going downhill fast and people have the variant for sure."

"You've seen infected people?" Vybes asked, taking a step back.

"Yes, men collapsing, sudden heart attacks, and the military freaking out, but we're fine. We've only seen it from a distance," Teddy said. "But things are breaking down, people are robbing each other and stuff."

"Robbing each other?" Vybes' friend gasped. Gretchen noticed she was swaying back and forth on the black heels of her boots and also missing her eyebrows.

"This is Candi," Vybes told the man. "And tell me your name one more time, sorry."

"Teddy. Yes, they're some bad seeds out there, ya know. Tings is breakin' down."

"I'm still looking for the tunnel." Gretchen said. "There's a section we haven't yet searched."

"The tunnel?" Candi said, "Yes, let's all go back to the tunnel."

Gretchen's jaw opened. "You know where the tunnel is?"

"She thinks you mean the breezeway," Vybes said.

"Is there a different tunnel?"

Gretchen didn't bother explaining. "Come with us."

"Wait." Vybes dropped down and opened his duffel bag. "I have something for you."

"What?" They didn't have time for this. They needed to find the tunnel and get underground before the shocks started again.

He pulled out a book and ripped a page from it. "Take this now. Put a tab on your tongue and keep it there. It protects somehow from the shocks. Trust me."

"Seriously?"

"Remember I told you we found some LSD. Well, it helps somehow. You won't get shocked. Just trust me."

"I'm on it right now," the other woman said.

Well, that explains a lot, Gretchen thought and took the piece of paper. "You're 100% sure? But wait, am I also going to trip?"

"Yes, but it's fine. Just do it. We were on it and everyone got shocked but us."

She glanced down at the page in her hand, and the world stopped. What in the name of God's great earth? She blinked. Did she have a concussion? She squinted at the image and held up the page. The paper contained an illustration of an intense white, ring of light floating in a snowy sky over a field of snow, and in the snow was a plane with a red maple leaf painted on it. Her breath caught in her chest. The bright ring in the picture looked like the same material as The Glow Stick. "What is this? Did you draw this?"

"We don't know. I know it's crazy, everything is crazy but..."

"Don't worry, it makes everything better," the red-head said.

Crazy doesn't even begin to explain this, she thought, but tore off a tab and put it in her mouth, then passed the picture to Teddy. He took it and did the same, then passed the paper back to Vybes.

Chapter Sixty-Three

FIERY VYBES

Vybes watched the pandemonium unfold. Teddy crashed to the ground. Then Gretchen fell. Their acid hadn't yet kicked in. The shocks were stinging them. People writhed on the ground. He ran with Candi and the dog to the backside of the Christmas Tree. Pressed against the window, tripping hard, he was almost unable to process reality. Peering through the fake pine needles, he could no longer see Teddy or Gretchen, and the air smelled like burning toast or melting rubber or something. Another gunshot cracked. Screams multiplied. The room grew hazy. "Something is on fire," he told Candi.

Then it was like he'd stepped on a landmine, and the second round of LSD shot energy through his feet and made him feel like he was levitating. He took Candi by the hand and inched around to the other side of the Christmas tree, but as they did, the source of the smoke revealed itself. Around the shopping area, people huddled by kiosks and under tables, all watching the same thing: the Christmas Tree.

The giant fake tree was on fire, burning from the top down. A petite woman with short black hair stood in front of it, her face glowing orange in the flames as she watched it burn. Sparks flew and branches broke off. Then Vybes spotted Teddy. He lay motionless on the floor to the side of the tree. Springing into action, he ran to the man, grabbed him, and pulled him out of the way. As he did, the stench of burning synthetic fibers invaded his nostrils and he could hear the tree's lights and ornaments popping and shattering in the heat.

"Come on." Candi was beside him, clutching the dog to her chest. "We have to get away from the smoke."

"Where is Gretchen? Gretchen," he yelled. But faster than he could comprehend, the entire tree combusted into flames. The petite woman collapsed into billowing black clouds. Glass and burning branches flew in all directions and the fire's heat scorched the exposed skin on his face. Candi fell to the ground as well, letting go of the dog, who scurried away, and in the fog of dark smoke, he saw her frantically batting at her legs and stomping her feet. She was on fire.

Leaving Teddy, he bolted to Candi, stripped off his jacket, and used it to suffocate the flames. Her boots and leggings were all but burned off and her calves were bleeding.

"I didn't feel it. I don't even feel a thing," she cried.

The smoke was making him gag. Gretchen reappeared and ran to Teddy. "Help me," she yelled as she struggled to drag Teddy's bulky body further from the encroaching flames.

He left Candi for a moment and ran to help. Gretchen put her ear to the man's mouth, checking to see if he was still breathing. "He's alive."

They moved Teddy further from the burning tree, pulling him by his shoulders, then Gretchen started CPR.

"Stop," Candi said, coming to kneel beside them. "You're doing it wrong." And to Vybes surprise, despite her burns, she started pushing down with all her body weight on the man's chest. After four hard pumps, Teddy sputtered to life. "Ahhh," he groaned, and clutched at his large gut.

It was then that Vybes saw the blood. "Oh my God, wait. He's been shot."

Candi gasped and pulled her hands away. Her palms were indeed wet and red. Gretchen lifted Teddy's shirt. Blood covered his protruding abdomen.

He moaned again in pain and held onto Gretchen's arm with his bloody hand. "My bag, I dropped it, my notebook. Please. Help me. I have to make it out of here." Teddy gasped again for air and blood bubbled from his lips.

"No. No," Gretchen cried, but his body convulsed and shook, then stopped moving. His hand fell from Gretchen's arm and his eyes rolled back into his head. In Vybes' tripping vision, the string creatures returned to the room, swimming like worms through the smoke and latching on like leeches to Teddy, their translucent bodies alive with flowing bolts of energy.

Vybes backed away from the man, pulling Candi with him. "Gretchen, he's dead."

"No, no." Gretchen shook Teddy's body. "Not you too." She was on one side of him with her fingers on his neck. Then she was shaking his shoulders again, sobbing.

"It's too late. Let's go."

"No," she screamed. "He knows the way. He's the only one who knows the way."

Teddy's abandoned bag lay open nearby, spilling out food and books, and at that moment, a raccoon darted out from behind them, snatched a donut hole, and scurried off. Vybes went to the bag and stuffed the scattered items back inside.

"The dog," Candi said, coming to him. "I have to find the dog." She took a Tim Bit from the bag and held it out, calling the animal's name. "Foxy, here Foxy." The pup snuck out from under a chair and Candi lifted him into her arms. Vybes couldn't stop coughing. The smoke was getting thicker. The room grew hotter and hotter. Besides some other bodies on the ground, everyone else was already gone. He slung Teddy's sack over his shoulder and said, "Come on," motioning for Gretchen to follow him.

The journalist didn't move. She stayed by the fallen man, crying, pressing her hands over his gunshot wound.

Vybes couldn't wait any longer. His lungs stung. It felt like he was inhaling plastic trash. As fire consumed the room, he fled with Candi, Teddy's sack, his duffle bag, and the dog.

Chapter Sixty-Four

CANDI CALL

Candi coughed and clung to Foxy in her arms as they burst into the next departure area. The smoke hadn't reached it yet. People milled around like zombies and leaned against the walls, coughing.

"Wait, wait for me," a voice yelled.

They stopped and Gretchen came staggering towards them. "That way," she said. "We were going that way."

They followed her into a curving hallway and then to another area of gates and shopping kiosks. The dog's little body shivered against her, but she couldn't feel her own legs. She stumbled, and Vybes caught her. She used one arm to hold on to him, otherwise she'd trip over her numb, burnt feet. The room swam with distorted shapes and snakes of moving light. She felt like a drunk person trying to drive.

"There." Grethen ran to a door behind a long counter and an area with metal detectors. "We have to get in here. I think it leads to the airport conference rooms and the director's office." She tried the door. It didn't open. Vybes tried to force it open with his body weight. Gretchen pulled a card from her pocket and swiped it at the door's access panel. Nothing happened. Vybes lunged at the door again with his shoulder. The smell of smoke followed them like a ghost.

"Try the card again," she said, trying to catch her breath, her mouth tasting like ash.

Gretchen ran the edge of the card across her lips, wiped it off, and swiped it.

Candi heard the click. They were in.

"This connects to offices," Gretchen said. "I'm pretty sure that's where the tunnel is."

Adrenaline swirled in Candi's body and, once more, she was floating like in a dream. Energy surged through her and her vision became an intense field of undulating clouds. The acid, or maybe her body's own fight-or-flight system renewed her strength. She stood up straighter and focused on her every step. She realized they were entering the damaged lounge. Someone had already pushed aside the barricade to where the plane had crashed. The walls were charred and rubble covered the floor. She shivered. It was freezing now, especially since part of her legs were now exposed.

Gretchen tore away some additional police tape blocking their path, and they walked across what little that was left of the destroyed lounge.

Candi no longer wondered where her friend Adrienne had been when she died, or where Chad's body had ended up. Nor did she care anymore about her blackened feet. Her mind was focused on one thing, and one thing only, the strings around them and The Glow Stick in the sky. She could hear the beings again and they were telling her it was time. But time for what? She didn't know. A temporary wall of plywood and plastic covered where the plane had smashed into the terminal. Still, a cold wind made its way inside, and outside the only window left in the lounge, the light from The Glow Stick illuminated the snow-smothered airport in an eerie, blue, twilight, and there was indeed a tunnel unlike any she'd ever seen—a glowing, white-rimmed portal with a metallic, reflective interior—like the inside of an air conditioner duct, but 1,000 times bigger. It hovered over the runway, right next to the submerged remaining half of the crashed plane.

Vibrations and dissonant organ-like sounds boomed over the landscape, and in her ears they sounded like whales singing, and the fibrous, illuminated giants with gangly string bodies stirred against the moonlight, their strumming, pulsing layers emitting more and more snowflakes into the air, frozen dust falling across beams of blue light. But instead of terror, she felt wonder. These creatures belonged here. They controlled the weather; they could fix the earth. They lived here too. She just couldn't see them before. This, she suddenly realized, is what humans deserved.

It's almost time.

Could Vybes hear it too?

She turned to the closest window. The ring of light spun in the sky and opened. Strings, thousands and thousands of luminous strings flowed out amidst snowflakes. They streamed in towards her, breaking the glass as they came, forcing the trio to retreat inward. No one bothered to scream. Outside the circle became a rod and ran into the ground like a bolt of electricity.

Transfixed by the winter giants, she moved amidst the creatures that flickered and shifted in the shadows. Their tentacles touched on her cheeks like human hair. Snow blew in and covered them along with blowing ash and smoke. She pressed Foxy tighter to her body, shielding him from the debris, covering his head with her jacket.

Beyond the window, the sky ring emitted another beam of light like a laser and she watched as another part of the terminal exploded. More screams and shattering glass filled the Canadian night like crashing church bells.

"Look," Vybes yelled, turning backwards. "People are jumping."

She pivoted to see dark figures leaping out the windows of another section of the terminal, screaming, stumbling in the snow. They sank like lemmings below its white surface.

"That way. Go that way," Gretchen shouted and pointed ahead.

Why weren't the sprinklers coming on? Candi wondered in a moment of lucidity. And how much longer did they have before the whole airport burned? Probably not long.

It's time. It said it again. A whisper through the snow.

Chapter Sixty-Five

GRETCHEN'S TRIP

Gretchen pressed forward in the smoky darkness as the snow and wind blew against her. They were near the press access area, where she'd gone outside before. She sucked in a breath of the cold air and it stung her throat as her tab of acid kicked in. *Woosh.*

The room throbbed. In a flash, the walls around her turned ancient, covered in primitive designs like cave paintings. She still couldn't believe Teddy was dead. To be accidentally shot in this mess, of all the things.

A dim expanse of foreign objects stretched before her, and the icy air burned her chapped, bleeding, stinging lips. She swallowed it like a popsicle. It hurt to breathe the icy air. She hoped the pain in her legs, neck, her chest, lungs, and throat was from internal damage caused by the fall and the shocks and not from the variant. The Glow Stick she could attempt to escape from, but if she was infected with the variant, well, there was no calling 911.

She gripped Teddy's ID badge, holding it tight in her hand in case she needed it again.

Even with her coat, boots, hats, sweatpants, gloves, all of it, she was freezing. The space smelled like fried socks. She hadn't taken acid in a very long time and had forgotten what it was like.

It was hard for her to get her bearings as the drug expanded its presence in her system.

The overhead lights were no longer working. Instead, the alien thing outside illuminated her path with an ominous bluish glow. Through the window, it hovered, round now, like a spinning black hole, an electric vortex with white-hot edges. She moved at a slow pace, making sure to check every wall and every floor tile because maybe the door to the tunnel was in the floor, maybe it wasn't a door at all, but an escape hatch. It was hard to see. Everything around her kept moving. The snow came faster, heavier. She couldn't focus. Where were the offices? Were they even going the right way?

Find the tunnel. Find the tunnel. She repeated it like a mantra as the cold air whipped across her cheeks. Gretchen's head hurt. Her mouth tasted like burnt hot dogs. Her eyes continued to scan every surface for a door. The airport pulsed with beings, with string-like creatures. I'm on acid, she remembered. It's just the acid. God, what a strange turn of events, but she couldn't stop searching. Not now. Not until they found the way out. It had to be here. It just had to.

She coughed harder and covered her face with her jacket. Gathering her strength, breathing through the fabric, she moved onward. Her heart sped up, beating faster and faster, making her fear she'd soon collapse. Growing warmer, panting, she turned around for a split second. Behind her, almost everything burned. Smoke billowed and flames licked at the furniture. It sucked out all the oxygen in the room. Even the snow wasn't enough to stop it. The last round of shocks hadn't hurt her, but it had broken all the windows and lit everything on fire.

Then she saw it: another door. She ran to it and swiped Teddy's card into the slot. The sign said "Secure Conference Room." This must be it, she thought, but the door didn't open. Shit, maybe Teddy didn't have the right clearance? Why would he, she realized. Fuck. They had to get the door open. The fire was closing in. Vybes and Candi pushed against the door. She tried again. Nothing. Mounted on the wall was a glass box with a fire extinguisher and an ax. Vybes punched the glass and yanked out the ax. "Take the fire extinguisher," he said to her, but she was already on it.

"Move," he yelled and started chopping a hole, not in the door, which appeared to be solid metal, but into the wall. He smashed through the drywall, through the installation and revealed a square gap in the metal frame. He chopped open the other side of the drywall to reveal a long table and beyond that, another doorway, this time, hanging open.

"Come on," Candi yelled. Gretchen sprayed the hole behind them with the fire extinguisher's foam then dropped the canister. They ran to the open door and she gasped. It was a stairwell, only going down. "That's it. It's the tunnel," she said. "It has to be."

Vybes pulled the door closed behind them and they descended the steps. She prayed the door was strong enough to hold the fire back.

Only three flights down, they reached another open doorway with a massive metal door like a bank vault. Had someone else already gone through? She wondered. Together, they stepped into a wide, dark passage, then using all their combined strength, swung the heavy door shut. As it clanked to a close, emergency light strips illuminated along a cement floor. Plastic sheeting covered the walls which stretched infinitely into the distance. Metal pipes ran above them along the ceiling. The underground chamber smelled moist, like wet dirt, but there was also another scent that she couldn't identify, motor oil maybe. It was dead quiet. Candi coughed and the sound echoed. Anxiety twisted in Gretchen's gut. What if it led to nowhere? The ceiling above them shook a little. What if it collapsed? But then again, what was their alternative? There was no other alternative.

In the dim light, under the power of the acid, a million things gleamed and shimmered and moved, but wait, she took a few more steps forward. Was she seeing things? She could hardly believe her eyes. Parked a ways in front of them was a golf-cart-sized vehicle, the kind crew drove around the airport.

"Oh man," Vybes said, hurrying to the machine. He threw what remained of Teddy's sack of bagels into the back cargo area and climbed into the back seat. "If this thing works, I'll start believing in God again." He slid into the drivers' seat and Candi climbed into the front beside him, opening her jacket a bit for Foxy to stick out his little head. The dog sniffed the air.

There were no keys for the vehicle, just a button that said push to start. "Come on baby Jesus," Vybes said, and pushed the button. The cart whirred to life.

"Fuck yeah!" Gretchen exclaimed.

"Time for another ride, Foxy," Candi said and pet the top of the dog's head.

"Okay, here we go. Hold on tight."

They jerked forward and drove, rolling over the tunnel's rough, cement floor, heading into the darkness. Gretchen leaned back, still breathing hard, gripping the roll bar of the cart. She sure hoped Vybes wasn't as fucked up as she was because there was no way in hell she could drive right now.

Above them, something rumbled. The ceiling shook. Particles of dirt dropped.

Gretchen closed her eyes and colors blurred and became scenes, shapes, even animals. Sounds like thunder rumbled around them. Vybes must have stepped harder on the gas because they accelerated and sped forward. She kept her eyes closed. She tried not to freak out. Above, it sounded like bombs dropping, like an earthquake, and behind her closed eyes, in the vision of her mind, she could see the scene.

A blazing arc shot like an arrow from The Glow Circle and formed a fiery blue ring above the airport. From this blazing circle emanated other spheres, big bubbles, baby planets hatching from an ice egg. The burning rings expanded. The heavens rattled, and the Toronto airport went white. Snow, snow, snow. It didn't stop.

Rings of light and strings of moving things like frozen sea anemones covering, covering—they covered everything.

If I make it out of this alive, she thought, I'm going to Montego Bay. Fuck this cold ass place, and she pushed away the nightmarish winter scene. She pictured a beach, a fruity drink. She pictured her family. She pictured Kevin leaving the hospital. She pictured having a working phone. She envisioned the end of the tunnel. Smiling handsome men with hot food. She even thought of kissing and hugging Sam. She held the images in her head. She let the acid make them dance. The tunnel rumbled again. Another loud blast. The cart wobbled. Her body jiggled. Foxy barked.

And then it went quiet.

Then they were alone underground with only the sound of their wheels turning. She loosened her grip and away they went, through the tunnel, towards an unknown destination—a man and two women, all tripping hard, a toy schnauzer, a book of LSD, a few bottles of water, Teddy's notebook of poems, and a garbage bag of stale, maple-flavored bagels, some TimBits, and one cold, hard half of a grilled-cheese sandwich.

Teddy's Final Refrain

Missed my connection.
    Some people never reach their destination.
    Some bodies are never found.
    Some storms never end
    Some women need men
    Some men need them more
    Some dreams never begin
    Some come true too soon
    There aren't always heroes
    Nor a clear foe,
    Sometimes it's just confusion
    Tsunamis and delusions
    People hoarding bombs behind curtains
    Blizzards and aliens
    Beef jerky that's really turkey

Will the future be naughty or nice?
    A bundle of switches or cloves and Allspice?

Just because things seem okay, doesn't mean they are.

Could be no more cookies for Santa and no more candy for the kids. No more good vibes.

No matter how smart, some people can't survive.

Not even when they try.

Following all the rules only works some of the time.

And like missing luggage, we may never know where things end up.

(Who made these rules anyway?)

My crystal ball seems a little cloudy after all.

So, walk gud, tek care, sleep warm in your bed tonight my friends! Until we meet again, I'm gone.

If you're reading this, it's already too late.

Bye, at least from Toronto.

(Wink wink, kiss kiss, smile with sunglasses emoji, moon, Saturn, shooting star, cookies, alien head, Santa, Christmas tree, fireball, palm-to-face.)

Epilogue

Gretchen Green, Candi Burns, and Vybes Bibi waited together in the green room of Chloe Logan's podcast studio amidst dressing mirrors, arcade games, rare books, boutique workout machines, vases full of candy, and movie posters. Gretchen wished she wasn't sweating so much. She clenched and unclenched her freshly done fake nails. Unlike Candi, she never wore acrylic nails, and they felt alien on her fingertips, but with 11 million people about to watch their story, she'd wanted to look tidy and put together. She swallowed a gulp of water, wetting her dry mouth. I'm doing this for you, Kevin, she thought, and for Teddy, who'd saved her life, and for everyone else who hadn't made it out alive.

Candi sat nearby in front of a mirrored vanity, wearing a pale blue, business casual, fitted dress that stopped at her knees to show off her new top of the line, artificial legs and feet. She smoothed her red hair in the mirror, and added pressed powder to her already perfect, made-up face. Her eyebrows had returned and Gretchen thought she looked better than ever—glowing, in fact. Likewise, Vybes wore an outfit made especially for the episode by an emerging designer, matched to the color of Candi's dress. It resembled a space suit with clouds protruding from the front and back, almost like angel wings. He lounged with his long legs sprawled over a leather sofa, scrolling on his phone, as calm as could be with two long French braids in his hair.

In black sneakers, black jeans, and a black t-shirt with her brother Kevin's face on it and the dates of his life, Gretchen paced a bit, trying to shake the nervousness out of her system. She came up behind Candi, catching an unwelcome glimpse of herself in the mirror. Despite almost starving to death in the tunnel, she'd regained all the weight plus some.

"You look great already. You don't have to add anything else," she told Candi.

"Do you think people will finally believe us after this?"

"Some will. Some never will."

"I'm so nervous."

"You've done plenty of interviews. This should be more relaxed than most. Everyone says Chloe's easy to talk to."

But this would be different. Gretchen knew that. The whole world was about to hear what really happened at the Toronto airport, and not just a sound bite or a few clips of their story, spun to match the accepted narrative: a rare, but natural weather event, but they'd hear the entire, uncensored thing. It was a tale only the survivors could tell, and that was them. Even the few people who'd managed to escape in the final days of the snowpocalypse, in private planes or military tanks, they'd either crashed and died or had disappeared and weren't coming forward. Plus, Candi was more than just nervous about the interview. She also had a special announcement, a secret only she and Gretchen knew. They hadn't even told the show's producers, but Candi was pregnant. Gretchen couldn't wait for the reveal. She knew it would make for great entertainment, get millions of extra views, and Vybes would freak out with joy when he heard his fiancé's surprise. Candi would probably cry and he'd probably start doing cartwheels or something wild.

Chloe Logan's assistant popped in. "Five minutes. Anything else I can help you with?"

They all said no.

Gretchen picked up the signed copy she'd prepared as a gift for Chloe of her debut book, *Snowtastrophe: A Journalist's True Escape from The Toronto Airport Disaster*, and tucked it under her arm. Maybe, if she got a chance, she'd read one of Teddy's poems, which she'd sprinkled throughout the book. There was one in particular, his final poem that she wanted to share.

Conversely, Vybes held the green velvet book, which they'd come to call, *The Art*. This would be the first time they revealed it to the world. While in the tunnel, they'd agreed that if they managed to survive, they'd keep the book a secret, otherwise it might end up rotting away in some government storage room.

Instead, they planned to give it to Logan who knew many scientists and people in power. She would not only love and appreciate what remained of the psychedelic, art-filled book, but also do the right thing with it.

The assistant returned, handed them all bottles of water and, with a wave of her hand, ushered them into the studio and to their chairs.

Gretchen's adrenaline skyrocketed, rushing from her racing heart to her shaking limbs.

"Everyone relax. This is going to be a blast. You guys are going to blow the world away," Logan's producer said, tipping his ball cap to them from behind his mixing board on the other side of the room.

She took a few deep breaths, trying to ground herself, to appreciate the moment, but it was too surreal. Her pulse kept its quick pace.

Then Chloe Logan herself walked in and Gretchen let out a gasp of air. The famous host was wearing a white, abominable snowman, yeti costume. It immediately broke the tense chill in the air and they all burst out laughing.

"So," Chloe said, removing her blue, sasquatch-like mask, and sitting down, "I don't think I need to do introductions. Everyone has seen y'all on TV and I've been dying to talk to you because I still can't believe the world is acting like this crazy ass shit didn't happen. Like an entire airport, full of humans, can be obliterated, and people want to just forget it. The government is like, I dunno uh huh uh huh, duh—nothing to see here folks, move along." She spoke in a mocking, clown voice. "Like how the fuck do people do that?"

A smile spread wide on Gretchen's round cheeks. That really was the craziest part, she thought, that aside from those who'd lost loved ones, most people acted like it had never happened at all. A few tried to study it, to explain it, but most didn't care. It was almost like they didn't believe it could ever happen again... or to them...

"You guys survived," Logan continued, slipping on her headphones. "You know what really happened. Was it aliens? Was it a weather attack? I want to hear every single detail and everything you think. I don't care if we're here for 10 hours. We *need* to know what *really* went down."

Gretchen grinned and glanced at the pair beside her. "Where do we even begin?"

"On the plane," Candi said. "That's when The Glow Stick first appeared."

THE END

Acknowledgments

Thank you for reading!

If you enjoyed this book, or even if you didn't, please leave a review on Amazon and Goodreads, or wherever you found this book.

And tremendous thanks to everyone who inspired or aided in the production of *Acid Christmas* and to my Reading Raccoon Crew! I love you folks so much!

Thank you Kayleigh and the BBBs for initially influenced me to write this twisted tale. Thank you Emmie Hamilton for your early story suggestions. Thank you Jonathan Koven, D.S. Davis, Sharon Dukett, Heather Knorr, Rochanda Ferrelli, and Rita Sotolongo for your edits to this book. Thank you Cherie Chapman for your cover design. Thank you Lainey Cameron and the entire Writers' Support Group for keeping me inspired and for helping me in more ways than I can count.

Thank you also to my mom, Agah, Katie, Patricia, Joyce, Jeffe, Randy, Bojana, Chantal, Mandi, Karisia, Sabrina, Anna, Dom, Franck, Ashley, Christian, Marina, Deanna, Gunter, Terry Fox (the schnauzer), the Raccoons of Toronto, and the late and great Gabs, you all contributed in bits and pieces to the spirit of this book.

Finally, thank you Tim Horton. I really do love your large hot Capp.

Also by Charlotte Dune

Cactus Friends: A Psychedelic Love Story

&

Mushroom Honeymoon

To read free short stories and essays by Charlotte Dune, please jump into Charlotte Dune's Lagoon: https://charlottedune.substack.com/

or use this QR code:

Hope to see you there!

About the Author

Charlotte Dune is a psychedelic fiction writer and the author of three novels and many non-fiction essays. Dune grew up reading science fiction books in a geodesic dome in rural western Virginia, roamed the globe with the US Foreign Service, worked on films in Canada, and now writes and lives in South Florida.

To learn more about Charlotte Dune, please visit CharlotteDune.com.

And if you would like to be on Charlotte Dune's **Reading Raccoon Review Crew (RRRC)** to offer feedback and beta read her new books before they are released, please join here: https://charlottedune.com/raccoon/

Thanks for reading!